A HERO'S HONOR

A RESOLUTION RANCH NOVEL
(BOOK 1)

TESSA LAYNE

Shady Layne Media
www.tessalayne.com

Copyright © 2017 by Tessa Layne
Paperback Edition ISBN-13: 978-0-9991980-0-1
Print Edition
Cover Art by Razzle Dazzle Design
Published by Shady Layne Media

This is a work of fiction. Names, characters, places, and incidents are products of copious amounts of wine, long walks, and the author's overactive imagination, or are used fictitiously. Any resemblance to actual events, locales, organizations, or persons, living or dead, is entirely coincidental.

Meet the Heroes of RESOLUTION RANCH

Inspired by the real work of Heroes & Horses... Chances are, someone you know, someone you *love* has served in the military. And chances are, they've struggled with re-entry into civilian life. The folks of Prairie are no different. With the biggest Army base in the country, Fort Riley, located in the heart of the Flint Hills, the war has come home to Prairie.

Join me as we finally discover Travis Kincaid's story and learn how he copes in the aftermath of a mission gone wrong. Meet Sterling, who never expected to return to Prairie after he left for West Point. Fall in love with Cash as he learns to trust himself again. Laugh with Jason and Braden as they meet and fall in love with the sassy ladies of Prairie. Same Flint Hills setting, same cast of friendly, funny, and heartwarming characters, same twists and surprises that will keep you up all night turning the pages.

A HERO'S HONOR – Travis Kincaid & Elaine Ryder
  (On Sale Now)
A HERO'S HEART – Sterling Walker & Emma Sinclaire
  (On Sale Jan 9th)
A HERO'S HAVEN – Cash Aiken & Kaycee Starr
  (Coming 2018)
A HERO'S HOME – Jason Case & Millie Prescott
  (Coming 2018)
A HERO'S HOPE – Braden McCall & Luci Cruz
  (Coming 2018)

A HERO'S HEART (On Sale Jan 9th)

The town superstar has just met his match
When retired Army Captain and Prairie's favorite son, Sterling Walker, returns home to join Restoration Ranch, he finds himself face to face with his biggest rival – Emma Sinclaire, the sole daughter of Prairie's oldest family – all grown up, gorgeous, and glaring daggers at him.

Will it be winner take all in this battle of hearts?
A rising star at Kansas City's internationally acclaimed Royal Fountain Media, Emma agrees to personally oversee the marketing and fundraising campaign for Resolution Ranch. But she never expected to come face to face with her high school nemesis, Sterling Walker, let alone have to work closely with him. As they face off across the boardroom, she can't deny her attraction to the smart, sexy, soldier who engages her in battle at every turn.

When a moment of carelessness threatens to shut down the fundraiser before it starts, Sterling will put everything on the line to protect Emma's reputation. Will it be enough to win Emma's heart for good? Or will the fallout be the ruin of Resolution Ranch?

WELCOME TO PRAIRIE!

Where the cowboys are sexy as sin, the women are smart and sassy, and everyone gets their Happily Ever After!

Prairie is a fictional small town in the heart of the Flint Hills, Kansas – the original Wild West. Here, you'll meet the Sinclaire family, descended from French fur-trappers and residents of the area since the 1850s. You'll also meet the Hansens and the Graces, who've been ranching in the Flint Hills since right before the Civil War.

You'll also meet the heroes of Resolution Ranch, the men and women who've put their bodies on the line serving our country at home and abroad.

Prairie embodies the best of western small town life. It's a community where family, kindness, and respect are treasured. Where people pull together in times of trial, and yes… where the Cowboy Code of Honor is alive and well.

Every novel is a stand-alone book where the characters get their HEA, but you'll get to know a cast of secondary characters along the way.

Get on the waiting list for Prairie Devil and the rest of the
Cowboys of the Flint Hills
tessalayne.com/newsletter

Additional books in the series:

COMING IN APRIL 2018 – PRAIRIE DEVIL

He's the Devil she shouldn't want

Colton Kincaid has a chip on his shoulder. Thrown out of the house when he was seventeen by his brother, Travis, he scrapped his way to the top of the rodeo circuit riding broncs, and never looked back. Until a chance encounter with hometown good girl Lydia Grace leaves him questioning everything and wanting a shot at redemption.

She's the Angel he can never have

All Lydia Grace needs is one break. After having her concepts stolen by a famous shoe designer, she returns home to Prairie to start a boot company on her own. But when her break comes in the form of Colton Kincaid, Prairie's homegrown bad boy and rodeo star, she wonders if she's gotten more than she's bargained for.

They say be careful what you wish for
To get her boot company off the ground, Lydia makes Colton an offer too good to refuse, but he ups the ante. Will the bargain she strikes bring her everything she's dreamed of and more, or did she just make a deal with the devil?

Help a Hero – Read a Cowboy
KISS ME COWBOY – A Box Set for Veterans
Six Western Romance authors have joined up to support their favorite charity – Heroes & Horses – and offer you this sexy box set with Six Full Length Cowboy Novels, filled with steamy kisses and HEA's. Grab your copy and help an American Hero today! All proceeds go to Heroes & Horses

Visit www.tessalayne.com for more titles & release info
Sign up for my Newsletter here
http://tessalayne.com/newsletter
Hang out with me! Join my Facebook Reader Group – Prairie Posse
facebook.com/groups/1390521967655100

CHAPTER 1

"Uh, Travis?" The sweet feminine voice that had haunted his dreams for months spoke as a coffee pot entered his line of sight. "Did you want some more coffee?"

He swung his gaze in the direction of her voice, meeting Elaine Ryder's big blue eyes staring at him with a hint of concern. It never stopped surprising him. How one morning she'd suddenly stopped avoiding his gaze and began meeting his eyes. As if, after two years, he'd finally passed some kind of muster.

It still rendered him stupid.

He grunted in reply to her offer of coffee, holding out his paper cup, missing the one Dottie used to hold for him at the diner. Missing the diner. But it was gone. Demolished with half the town in six minutes of devastation wrought by an EF4 tornado. All they had now was a food truck and a handful of picnic tables set up across the street from the flattened remains of the diner.

Elaine reached to steady his hand as she poured, a new part of their daily ritual thanks to the tornado, and one he wouldn't complain about. Or the zing that snaked up his arm and spiraled down to his cock. Every. Single. Time.

Across from him, his deputy chief and closest friend, Weston Tucker, made a disapproving noise in the back of his throat as soon as she left. "Real smooth, dickhead. No wonder you don't get anywhere with the ladies. Usually, when you like someone, you engage them in conversation. Not growl at them."

"You know I don't date women in town," he gritted out. How many times had they been over this?

"Or anyone, because of your damned rules." Weston held up a finger. "Because there's the age requirement," he ticked off on another finger. "And how could I forget the education clause, and the no-sleeping-in rule?" He held up another hand. "Shall I go on? No one divorced or with kids, no one in the military or at work. And you practically have to break down a door to assure yourself it's really locked. Maybe getting laid would help you lighten up. It would at least fix your crappy attitude."

"My attitude is just fine," he snapped.

Weston laughed, a rich belly laugh that rang across the crowded picnic tables. "Keep telling yourself that, Chief. Keep telling yourself that." His face turned serious. "You about bit Elaine's head off. You may be inept with the ladies, but you're usually not an asshole. What gives?"

How could he explain? Even to his best friend? Travis contemplated the dark liquid in his cup, as the memory of his latest bad dream shuddered through him. "It's nothing."

"Let me guess. You overslept again?" Weston's face softened briefly. "What was it this time? Up all night thinking about Elaine?" he teased gently.

"If only. More like pulling Warren out of the rubble, except it's not his face I see, it's my brother's. Or McCall. Or Hamm."

"When was the last time you talked to someone?"

Travis shrugged. He'd done plenty of time on a couch, and as far as he was concerned there came a point when it was just a crutch for crybabies.

"I know someone good." Weston signaled Elaine for a refill.

"I'll let you know." Travis took a big gulp of the still hot coffee, trying not to wince as it scalded his throat going down. It was stupid, he knew. Weak. He wanted to feel her hand against his again. His coffee consumption had quadrupled since the tornado. But he couldn't help it. He craved her gentle touch. The innocence of it. That fleeting contact did more to ground him than any of the rules he'd imposed on himself in the years since he'd left his SEAL unit.

"Don't be an asshole this time," Weston spoke low, eyes crinkling with mirth. "Use your words, big guy."

Travis took the opportunity to peruse her as she stood over Weston's cup and poured. She was on the short side, no more than five-five. Slender, but with enough curves to make his mouth water. He'd only ever seen her in what she wore right now – black Converse, slim fitting jeans, and a Dottie's Diner tee. She had three. A black one, a pink one, and his favorite because it brought out the blue in her eyes, the blue one she wore today. Even though it was slightly baggy, it didn't disguise her high, perky breasts or cover up the luscious curve of her ass. An ass he longed to cup as he pulled her close.

Weston cleared his throat, and Travis dragged his eyes to the sound. Weston rolled his eyes and smirked, then mouthed the word *dumbass*. Travis straightened and flicked a glance at Elaine.

Shit.

Pink splashed across her cheeks. Something he'd love if he hadn't been caught staring, because it made her eyes sparkle. And was that the barest hint of a smile? She rounded the table and opened her hand, silently asking for his cup. "Thanks, Elaine." He forced his voice into a normal register as he handed over his cup, embracing the zing that traveled up from his fingers when her hand brushed his.

"How's Dax doing?" Weston asked, finally rescuing him.

A look of worry crossed Elaine's face. She shrugged and gripped the coffee pot a little tighter. "As good as can be expected, I guess."

Her voice was so soft and sweet. It slid over Travis and enveloped him like a warm blanket.

"Where's he right now?"

Leave it to Weston to keep the conversation going. Weston was right. He needed to do a better job of talking with her. It was his job, for chrissakes. But at least where Elaine was concerned, Weston had appointed himself the unofficial public relations officer.

Elaine tilted her head toward the center of the park. "Over at the playground with a few of the boys from his class."

Pride surged through Travis as he glanced in the direction of the playground. In the early aftermath of the tornado, the community had determined their top priority would be rebuilding the playground so the town's children would have a safe place to play during clean-up efforts. It had been the perfect project to bring everyone together around a common purpose, becoming a touchstone of inspiration for the long months of recovery that lay ahead.

Say something, dumbass. Anything. He cleared his throat. "Well, ah…" Fuck. Why in the hell was he so tongue-tied?

"You'll have to excuse Travis, here." Weston smiled reassuringly at Elaine. "He's a little short on sleep. He's not usually such a caveman."

She swung her baby blues to him, scrutinizing him with the same worry he'd seen on her face when he'd reunited her with Dax after the tornado. In spite of his discomfort, something in him growled to life under her attention. Made him sit a little taller.

"Do you prefer tea?" she asked in a rush. "Or water? Sometimes when I'm sleep deprived, coffee just makes it worse."

Her concern warmed him. And for the first time that day, a genuine smile tilted up the corners of his mouth. "I'm fine, thanks."

Once she'd moved away, he scowled across the table at Weston, who sat shaking with suppressed laughter. "Smooth," he chortled. "You'll have to do a better job talking with the ladies if you're going to run for county sheriff."

"No way. We've got enough to deal with here. I don't need to run for sheriff."

"Have you seen who's filed?" Weston's voice filled with disgust.

Travis shook his head. "Don't care. Williams only had, what, eighteen months left? So long as the new guy follows in his footsteps and stays out of our way, we'll be fine."

Weston made a disapproving noise. "This guy's an asshat. Travis. None of the cops I've talked to over in Marion like him."

"So he's an asshat. As long as he does his job, who cares?"

Weston leaned forward. "Why not run? You've got the pedigree."

"You do, too."

"Maybe I want your job." Weston grinned and stroked the scruff covering his chin.

"Give me a better reason."

"Fine. Crime's down since you became chief. Sense of community is up. And you need a new project."

Weston had him there. He did need something new. He'd been feeling itchy for months, even before the tornado hit. Like it was time to make a shift. Problem was, to what? He was settled here. And while his long-term dream was to get the ranch up and running again, he didn't have the people or the capital tucked away to do it for a few more years. "I'll consider it."

"Hey Travis, you gotta sec?" Hope Sinclaire swung a leg over the bench and took a seat.

"You bet." Anything to stop talking about this county sheriff business. And get his mind off Elaine.

"I'm worried about Dax Ryder."

Weren't they all? The little boy hadn't been the same since they'd pulled him and Warren Hansen out of the rubble of the tornado. Granted, it hadn't even been two months, but the kid was obviously traumatized. And Hope's uncle, Warren, had died protecting him. "Talk to me."

"We've all invited Elaine and Dax out to the ranch to work with the horses, but they haven't come. I don't know why. But I thought since you're one of the only adults Dax seems comfortable with at the moment, maybe you could offer to bring them out?"

Weston spoke up. "That would be a great photo-op for someone running for sheriff."

"Shut up, Wes. I'm not doing that."

"The horses or the photo-op?"

Travis shot Weston a warning glare and turned back to Hope. "When?"

"Anytime. I've been studying more cases where trauma victims are positively impacted by working with horses. I think it could help him."

"It helped me when I was in a bad spot a few years ago," Weston volunteered.

"When was this?" Travis asked, intrigued. Weston hadn't spoken much about the time before he'd moved to Prairie. And Travis had been surprised he'd taken the job offer. Weston hadn't grown up out west, but he'd taken to the western life like a fish to water.

"Before you called me to come work for you. There's a program in Montana at the Triple Bar H Ranch called Horses Helping Heroes. You work with horses, training them, and caring for them. But it's really about giving you coping skills again. A lot of their guys have gone on to be farriers, or guides, or work on ranches."

"Exactly." Hope agreed emphatically, her signature strawberry blonde braids swinging behind her. "Horses communicate with you in ways we don't yet understand. Which is why I think it's really important we get Dax out to the ranch. I think we can help him."

Weston stood.

"Where you going?"

A glint of challenge entered his eye. "I thought I'd go talk to Elaine. Seeing's how you're tongue-tied around her."

Asshole. "I'll do it." Travis swung a leg over the bench and stood, ignoring Weston's soft chuckle behind him. He could talk to Elaine. He could talk to anyone. She was just like anyone else in town. And it wasn't like he was asking her on a date. This was to help Dax.

CHAPTER 2

ELAINE WALKED AWAY from the table where Travis and Weston were sitting, clutching the coffee pot to keep it from shaking. Why was she so jumpy this morning? She'd nearly dumped a plate of food on Anders from the Feed 'n Seed. And when she'd tried to apologize, she realized she didn't even know his last name.

Prairie was funny that way. Everyone was on a first name basis. Anders' Feed 'n Seed. Emmaline's Dress Shop. Dottie's Diner. A sign of true friendship, of *intimacy,* was when you knew someone well enough they told you their last name. And she was a nobody. Hardly memorable except to a select few women Dottie had introduced Elaine to during her time at the diner.

The shining exception to that unspoken rule was Travis Kincaid. Everyone worshipped Travis Kincaid. The man practically walked on water. And who could blame people for thinking that? He was the perfect police chief. Big. Strong. Imposing.

But he had kind eyes behind his aviators. She'd seen them. And she'd learned enough in her short time on earth that she knew people's eyes never lied. You could sum up a man in less time than it took to snap your fingers – just by looking him in the eyes. And the first time she'd looked Travis in the eyes, she couldn't look away. There was pain in his eyes, for sure. And way too much brooding. How could there not be after what Prairie had experienced? And rumor had it he was a former Navy SEAL. So he must have experienced the horrors of war, too. In spite of that, when he wasn't brooding and preoccupied, looking like the weight of the world was on his shoulders, his eyes radiated confidence. Kindness.

And the man had a devastating smile. It had only been directed her way a few times in the last two years, but oh, my. She'd turned to a puddle on the spot. In fact, she'd been surprised her clothes hadn't started smoking.

She let out a small sigh as she replaced the coffee pot on the portable warmer Dottie had set up to the side of the food truck. Travis Kincaid was so far out of her league it wasn't even funny. She had a better chance of winning the lottery than getting someone like Travis to notice her, let alone want to be with her. "Stop it, Elaine. You have too many problems as it is." Romance would only make it worse. Especially with a cop. A relationship with a lawman would invite scrutiny where she didn't want it.

A table piled with the remains of several eaters' meals caught her attention. The trash cans were only steps from the tables, but she insisted on bussing the dishes herself. It made her feel useful. Dottie should've let her go along with the line cook. But she had to have a job, and Dottie had insisted she stay on. She stacked the disposable plates, taking care that nothing spilled on her shirt. Turning, she nearly slammed into the object of her late-night fantasies.

"Let me." His voice had entirely too much sex appeal, and it fuzzed her brain as she stood rooted to the spot. Large, strong hands took the trash from her, but he didn't move, and neither did she. Elaine dragged her eyes up over his massive chest, made more so by the bulletproof vest that was part of his daily attire. She'd rarely seen him out of uniform. But those few occasions had fueled her imagination to fill in the blanks. The man was a wall of muscle.

She continued her upward perusal over his strong jaw, to his full mouth, which at the moment held a shadow of a smile, landing on his hazel eyes alight with an intensity that snagged her breath in the back of her throat. She couldn't look away.

He turned, breaking whatever hung delicately suspended between them, and walked the dishes through the cluster of tables to the trash. But instead of moving on like she expected, he swiveled and caught her eye again, holding her gaze like a tractor beam as he crossed back to her. A tingle started across her shoulders and skittered in waves down through her body to settle in an ache at her core. She clenched her thighs, trying to contain the sensation. When she opened her mouth to speak, nothing came out.

Again.

Sure, she'd had a crush on him since he walked into Dottie's on her first day nearly two years ago. But since the tornado, she'd been giddy and jittery around him like she'd drunk too much coffee. She'd made such a fool of herself that afternoon, collapsing into him, hysterical with relief that Dax was safe. His arms had come around her, sure and strong. Comforting. As if he truly cared about her.

But today, something was different. She'd felt it as soon as she'd brushed against him while pouring his coffee. She couldn't put her finger on it, at least not yet. Of course, it had nothing to do with the fact that she'd sensed Travis's eyes on her everywhere she moved this morning. Tracking her like a cat watches its prey before it pounces. It made her heart pound in ways it never had before. Not from fear, but from…

anticipation.

"Thanks," she stuttered when her voice decided to function.

"Happy to help."

He wasn't moving. She heated under his intense scrutiny, nipples pulling tight. "Is something wrong?" Dread momentarily refocused her thoughts, tightening her throat as her hopes sank like a rock. That must be it. Travis didn't make small talk. He must know. Maybe Dottie had let it slip. Well, if he did, he did. She couldn't change her past, and while she might be ashamed of who she was when she was younger, she wasn't ashamed of who she was now. At least not much.

His staring unnerved her. Was this some kind of ninja mind trick to get her to start singing like a canary? Her skin itched as a riot of feelings warred for supremacy inside her. Worry might be there, just below the surface, but it was eclipsed by an equally primal and physical response. The light in his eyes made her want things that were not for her. "Travis?"

She swore she saw him shake himself.

"Hope stopped me this morning and mentioned you and Dax haven't been out to their stables yet."

The Hansens had been so kind to her since the tornado, paying special attention to Dax even though it was their uncle, and Maddie Sinclaire's father, who died keeping her son safe. She was indebted to them for life. She had no intention of taking further advantage.

She shook her head and shrugged, moving to clear another table. Travis followed. She glanced his direction but avoided his eyes. "I'm already the town charity case. I just can't."

He made a scoffing noise in the back of his throat.

"Don't get me wrong. I'm incredibly grateful for everyone's kindness." Especially Dottie's. She'd be lost without the woman. Or worse. Even though the diner job on its own wasn't enough to make ends meet. With the library and her second job gone in the tornado too, she'd have to muddle through until the town rebuilt. "I have to stand on my own two feet."

Travis took another pile of plates from her hands and waited patiently while she collected the rest of the trash from the table, then followed her to the barrel. "You've been standing on your own two feet plenty. You ever think people might worry about you?"

"Ha." She hadn't meant for the bitter laugh to escape, but it had.

Travis's hand came down on her shoulder, and he spun her to face him, his other hand coming down opposite. That wasn't a thrill rocketing down her spine. Nope. She made the mistake of looking up, only to be pinned by his eyes doing their ninja mind trick thing again.

"What gives, Elaine? Why won't you go?"

Bitterness rose through her, lodging in the back of her throat. "You don't get it, do you? You think it's pride, or-or guilt, or-or… I don't know, something else. How about I don't own a car? I don't even know how to drive. And even if I had one, or Dax had one, I'd never bring a bike within fifty feet of Highway 30. Not with no shoulder and too many construction trucks on it these days."

There. Let him chew on that.

He wanted to know what it was? Poverty. Plain and simple. And the humiliation that accompanied it. She shut her eyes, willing away the hot pricks that poked at her eyelids. She scrimped and scratched, and she couldn't even get her son a bike, let alone the latest Transformer he always seemed to be begging for. And phones, tablets, or laptops? Forget it. She'd been studying for her GED at the library, and now that dream was destroyed, too. Just once, she wanted to be the one to get her son something nice, take him someplace nice.

"I'll take you."

"You?" Her stomach pitched.

Travis made an exaggerated effort of looking first left, then right. Turning around, before throwing her one of those devastating smiles. "I don't see anyone else."

The word *Yes* sprang up, ready to burst from the back of her throat, but she reined it in, shaking her head. "That's very kind of you, but you don't need to do that."

Her libido protested mightily.

God, she'd give anything to spend an hour with him when neither of them was on the clock. But, no. Saying yes was a bad, bad, bad idea. Besides, women like her didn't get to have men like Travis. Kind. Fair. Trustworthy.

"It's no problem at all. More importantly, I think it will be good for Dax."

Of course. For a split second she'd allowed herself to think he might be asking because he was interested in her. She ignored the little ache that lodged at the bottom of her chest. Of course, he was asking for Dax. Just like a good, upstanding cop. And that was sweet, really. Dax worshipped Travis. He was the only other adult besides herself and Dottie that Dax would talk to right now. So it went without thinking that Travis would naturally take an interest in Dax.

But that still didn't mean she could take advantage of the Hansens' offer. "You probably don't have a car seat. Dax is still in a booster seat."

Travis seemed unfazed. "Not a problem."

"He's never ridden a horse before."

"Also not a problem. Hope thinks it will help him."

Temptation won out. And curiosity. If Hope thought horses could help her son get back to being the rambunctious, curious, funny kid he'd been before the tornado, she'd give it a try. "I do worry about him."

"Good. I'll pick you up tomorrow morning."

"I'm so sorry, but I work tomorrow."

"I'll work it out with Dottie."

"But–"

Travis held up a finger. "No buts. I'll see you at nine."

CHAPTER 3

TRAVIS PACED BACK and forth in front of the large stone fireplace that anchored the great room of the Kincaid family home. Three paces across, turn, three paces back, glance at his watch, then at the booster seat on the floor by the door, then another turn and the pattern began again.

Where in the hell was Weston? Weston was going to make him late. And he hated being late. Almost as much as he hated oversleeping. As soon as he heard Weston's truck roar into the yard, he was out the door, booster seat in hand. By the time Weston's boots hit the porch step, Travis had locked the deadbolt and was making a show of checking his watch.

"You're gonna make me late."

Weston snorted. "It's just now eight-thirty. How long is it going to take you to drive through town? A whole ten minutes?"

"To the FEMA park?" Most of the FEMA trailers had been placed in the KOA at the edge of town. "Thirteen minutes and twenty-six seconds."

"But who's counting?"

"You know we've had to take a few late-night calls out there," he grumbled. Just one of many reasons why Travis had ordered extra patrols through the FEMA park. It had nothing to do that he might be worried about the safety of a certain single mom and her son.

Weston eyed the booster seat. "I see someone's been busy. Where'd you get that?"

Travis shrugged. "Drove into Manhattan. I picked up several for the station. Probably something we should have on hand for emergencies."

Weston quirked a smile. "Probably. But I was talking about *that*." He tilted his chin at the Transformer tucked under his thumb.

Why was Weston staring at him like he had grown an extra head? "What? Kid needs a toy and I sure as hell wasn't going to get him a teddy bear." He was off his game this morning. Unsettled. Distracted. He wasn't even like this before a mission. Sure, he might feel the adrenaline thrumming in his fingers and toes, but it only heightened his awareness. Made him more focused. This morning, the thrumming came from an entirely different place and he needed to shut it down fast.

Travis tossed the keys to the beat-up '76 Chevy truck that he still thought of as his dad's over to Weston. "Trade me."

Weston easily caught the keys and jammed them in his pocket, chuckling and shaking his head. "No way, man. I'm coming along for the ride."

What? He couldn't say why that irritated the shit out of him. He'd fallen asleep last night mulling over all the potential topics of conversation with Elaine. But if Weston was along, judging every word he uttered, he was screwed. He'd fuck it up like he had the day before. "I don't need a chaperone."

"I didn't think this was a date."

The fucker was already laughing at him. "It's not."

"Then what's the big problem?"

Three's a crowd. But he couldn't say that, even though every cell in his body shouted it. Because he wasn't interested in Elaine. Couldn't be interested in a lady like her. He opened his mouth to explain, but then snapped it shut. It wasn't worth the ribbing he'd have to endure.

Weston placed his hands on his hips and dropped his head back, laughing. "You got it bad, man. Just admit it."

"Fuck you."

"I love you too, champ."

"I know why you're doing this."

"Yeah?"

"Once a swim buddy always a swim buddy."

Weston huffed out a laugh. "Maybe something like that."

There was a reason Weston was the first person Travis had called when he'd become police chief. Weston had been there for him in some of his lowest moments during BUD/S training. And a bond forged in the cold, sleep-deprived waters off of Coronado was never broken. "Come on, then."

As they pulled into the FEMA park, the knot in Travis's stomach tightened. There were too many people in town post-tornado to keep track of. Between builders, inspectors, and demolition crews, he no longer recognized every face. It was hard to know who was a part of the recovery effort and who was just passing through town. It set him on edge. He pointed Weston to Elaine's trailer.

Weston slid him a knowing glance.

Travis squirmed in his seat, drumming his fingers on the console. Why wouldn't he know where Elaine lived? He also knew that the Waldrons lived three houses down with their son, Davie, who was the same age as Dax. So what?

Weston pulled the truck to a stop and set the brake, turning to him. "I'll wait here. And be cool, man. Remember to tell her she looks nice."

"It's not a date," Travis grumbled as he hopped out of the

truck. As he approached the door, he pulled up short, stomach lurching. The door stood ajar six inches. Shit. Had someone broken in? Were they safe? What if the intruder was armed? His brain flew through half a dozen ugly scenarios and he turned back to Weston, giving him the silent signal to circle around.

Weston's eyes grew wide with concern. Travis signaled again, going into full-on stealth mode. Weston slipped out of the truck, and ducked around the far side of the trailer, shaking his head as he went. Silently, he approached the door, scanning left and right, cocking his ear for any sounds of trouble. His fingers itched to pull his weapon, but in a small space it was too dangerous. He'd have to rely on his hand-to-hand skills if Elaine was in trouble. He could use the Transformer he clutched as a projectile if necessary. Blood pounding in his ears, he gave the door a little push, breathing a silent prayer of thanks that the door didn't squeak as it fell open wider. Slowly, he stepped in, quickly scanning the empty room for signs of danger. Nothing. A tiny space with a short hall to the left past the tiny kitchen. In front of him a small table and chairs. To his right, a couch and a folding door. Where were they?

He pivoted toward the noise he heard on his left, the tight knot between his shoulders unspooling when he saw Dax standing at the edge of the short hall. "Why was the door open?" he growled.

"Why wouldn't it be?" Elaine asked, her normally soft voice sharp with surprise.

The sight of her freshly showered, with still damp hair, turned something liquid inside him. So fresh. So sweet. So kissable.

He recognized her jeans and black Converse. Her shirt

was simple – a white cotton pullover with a wide scoop neck revealing her collarbone and a splash of freckles. It was cut closer than her Dottie's tee-shirts, skimming her ribs and stopping just above the curve of her hip. He liked it much better than her work uniform.

And he'd never seen her hair down before. It was always pulled back into a ponytail at Dottie's. It was wavy and hung just below her shoulders. His palm itched. What would her hair feel like sliding across it? Silky and fine like gossamer? Thick and heavy like satin rope? He shut down the stirring low in his belly the only way he knew how. "Someone could walk in off the streets," he growled again, voice rough, but not from impatience.

She rolled her eyes and stepped around him. "I know pretty much everyone in the park. Who's it gonna be? Waldrons? Bateses? Oh, let me guess. Angelina Sanchez who's *seventy-six?* Besides." She waved a hand around the tiny space. "It's not like I have anything worth taking."

Travis scanned the small room again. Not even a TV. Damn. He'd gone Captain Caveman, and it had been completely unnecessary. Maybe he did need a chaperone. He crossed his arms over his chest. "Still. You should always keep the door locked."

Elaine made a face as she grabbed a glass from the cupboard, filling it with water and handing it to Dax. "So someone can kick in the door and take… oh, I don't know… my coffee maker? Puhleeze."

"What's that?" Dax asked, pointing to the Transformer still encased in his hand.

Shit. What an ass. He squatted low so he was eye level with the little boy. "You excited for today?"

Dax looked uncertain.

Travis held out the Transformer. "I thought this might help. So you can have a friend with you if you get scared."

Dax took it, his eyes brightening. "Mommy says horses aren't scary."

"They're friendly. I think you'll like them."

"Dax," Elaine cut in. "What do you tell Officer Kincaid?"

Travis shook his head, an ache forming in his throat at the formality of it. "Just Travis, okay?"

Dax nodded, his eyes in big circles as a smile brightened his face. "Thanks." He drained his glass and held it out for Elaine, who took it and placed it in the sink.

"All right, kiddo. Outside." Elaine smiled indulgently and ruffled her son's hair.

The ache in Travis's throat grew. There was pure love on her face, and it lit her up, smoothing out the worry lines that were too many on a face so young. His stomach flip-flopped at the sight of it. Elaine gave him a funny look as she stepped around him and paused in the threshold. "Are you coming?"

He stood. "Are you going to lock the door?"

She made a scoffing noise and, shaking her head, disappeared down the steps. He followed, quickening his pace to catch up with her. "You should lock the door."

"Don't want to."

He dragged his eyes away from her full lower lip, which now jutted out as she scowled at him. So. Cute. He fisted his hand to keep from reaching a thumb out to touch it. "It keeps you safe. And bad people out."

"Or good people locked in. No thank you."

Weston interrupted their standoff. "Are you two going to stand there arguing, or are we going to go ride horses?"

CHAPTER 4

S HE WASN'T USED to being bossed. She'd been on her own for too long to take orders from anyone except herself. And she damned well wasn't going to lock her door. No way, no how. She'd never let herself become trapped in a small space again. Not if she could help it. He was lucky he was so damned handsome.

Travis looked even better out of uniform than she remembered. Her heart had taken up residence in her throat when she'd come out of her bedroom to see him towering in the entryway, looking delicious in worn denims and a soft plaid shirt with the sleeves rolled up. She hadn't realized until that instant that it was possible to go wet from staring at someone's forearms.

Then he'd had to go and give Dax a Transformer. One that he'd been begging her to buy for weeks. And the way Travis always got down on eye level when he spoke to Dax? Melted her. She wasn't sure she had insides anymore. They'd turned to goo. Not to mention, he was standing so close she could smell his aftershave. A piney, masculine scent that did a second number on her panties.

This isn't a date. This isn't about you.

With a resigned huff, she turned and held her hand out to Dax. "You ready to be a cowboy today?" Her heart twisted at the fear shining back at her. He'd never been afraid of anything before the tornado. He'd been one-hundred percent rambunctious and too curious for his own good. She knelt down and pulled him into a hug. "It's okay, sweetie. No one's going to get hurt. I promise. And Travis and Weston are here, right?" Dax nodded, flicking a glance at the men behind her. "Would Travis let you get hurt?" Her throat tightened that she had to say it, that she could no longer reassure her son on her own that he would be safe. Guilt stabbed at her. She never should've given him the money to go to the Five 'n Dime that afternoon. But he'd done it a thousand times. And he felt like one of the big boys, going half a block down the street on his own. "And I'll be there too, sweetheart. Mama's not going anywhere. Will you try?"

"Can I ride with him?" He shook the Transformer clutched in his hand.

"Gotta use both hands for the reins," Travis answered. "But I can keep him in my pocket for you."

That was enough for Dax. He nodded and moved to the truck. Travis followed him around to the passenger side. "Do you know how to buckle him in?" Elaine called as she hurried to catch up.

Travis shot her a look of exasperation, but his eyes were filled with a gentle humor. "Learned that the first week of police academy."

"Just checking." She placed a foot on the running board.

Travis's hand wrapped around her elbow. A zing of electricity went straight to her belly. "More room up front."

"Even with three of us?"

Weston opened the driver's door. "Might as well call this truck a Cadillac."

But that would mean… at least fifteen minutes of being pressed up against Travis. Her body hummed with glee. "Oh I don't mind sitting back with Dax. Really. It's no problem."

Travis didn't answer. He pushed the seat back and climbed in the middle, and turned, extending his hand. "More room for you on the outside." He beckoned, giving her a slow smile. "C'mon. I promise I won't bite."

Too bad. A shiver ran down her spine at the thought of a few places she wouldn't mind being bitten. Or at least licked. She took his hand and allowed him to help her up into the cab. Their fingers brushed again as she reached to buckle herself. She glanced at him through her lashes. This had to be uncomfortable for him sitting in the middle.

He stretched his hand across the back of her seat and craned his head to look at Dax. "You okay back there, buddy?"

Dax gave him a thumbs up and a smile. Travis turned back to face front as Weston pulled the truck around the u-shaped street, but he didn't remove his hand. Every cell in her body longed to burrow into his strong embrace, to tuck herself next to him and lose herself in his masculine scent. But she couldn't do that. Not in front of Dax and not with him. She squeezed her knees together, putting an inch of distance between their legs. If she didn't, she'd rub up against him like a cat in heat.

As if sensing her discomfort, Travis slid a look at her, the barest hint of a smile tugging at the corner of his mouth. Then he turned back to Dax. "I can't wait for you to learn how to ride a horse today. I was about your age when I learned to ride on my own. Although my dad took me out on his lap all the time."

"I don't have a dad," Dax answered matter-of-factly.

A stone dropped through Elaine's stomach as she braced for the inevitable questions. Leave it to her son to throw the awkward wrench into the conversation. Although relief still coursed through her that Dax's father was out of the picture for good. She shuddered to think what it would be like for her son now if the man were still alive.

Travis shot her a questioning glance, as if to say, what do I do now?

"That's okay," Weston offered from the driver's seat. "Travis doesn't have a dad anymore either."

Elaine gave a shaky laugh, relieved that Weston had saved her from a complicated and uncomfortable explanation. "That makes three of us."

"We're the same," came the small voice from the back seat.

"Yeah, sweetie. We are."

By the time they pulled to a stop in front of the Hansens' farmhouse, Elaine ached from holding her body so still. She grabbed the door and hopped out as soon as Weston cut the engine, shaking the excess energy from her hands as soon as her feet touched the ground. Travis unfolded himself, and before she could protest, had reached in to pull Dax out of the back seat. Taking the boy's hand, Travis led Dax down to where the horses waited in the corral.

Weston flashed her a quick grin and followed.

It was sweet, the way the men had taken an interest in Dax. And good for Dax. He needed positive role models in his life. Lord knows, she could have benefitted from one. Anyone. She ambled after the men to where Hope was waiting for them by the fence. Travis had Dax in his arms, holding him up so he could touch the horse's nose. The smile on Dax's face said it all. Warmth flooded her, and she blinked rapidly. She'd give anything to see the old Dax again.

Travis put down Dax, and Hope bent with an extended

hand. "I see you already met Lucy. Would you like to ride her?"

Dax slipped his hand into Travis's and leaned into him. In answer, Travis wrapped his arm protectively around Dax.

"Mommy's right behind you," she called out. She was the parent here. It wasn't Travis's job to provide that kind of support. She started forward, but Weston put a restraining arm in front of her.

"He's going to be just fine. Travis grew up on horseback."

"But–"

Weston silenced her with a shake of his head. "This is good for Travis, too."

Just before they entered the ring, Travis bent over and said something to Dax. Dax looked back and gave her two thumbs up, while Travis tucked the Transformer into his shirt pocket. It was ridiculous how sexy he looked with that thing sticking out of his chest pocket.

But as she and Weston moved to the fence, her palms got sweaty. Lucy was a *big* horse. And Dax was so small. Her breathing grew quick and shallow. Seeing Dax next to Travis, next to the tall fence, and in front of a horse nearly twice his size only reminded her how lucky he'd been to come out of the tornado alive. She clutched the railing to stop her hands from shaking.

Hope looked over their direction and hurried over. Was it that obvious she was terrified? Hope flashed her an easy smile. "You have nothing to worry about. Lucy is one of our gentlest mares. She's been through this process hundreds of times. I'm going to be taking them through some exercises with Lucy that will facilitate bonding for both of them."

Elaine nodded, her voice lost somewhere in the back of her throat. Hope reached out, giving her arm a squeeze through the bars. "I can only imagine how you're feeling. I want to assure you, working with horses can help him. There's a true connection between horses and humans. They can sense our innermost thoughts, help us bring them to the surface. They accept us just as we are. And there's no feeling in the world like when a horse joins up with you."

"It's true," Weston chimed in. "I spent time with an organization in Montana working with horses. Changed my life. They'll be okay. Better than okay."

Elaine stood at the rails for the better part of an hour, transfixed, while Hope showed Dax how to hold a lead line, and with Travis's help took him through the steps necessary for the horse to follow him. She swore Dax grew two inches taller when he realized the horse was following him around the pen.

"Good job, Dax," Travis called out quietly.

Her chest hitched at the smile Dax returned to Travis.

"Okay, Dax. I'm gonna saddle up Lucy now. Would you like to ride her?"

The fear returned to his eyes, and he shook his head. Elaine sighed heavily. Two steps forward, three steps back.

"He'll get there," Weston said, keeping his eyes on the pair in the ring. "It's not gonna happen overnight."

Across the ring, Travis got low and spoke to Dax, who then nodded and stepped back. Travis clicked at Lucy, and the horse followed him to the center of the arena. In a fluid motion, Travis mounted up. Weston was right, Travis was a natural on horseback. Holding the reins in one hand, he looked like the quintessential cowboy – worn hat, faded boots, worn denim that clung to his muscled thighs. Elaine didn't realize she'd sighed until Weston shot her a funny look. She quickly schooled her features and ignored the goosebumps cascading down her chest.

Travis wheeled Lucy around and stopped in front of Hope and Dax. With Hope's help, he pulled Dax up in front of him and settled him in the saddle. Elaine's breath caught. Not for the first time, she wished she had a camera to capture the moment. Travis relaxed and smiling, with one arm slung across a beaming Dax's middle.

"Perfect photo-op for a future county sheriff," Weston called out.

Travis's jaw set and he shook his head once.

Weston whipped out his phone and snapped a picture. "Don't worry, I'll only use the picture if you give your permission."

"For what?"

"A warm and fuzzy mailer when Travis runs for sheriff."

"Oh." Her blood ran cold. "He's running for county sheriff?" she repeated when she found her voice again.

"He will. Mark my words."

And he'd win, too. Because Travis was great at everything. She should know better than to dream. But seeing Travis with Dax had, for a brief moment, made her imagine what it would be like to be part of a family. What it would be like to have a father figure. Regret stuck in her throat. A sour reminder that other people belonged in nice families, not her.

Hope held Lucy's halter while Travis dismounted and left the pen, and then she started leading Lucy in a circle while Dax held onto the saddle. Travis joined Elaine at the rail. "He's a good kid."

She nodded, her tongue too thick to speak. Swallowing hard, she dug deep. She and Dax were a family, and that's what mattered. "Yeah. The best."

After they'd circled the arena a dozen times, Hope helped Dax dismount. Elaine swept him up in a hug when he came around to where they stood waiting. "I'm so *proud* of you.

You were so brave in there. Did you have fun?"

He nodded. "Hope said I could go up to the house and get some cookies?"

"You bet. Did you say thanks?"

He rolled his eyes. "Not yet, I didn't eat them."

Elaine covered a laugh. It was nice to see a little of his sass back. Dax hustled up the hill, a hint of a bounce in his step. Maybe someday soon the full bounce would return. Kids his age still bounced when they walked, and the knot of worry for her son wouldn't unravel until she saw him bouncing again.

Hope joined them at the rail. "I hope you'll let him come again, Elaine. I think we can make good progress with him. And you two," she eyed the men. "Why not help me train the next round of mustangs I'm bringing up from the BLM auction next weekend?"

"I'm out." Weston clapped Travis on the shoulder. "I'll be covering for the candidate, but Travis is in, so long as we can use some photos for his campaign."

"Would you stop saying I'm running?" Travis ground out. "I only said I'd think about it."

"Marion County loves a rancher, and what better image to convey that the next county sheriff is a man of the people? Lawson ain't that."

"Except that it's wrong. I haven't ranched since before I went into the Navy."

Weston rolled his eyes. "You've got the heart of a rancher. That's what matters."

"But it's about law enforcement. Not ranching."

"Everyone knows that Travis Kincaid is a rule-keeper through and through. Not. Worried."

A weight pressed on Elaine's chest. She'd broken more rules than she cared to count.

CHAPTER 5

A T ELEVEN ON the nose, Travis pushed back from his desk at the station. "I'm going for coffee," he said as he passed Jeanine, his right-hand assistant and dispatcher.

"I'll catch up," called Weston from his spot where he stood holding up the wall while flirting with Jeanine. Good luck with that. She was a tough nut to crack. She'd been at the station longer than he had, and he'd seen countless guys vie for her attention over the years. It was downright entertaining the way she could reduce even the toughest cops to a puddle with a witty insult.

Travis pushed out the door and into the humid mid-day sun. He'd sweat through his uniform on the walk over. But it could be worse. He could be on a jungle floor in Kevlar in Colombia. No thanks. He kept fresh shirts at the station for just this purpose. Donning his aviators, he started across the street. The three-block walk took no more than five minutes, and he scanned the area for Elaine as soon as the picnic tables came into view.

What shirt would she be wearing today? He stopped at the corner of the food truck as soon as he spotted her. Pink. She bent to pick up trash from a table, and he ignored the rush of blood that bypassed his brain and dove straight to his balls. But what struck him today and didn't sit well with him was the way she pulled on her shoulder after she dumped the garbage in the barrel. It hit him with the force of a charging bull. Fuck him for never noticing before. She was exhausted. He could see it now. Plain as day. The pinch at her shoulder blades, the slump of her shoulders when she thought no one was looking. He pushed off the corner and moved to intercept her. "Here," he said gruffly as she turned his direction, her hands full of paper plates and cups, the top one filled with plastic silverware and napkins. "Let me." He took them from her and made the trip to the barrel. "Why doesn't Dottie make a big sign telling everyone to pick up their trash?"

"Because then I'd be out of a job," Elaine answered quietly.

Come to think of it, why *had* Dottie kept Elaine on? Elaine was right. There was nothing for her to do here but pick up trash and pour coffee refills. And when push came to shove, people could do that themselves too.

"But thanks for your help." She smiled shyly at him, pink staining her cheeks the same color as her shirt. "I'll grab your coffee." Air stuck in his lungs. The pink shirt was his new favorite color.

He should move to a table. Have a seat. But instead, he stayed planted in the middle of the picnic area, tracking Elaine as she wove through the tables to the coffee maker, and then carefully made her way back. He'd almost hugged her the other day, when they'd dropped her off. But in the end, he'd forced himself to take a step back even though every cell in his body yelled at him to move forward. The urge came over him again. Pull her flush, so he could feel her softness molding against him. Instead, he held himself still, bracing for the zing of contact when she handed him his cup.

Her eyes flew to his when they touched, and she froze as he wrapped his hands around hers. Chickory. Her eyes were as blue as the wild chickory that grew in the ditches alongside the highway. He zeroed in on her mouth, noticing for the first time tiny lines of tension, as if she worried too much when she was alone. Could he kiss that tension away? Suck on that sweet lower lip until she cried out from the madness of it all? And the corded muscle at her neck… would that soften after an orgasm or four? God, he was half hard at the thought.

No. No. No.

Too young. Single Parent. Keeps the doors unlocked. The laundry list torpedoed through his head. Reluctantly he released her, taking the cup. He was doing the right thing by staying away, but why did it leave him so deflated and generally pissed off?

"Tell me again why you're making a third career out of being a stalker instead of asking the girl out?" Weston asked after Elaine had moved away.

He'd been so focused on Elaine's mouth, he hadn't even noticed Weston approaching. So much for being alert to danger. Elaine had his senses befuddled and turned upside down. Travis took a gulp of the scalding coffee, the burn jolting his mind away from his cock. Too much more of this, and his taste buds would be gone.

Weston crossed his arms, looking pissed. "Well? I'm waiting."

"You really want me to say? Out loud?"

"Yes," he snapped. "I want you to hear with your own ears how stupid your reasons are. Go on."

Weston could push all he wanted on this one. He wasn't giving in. "Fine. For starters, she's a resident. She's too young. She refuses to lock her doors."

Weston glared at him and scoffed. "This has nothing to do with Elaine and everything to do with shit you still can't let go of. When you gonna stop carrying those guys around with you like a ball and chain?"

He grimaced at the analogy. He'd carry his fallen friends as long as he needed. "It was my fault. I was lead."

"Bullshit," Weston spat. "We all thought that kid was safe. You just happened to be the one who voiced it."

"Because I was lead," he gritted. "And I gave the order to let him go, and we lost half the team because of it." And what made him sick, what he couldn't reconcile in the punishing quiet of a lonely dark night, was that the scared look in the young boy's eyes was the same damned look he'd seen in Colton's eyes the night he'd kicked his brother off the ranch. He'd been a heartless bastard that night, and in some fucked up way the Universe had of evening the score, he'd taken a look at that scared kid halfway around the world, and thought of his brother. His guilt had killed his teammates. Fuck. That.

Weston's voice softened. "Can't you see how this is eating you up? Stopping you from living in the here and now? It's time to shake things up. Run for sheriff."

"Who's running for sheriff?" Dottie asked as she held out the coffee pot.

Travis clenched his jaw. Jesus, that woman had the hearing of an owl at midnight.

Weston pushed his shoulder. "Travis is."

Dottie looked him over, a critical light in her eye. "Lord knows you'd be a sight better than that Lawson."

That got his attention. Why would Dottie have an opinion about Lawson? Furthermore, why was it bad? You had to be a real chump to get on Dottie's bad side. Then again, the diner had been like a newsstand. Maybe Dottie had heard something. It was why he made a point of coming in around lunchtime every day and sitting at the counter. All he had to do was sip his coffee and listen to the chatter. It had nothing to do with the pretty young woman in the pink shirt and the jeans that perfectly framed her curves currently scrubbing the picnic table.

"You'll need a treasurer to file, and there's your lady," Dottie tilted her chin in Elaine's direction. "I've never seen a girl as good with numbers as she is."

Travis's head snapped up and he looked over to Weston. He looked like the Goddamned Cheshire Cat. "I suppose you knew this too?"

Weston shrugged, grinning shamelessly. "I suspected. Haven't you seen her add a bill and calculate tax in her head? Perfect every time. And she can do it faster than I can with a calculator." He shook his head and tsked. "For someone who can calculate bullet speed and wind drift and hit a target dead on from 200 yards, you're remarkably clueless. Oh, wait…"

Weston was going in for the kill. He could feel it.

"Maybe it's because you were too focused on the sway of her hips to notice anything like her math skills."

And bullseye. Dottie swung the weight of her gaze toward him, eyes narrowed. "I always suspected, but I couldn't say for sure. You make her your treasurer, Travis. Lord knows I can't pay her much of anything right now, and her second job disappeared when the library got destroyed. But–" She wagged a finger at him "You be good to her. That girl has had enough trouble thrown at her for three lifetimes. I don't want to hear you've behaved badly."

There were few things as uncomfortable in life as being scolded by Dottie. "I will be a perfect gentleman." Even if it killed him. "But what does a campaign treasurer do?"

"In a small race like this, keep track of your expenditures and receipts," Weston answered. "Help you budget. They can help with fundraising."

"Fundraising." What in the hell was he getting himself into?

"You're going to have to raise money. Ask for donations."

"Oh hell no. Not while we're recovering. I'll pay for it myself. *If* I do it."

"I can look into the campaign finance laws here, but you can probably do that too, although campaigns can get pretty expensive."

"How much are we talking?"

"Forty, maybe fifty grand for a county race."

Travis's stomach pitched. "You're kidding."

Weston shook his head. "Welcome to politics."

He had a nest egg that would more than cover the expense. But he'd always imagined using it to refurbish the ranch and get it running again once he retired from the police force. He'd do it now, but you couldn't be a ranch of one. So he'd continued setting something aside each month for someday. But what if someday never came? Should he pull some of it now? Challenge this Lawson character? Lawson's name sounded familiar, but he couldn't place it.

Dottie and Weston waited expectantly. Was he supposed to tell them now? No way. He wasn't doing that. But he wasn't comfortable saying flat out no either. "I'm not saying yes, but I'll think about it."

Dottie clapped her hands. "Good. I want to see Steve Lawson get what's coming to him."

Weston gave him a look that spoke volumes. He was so screwed.

CHAPTER 6

TRAVIS STOOD AT the top of Main Street where Dottie's Diner belonged, scanning for possible trouble spots. Normally the view from Dottie's down Main Street brought a smile to his face. You couldn't get more America & Apple Pie than Prairie on the Fourth of July. In past years, Main was decked out in red, white, and blue bunting, with flower baskets hanging from the light posts. This year, the contrast couldn't be more stark. No bunting. Not even light posts. Only a road bordered with cleared lots waiting to rebuild. But the city council had been adamant the parade go on as usual. So demolition teams had worked double shifts alongside residents to remove the last of the rubble. Prairie might be down, but she certainly wasn't out, and the upside of their work was that construction would be ready to begin July 5th.

He reached for one of Dottie's famous biscuits piled high on the hospitality table and coated it liberally with strawberry jam before popping it into his mouth. A quick glance at his watch confirmed that parade participants would start arriving any minute. The mayor's office projected double the usual crowd this year. But double the people meant a headache for logistics and crowd control. He hated doing it on a holiday, but he'd called the whole squad to work double shifts today.

Thanks to the storm, people were curious about Prairie's recovery. He couldn't blame them. Seeing the town pull together had been nothing short of miraculous. In past years, they'd struggled to find volunteers to help place baskets of small American flags along the parade route. This year, they'd come out of the woodwork and were finished by the time the sun peeked over the hills.

Gunnar Hansen pulled into the lot towing a horse trailer and rolled to a stop, elbow hanging out the window and shaking his head. "Still can't get used to it."

"Me either. Although I like this view better than the one right after the tornado."

Gunnar grimaced, grief momentarily flickering across his face. "Me too. Me too. And we'll like it even better next year."

"We will. Now let's get those horses unloaded. I appreciate you letting us use them this morning."

Gunnar flashed him a smile. "Happy to help Prairie's finest keep up their image."

They walked around back, unloaded the horses and led them to a makeshift corral they'd erected where the building next door to Dottie's had once stood. Gunnar tossed a saddle blanket over the horse closest. "This is Buzz, and the horse you're saddling is Ricky. They're our largest animals. Ricky is a bit more lively than Buzz, so I'd recommend him for you."

"You don't think I can handle a feisty horse?" Weston asked, joining them.

"You're a pretty good rider for a city boy," Travis acknowledged.

"Thank Horses Helping Heroes."

"I'm gonna move the trailer outta the way. See you day after tomorrow when Hope gets back?"

"Not me." Weston shook his head. "Boss-man put me on shift so he could go play cowboy."

"Perks of being the boss." Travis grinned.

"Catch you then." Gunnar hopped into the cab and pulled out onto Main.

Travis checked his watch again. "Time to get this show on the road. Traffic cones set up?"

Weston nodded. "Volunteers are directing traffic, and I've got three guys on the outskirts."

"Good. See you back here for the start?"

Weston gave him a mock salute and turned. Travis headed down the street, scanning for potential threats. There never was one, but he couldn't help it. He was always on high alert when the crowds were big. People had begun to line the streets with lawn chairs and picnic blankets. Music blared from a speaker system by the 'grandstand' – basically a set of choir risers someone had pulled from one of the local churches with a few folding tables covered in bunting and a PA system. As usual, the Mayor, Wilson Watson, would be acting as emcee.

When he finished checking the parade route, he circled back to the staging area via the food truck. But not to check on Elaine or scan the playground for Dax. He was just making sure everything was under control. He immediately spotted Elaine looking harried. The truck was crowded with out of towners. The picnic benches were full up, with many eating while standing. Elaine was flipping them as fast as she could. He checked his watch. Twenty minutes before he and Weston had to mount up. He made a beeline for her through the crowd, tapping her shoulder and bracing himself for the zing of electricity. "How can I help?"

Her eyes brightened, and his throat squeezed tight. "You sure it won't tarnish your image?"

"Makes me more approachable." It was true. People were naturally afraid of the uniform, so doing things like helping bus tables, petting dogs, or stopping by the playground went a long way to build relationships in the community.

"Great. Can you change the trash barrels? They're overflowing."

"On it." He made his way to the trash cans, stopping behind the food truck first to pull fresh bags out of a locker that had been salvaged from the part of the school damaged by the tornado, and which now acted as a utility closet for the food truck.

Armed with rubber gloves and fresh bags, he mashed the trash into the can, knotted the bag and replaced it with a new one. Grabbing all four bags, he crossed to the dumpster and tossed them in, followed by the rubber gloves. Making a mental note to ask the rest of the squad to check on the cans throughout the morning, he skirted the throng, catching Elaine's eye and waving. *Thank you*, she mouthed, bestowing another smile on him that warmed him more than Dottie's coffee on a cold day. Surely Dottie would close down the truck for the parade? He'd hate for Elaine and Dax to miss it.

Just as he arrived at the staging area, a commotion sprang up on the far side of the lot. Weaving through clowns, 4-H-ers, trick riders, and a marching band from one of the big high schools in Kansas City, he discovered the source of the problem. A large man in a navy suit and white straw cowboy hat stood arguing with a tiny woman in a traditional Mexican gaucho costume.

"What's the problem?"

The woman, Luci Cruz, turned to him, eyes flashing. "This man's car is spooking my horses."

The man also turned to him with a smile that didn't reach his eyes. "I was just explaining to the little lady that she needs to move her horses."

Travis bit back a chuckle. Little lady, huh? Nobody called Luci Cruz little lady.

"*Este cabrón que finge ser un vaquero dice que estamos robando su sombra. Pero, mira! Él está en el lugar equivocado.*" She waved her parade number at him.

"*Tranquila, hermanita,*" he answered, grateful for the cover of a second language. The guy looked familiar, but Travis couldn't place him. Whoever he was, he had the false air of a used car salesman. "*Me ocuparé de este imbécil.*"

Lucy crossed her arms, scowling. "*Simplemente no quiere caminar detrás de la mierda de caballo.*"

A rough laugh escaped Travis before he could stop it. Probably. Wouldn't want to mess up his too shiny boots. He turned to the man and extended his hand. "Can I see your parade number?"

The smile left the man's face for a fraction of a second. "No need for that. The little lady just needs to move her horses over with the others."

This triggered another round of Spanish from Luci, which only increased the man's scowl. If this guy was going to be an asshole, he could be a bigger one. "Luci is in the right place. Your paper please." His voice came out clipped.

"Lee, find that damned piece of paper." The man shouted angrily at the driver of the shiny red convertible, decked out with American flags and spinning silver pinwheels. God, the thing was as gaudy and fake as he was. Who was this guy? He dressed like he was from Texas, not Kansas. Or going to a wedding. But everyone in these parts wore their best black Stetsons to a wedding. Travis dropped his gaze to the car door. STEVE LAWSON for COUNTY SHERIFF, it read in bold letters. No wonder the guy was trying to hang onto his temper. You couldn't be an asshole in public if you were running for office. And all of a sudden, the loose end that had been flitting around his head slipped into place. He *had* met Lawson once before. Well, seen him. And he hadn't liked him then either. The guy had given a speech at a Police Union conference in Topeka a few years back. He'd come across then as a know-it-all blowhard with a mean streak, and from the looks of it, he hadn't evolved.

Travis stepped up to the driver, who reluctantly handed over the paper. Biting his cheek so he didn't grin, he turned to Lawson. "Turns out you belong in the lot across the street." Travis waved to an empty lot on the other side of Second Street, which ran parallel to Main.

The smarmy smile was back. "Surely, Travis." The man's eyes drifted to his name tag. "You can let us stay here a bit longer? I'd be mighty grateful."

So this guy was pouring on the charm because of the badge? And he was treating Luci Cruz like dirt? Travis's stomach churned. Fuck this asshole and the horse he rode in on. If he even knew how to ride a horse. Travis clenched his jaw, breathing in through his nose before he spoke as firmly as he could. "Sorry. That's not how we roll here. Wouldn't be fair to the rest of the participants. You'll have to vacate the spot." Travis gave him a tight smile.

Lawson's eyes flared angrily for a brief second, then the cool mask was back in place. "I understand."

Good.

Travis crossed his arms and stood his ground, pointedly watching the convertible back out of the shade and onto Second, before flipping a U-turn into the far lot and rolling into its proper spot behind the Future Farmers of America trailer and a half dozen kids on horseback.

Luci shot him a grateful smile. "Thanks, Travis. Saul here

thanks you too." She patted her sleek, black Arabian decked out in antique silver.

"Anytime, Luci. Tell your folks I said hi."

"You bet," she called out as he turned back across the lot to find Weston waiting with their borrowed horses.

"Let's get this show on the road."

Weston shot him an easy grin and handed him his black Stetson. He didn't wear it much anymore, but after his run-in with Lawson, he was glad they'd decided to ride the parade route on horseback this year, instead of in their vehicles with the lights on. He swung up onto Ricky. Weston handed up a big sack of candy before mounting Buzz. Together they wheeled the horses around and trotted through to the front of the line. They would lead off, followed by the VFW color guard and the marching band, which would stop at the grandstand to play the national anthem.

They started slowly down the street to the cheers and claps of the townspeople, throwing candy as they went. "Hey Kincaid," a voice called from the side. "You gonna run for sheriff?"

"Yes," Weston hollered at the same time he said, "We'll see." Their mixed response drew laughter and applause.

"I met Lawson just now," Travis muttered under his breath. "Dottie was right, the guy's a total douchebag."

"So, run already."

Travis threw some candy to a group of little girls. "I was saving that money to restart the ranch someday."

"So ask for donations then. People would give you money in a heartbeat."

"No," he gritted through a plastered-on smile. "I can't ask them to support me when half these folks don't have jobs right now. Not. Happening."

41

"So you're saying you'd rather Lawson be your new boss?"

"Fuck you, asshole."

"Just callin' it like it is."

"Travis! Hey, Travis!"

Travis turned in the direction of Dax's voice, smiling for his favorite seven-year-old. Dax stood jumping up and down, his new Transformer clutched in his hand. Seeing the boy with a genuine smile on his face warmed him. "Hey there, buddy. Want some candy?"

Dax nodded eagerly, but it was the indulgent smile from the woman behind Dax that heated his belly. He tossed a handful of candy in Dax's direction as an idea popped into his head. If only Elaine would agree to it.

CHAPTER 7

BY THE TIME the parade and cleanup were over, and the participants had scattered, it was nearly lunchtime. Dottie's food truck was sure to be hopping. "Meet you back at the station?" Travis asked Weston. "I'll grab us lunch."

Weston arched a brow. "You're in uniform. Make sure that's all you grab."

"Fuck you, asshole." As if he'd ever grab Elaine's ass. Well, he would if they were dating, but only at home, and since they were never going to date, it was a moot point. He flipped a middle finger over his shoulder as Weston's laughter carried through the air behind him.

In spite of Weston's constant badgering, he had to admit he felt pretty good about today. He'd seen genuine hope on people's faces as he and Weston had ridden down the street. And he was damned glad he'd played a part in that. Prairie had been a nice small town before the tornado, but the blank canvas of rebuilding had triggered people's imaginations. There would be new shops and restaurants in a year. And a clinic. Prairie was poised to become a *great* town. A shining example of what happened to places when people pulled together.

His mood darkened the second he laid eyes on Elaine looking terrified and shrinking from a leering Steve Lawson. The only time he'd seen her look that scared was the afternoon of the tornado. He never wanted to see her looking like that again.

Seeing Lawson crowding her space unleashed something deep and dark inside him. His stomach hardened into a tight knot as his legs propelled him forward quickly and silently. His chest burned, sending adrenaline down to his fingertips, which made his palm itch like it did before he squeezed the trigger on a kill target.

It took everything inside him not to punch the guy's lights out. Instead, he ground his teeth together and forced his mouth into a smile. As soon as he reached Elaine, he placed a hand on the small of her back and pulled her close, positioning his body so he stood between her and Lawson. Then he bent and kissed the top of her head. She shivered and leaned into him.

In the course of half a second, his senses were flooded with the faint aroma of her floral shampoo, and awareness shot right to his dick. Okay, so maybe that wasn't the smartest thing to do, but he wanted to make sure Lawson got the message loud and clear that Elaine was off limits. Maybe it was testosterone, maybe it was adrenaline. Who knew? But he wasn't about to leave Elaine in the clutches of this asshole, and if it helped to kiss her head, he'd do it. But that didn't mean he'd ever let things go further between them. "Something I can help you with?" He zeroed his attention in on Lawson.

Lawson's facade slipped a fraction as his eyes went cold. Travis had to hand it to him. The guy was a pro. He wouldn't easily be provoked into doing or saying something stupid. The fake smile was back, as was the politician's voice. "I was just introducing myself to the lady. Good opportunity to meet the people of this great town. You probably saw this morning that I'm running for sheriff."

Travis's stomach churned at the way the lie slipped out of the man's mouth. He could stomach a lot of things, but lying wasn't one of them. "I know who you are," Travis answered, letting his voice get steely and focusing his gaze on the man. "I should have introduced myself this morning. I'm Travis Kincaid. Prairie's police chief, and your opponent."

Lawson's eyes widened slightly, just enough to give away his surprise. Although, of the three of them, Travis was arguably the most surprised at the bomb he'd just dropped. What did Dottie always say? In for a penny, in for a pound? His stomach felt just like it had the first time he'd jumped out of a plane at twenty-thousand. He was damn well gonna make sure he landed in one piece. He gave Elaine a reassuring squeeze. "And this is Elaine Ryder, my treasurer."

She squeaked and stiffened.

"Elaine, is it?" Menace flashed in Lawson's eyes, and then, just as quickly, disappeared.

Every cell in Travis's body went on alert. Lawson was trouble. He knew it. So much so, he'd double down on his last dollar at a poker table with the Sinclaire brothers.

Lawson took Elaine's hand, bowed slightly, and kissed the back. "A pleasure meeting you, *Elaine*."

Revulsion slithered through Travis, and he clenched his fist at his side, refraining from forcefully removing the man only because he'd gone and jumped into a political campaign without thinking about the consequences. Not his best moment.

Lawson turned to him, his eyes glittering points. "I'll see you on the campaign trail, Kincaid. Good luck." He spun on his heel and stalked off, not bothering to *meet the people*.

Elaine turned to him, eyes sparking in anger, cheeks pink. He should be thinking of how to fix this, but instead the air in his lungs turned to ash and he couldn't breathe, let alone think. He'd never seen Elaine this way, all riled up and intense. Awareness shot through him leaving a trail of fried synapses on the way to his cock. Holy smokes, did his cock like this side of her.

Elaine was the kind of woman who hated to be the center of attention. And for two years, she'd done an excellent job of blending in with the decor at Dottie's. If he had to guess, he bet half the folks who came into the diner didn't even know her name. Of course post-tornado, *everyone* knew who Elaine and Dax were, and he'd seen her discomfort at the attention. Seeing her outraged and not caring who saw, was a revelation.

"What do you think you're doing?"

He couldn't help smiling, even if it made her madder. She was so damned cute.

"Running for sheriff?"

She rolled her eyes and crossed her arms. "And apparently, I'm your treasurer," she answered, lower lip jutting out. "How about you explain that?"

Her tone was meant to intimidate. She was as puffed up as an angry prairie chicken, and the only effect it had was to heighten his desire. Tingles raced down his spine, and he could only focus on that sweet lower lip.

"Well?" She tapped her foot.

Pull yourself together, asshole.

"Dottie and Weston both mentioned you're a whiz with numbers, and I need a treasurer to file."

"Then find somebody else."

"But I want you."

Her eyes widened in surprise as his words sank in. Then went dark as her mouth opened enough for her tongue to slip out and wet the lower lip he couldn't stop staring at.

46

Shit.

As the silence spun out between them, the reasons why he was the world's biggest idiot came at him like bullets on a live fire range. What was he thinking? He should have thought this through. Anyone but Elaine. What happened to his rule about mixing business and pleasure? Relationships with townspeople? Fuck. His tongue had a mind of his own. Or maybe it was his cock. "I want you…" He swallowed, willing the words to form in his brain. "To be my treasurer."

Elaine rolled her lips together, shaking her head. "I don't have time."

It was for the best. At least one of them was thinking with the right brain. "Dottie can give you all the time you need. And I can pay you."

Great. There went more of his nest-egg.

"Oh?" A hungry look entered her eyes.

An ache hit Travis in the throat. Sure, they'd had it tough growing up. But they'd never gone hungry. He raked his eyes over her, stomach rumbling at the thought of going hungry. She looked healthy, and Dax did too. Likely thanks to Dottie – the woman was a saint.

"Yeah." He nodded. "It won't be much, but if you can be my treasurer and… er… help me with campaigning, I could pay you." How much did someone pay a person? He had no idea. "Two thousand dollars a month for the duration?"

"Two *thousand?*" Her voice pitched high at the end.

"Is that enough?" Shit. He raked his fingers through his hair. Getting her to say yes suddenly meant everything. "I know it's only for a few months, but I'll make sure it doesn't interfere with your work for Dottie." Especially if Dottie was feeding them. Elaine looked torn, and the air squeezed from his lungs. Surely she wouldn't turn him down?

Regret filled her eyes and she shook her head. "That's very generous of you... but no. I'm sorry."

"Three thousand." This was the dumbest thing he'd ever done. He should be relieved she turned him down. But the ache in his chest only grew.

She shook her head and giggled. A bubbly, sweet sound that went ricocheting through his body like sparks of electricity. Lighting him up. "It's not about the money."

Damn. Was it him? His stomach sank. "What is it?" He was almost afraid to ask. But he had to know.

A pained expression crossed her face. "I... it's just..." She sighed heavily, shoulders sagging. "I don't know anything about politics, except that I don't like politicians."

Oh, *that*. Relief washed over him. "That makes two of us. You're smart, and we can learn together." He reached for her hand, encasing it in his own, struck by how tiny it was. But his eyes were drawn upward by a faint pattern of light, feathery scars on the inside of her left forearm. His insides tilted. He'd seen marks like that before. But usually red and raw. What had happened in her life that she'd cut herself? He traced a finger over the pattern, a knot of nails poking at the base of his throat.

"Travis, I–" She tugged on her hand.

He should walk away right now. Ask Bob the accountant, or Anders from the Feed 'n Seed. Anyone but her. "Please, Elaine?" He reached for her hand again, unable to keep himself from touching her. "I want you... your help," he added lamely. Someone put an out of order sign on his brain. At least Weston wasn't here to laugh his ass off at him while he was making a fool of himself.

"I... let me think about it."

"Can you let me know at the fireworks tonight?"

"Tonight?" Her eyes grew wide. "But we're not going."

"Why not?" Everyone went to the fireworks. Why wouldn't she, especially with Dax? "Dax would love them."

A flush started at her neck and crept up, flaming her face, turning her eyes to embers. She yanked her hand back. "The fairgrounds are two miles outside of town on unsafe roads. How exactly am I to get there?"

Right. What an idiot. "I'm sorry. I wasn't thinking."

"Not a good trait for a man running for sheriff," she snapped, eyes still sparking.

He liked her inner firebrand, even as he scrambled to dig himself out of the idiot hole. Then it hit him. "I have to be at the fairgrounds at four. Meet me here and I can have Jeanine take you. Unless you don't mind riding in the police car."

She blew out a breath and scraped the dirt with a toe. She shook her head and pinched the bridge of her nose. But a little smile tilted up the corner of her mouth.

"Sure. Why not? I'm sure Dax will be delighted." She sounded more resigned than excited, but he'd take it. Warmth rushed through him. And triumph. God, he felt like he'd just scaled a mountain.

"Elaine?"

There was that small smile again. The one that made his heart beat irregularly. "Yes?" Her voice had gone husky.

"Thank you." Before he could stop himself, he traced a thumb down her jaw and paused. Her chin tilted ever so slightly up. Blood pounded in his ears. It would be so easy to bridge the distance, so easy to give into the desire pumping through him and take a tiny taste. Her eyelids fluttered.

Smothering a groan, he pulled himself back from the brink and dropped his hand, turning away before he did something really stupid like kiss her. "I'll see you at four," he tossed over his shoulder as he headed for the station.

Coward.

CHAPTER 8

THE AFTERNOON PASSED in a blur. For the first time since the tornado, Elaine was grateful she wasn't doing more than bussing tables and refilling drinks. She'd gone cold as ice when Steve Lawson's red convertible drove down the parade route, and she still hadn't recovered, even with the heat of the day. Her luck couldn't be worse. Steve Lawson was the worst kind of cop. Sneaky. Manipulative. And worst of all, vindictive. She'd been given a chance at a fresh start here, and he could bring it crashing down around her. Her stomach churned at the thought.

Thank God Dax had been at the playground when he'd come prowling around the food truck. He'd have recognized her for sure, even without pink hair. As it was, Travis had pretty much saved her, but given the pissing match she'd witnessed between the two men, Lawson would be back. Especially now that Travis had announced he was running for sheriff. Lawson never lost, and the look of menace in his eye had been more frightening than the sound of the tornado when she'd been huddled in the diner's storeroom.

She should turn down Travis's offer. Put as much distance between them as possible. Maybe it would keep him safe from Lawson. Although who was she fooling? That wouldn't stop Lawson from going after Travis. Travis had thrown down the gauntlet, and Lawson wouldn't stop until he'd won. And if

Lawson remembered her, it wouldn't matter how far away she went, he'd still figure out a way to make her life a living hell.

From that standpoint, maybe accepting Travis's offer was a good idea. Lawson only backed down because Travis had rescued her. Lawson might leave her alone if Travis was around all the time. A shiver rippled across Elaine's shoulders as she carried a pile of plates to the trash bins. She chewed on the corner of her lip as she wiped down a table. Two-thousand dollars a month. The air whooshed out of her lungs just thinking about it. Even if she only worked for him one month, she'd be able to exhale a little more easily. And after two? Maybe she could go to community college after she earned her GED. For the first time, she wouldn't have to rely on the principal's charity for Dax's school supplies. Maybe she could even buy a phone.

There was only one big problem with that fantasy.

Travis.

Her knees turned to rubber when he'd kissed her head. She'd almost fainted when he nearly kissed her mouth. She'd been so close to melting into him, overwhelmed by the scent of him. How could she work with him when the effect he had on her was so powerful? She'd make a math mistake. Or do something dumb, like throw herself at him. Her shoulders sagged as she moved to wipe down another table. No, she'd have to turn him down. It didn't matter that he said he'd wanted her. A jagged ball of regret formed in her stomach. She'd never be so lucky in life, or in love. People like her never got what they wanted anyway. She'd have to content herself with pouring Travis coffee every day.

"Is Travis here yet?" Dax came bounding up still clutching his Transformer.

"No, sweetie. He'll be here soon."

A moment later, Elaine felt a presence behind her. Without turning to look, she knew it was Travis. How did he do that? Sneak up so quietly? Wiping her hands on her jeans, she took a fortifying breath, bracing for the onslaught of attraction that would sizzle through her body when she turned.

"You ready?"

She started when his hand landed on the small of her back and sent sparks zinging up her spine. She turned, the greeting she'd prepared sticking in her throat when he smiled. His aviators were tucked in his pocket, and he was close enough she could see the gold flecks in his hazel eyes. Heat flickered in his eyes, and her nipples tightened and pebbled in response. She went still, unsure of what to do next.

"Travis!" Dax bounded up, and Travis stepped back, dropping his hand.

He turned his megawatt smile to her son. "I see you've brought your friend with you."

"His name is Travis."

A look of confusion, then surprise flashed across Travis's face.

Oh, God. She shut her eyes as heat crawled up her neck. "In case you weren't sure about your superhero status." She smiled faintly.

Travis chuckled, then squatted down, ruffling Dax's hair. "Hey, that's great. Maybe you should call him T, so I don't get mixed up."

"Okay." Dax shrugged, and flew his Transformer in front of him.

"How would you like to ride in the back of a police car?"

"Yeah!" Dax crowed. "I wanna ride where the bad guys go."

"Well, come on then." Travis stood and turned the weight

of his gaze back to her, making her insides swim. "All set?"

Her mouth had gone dry, so she nodded. "I'll let Dottie know I'm leaving," she mumbled, ducking her head. Heat flamed her face as she hurried around the corner of the truck to where Dottie was wiping down the counter inside the window.

"High time you got out of here, sweetie pie. Travis taking you two to the fireworks?"

How did she know? She should know better than to wonder. Dottie knew everything. "Yeah. I'll be back first thing in the morning."

Dottie leaned out the window. "One more thing, Elaine."

"Yes?"

"I recommended Travis hire you to help him run for sheriff. If he asks you, you take it. He'll make it worth your while."

If she only knew.

She'd never be able to turn down the job now. She'd never hear the end of it if she did. Dottie had no idea she had a crush on Travis. She'd simply have to put on her big girl panties and suck it up. "Thanks, Dottie. I appreciate it." Dottie only had her best interests at heart. She gave the older woman a smile and turned, unable to stop a grin from splitting her face at the picture of Travis and Dax in the throes of a thumb war. Did the man have to be so adorable with her son? It was unfair.

Travis flashed her a smile. "Let's go."

Oh yes, her panties sang. When he placed his hand at the small of her back again, thumb rubbing across her spine, a rush of heat flooded her, slicking what remained of the fabric between her legs.

Travis pulled a booster seat out of the trunk and placed it

in the back. "Hop on in, kiddo. I'll get you buckled."

Dax bounded into the car, barely keeping still while Travis pulled the seatbelt across him.

"Do you want me to sit in the back with you, sweetie?"

Travis slid a look her direction. "He'll be fine back here."

"What if he gets scared?"

His eyebrows furrowed. "It's only a few minutes. But we can stop." He placed a reassuring hand on her shoulder, giving her a squeeze. "He'll be fine."

Her hands grew clammy.

She couldn't sit up front with Travis. But the thought of sitting in the back of a police car again twisted her stomach in knots. She'd do it for Dax, though. "Dax?" He looked like he was having the time of his life in the back seat.

Travis's voice cut through her confusion. "I'm gonna have your mom sit up front with me. Is that okay, buddy?"

Dax shrugged. "Sure."

Great. Thrown under the bus by a seven-year-old. She slipped in the passenger door Travis held open for her, folding her hands close once she'd buckled herself in. She hadn't missed the question in Travis's eyes when she'd caught him staring at the scars on her arm earlier. Over the last two years, there were days she forgot they were there, a permanent and painful reminder of another life. A different Elaine. She made sure no one ever noticed them, but Travis never missed a detail, and she'd let her guard down, thrown off by Steve Lawson and Travis's offer.

"What about you, Elaine?"

"Mmm?"

"When was the last time you were at a midway?"

She swallowed, avoiding his intense gaze. *This isn't an interrogation.* Just conversation. She shrugged. "A long time. I don't remember." And she couldn't. She'd blocked out so much of the past, she had a hard time even remembering the good things.

"So it's like the first time for you, too."

"Sure." She liked that. A fresh start.

"Good thing I brought some of Mike McAllister's root beers with me. We can enjoy them while we walk the midway."

"I thought you had to work?"

"I do. But I have enough time before things get crazy, I'd like to show you around."

Her pulse took off to the races. How could she concentrate with Travis right next to her? One whiff of his spicy cologne and she was reduced to a quivering mass of jello. But the worst part would be when he saw her meager ticket supply.

She'd brought enough tip money to buy two rolls of tickets, even though it would mean ramen and tuna helper for the next week. She wanted Dax to have fun, even if they could only pick a few rides. He'd been so serious since the tornado, and he was obviously excited right now. She missed his little boy laugh and his boundless energy.

Travis reached the ticket booth first, angling his body so she couldn't step up with him. Elaine craned her neck trying to see, but he was too big. Her heart plummeted when he turned with a fistful of tickets and handed them to Dax. Dax's eyes went wide with excitement.

She laid a hand on his arm, ignoring the heat that raced up her arm. "Travis." She kept her voice low and firm. "I can't let you do this. There's no need."

"There absolutely is." His tone of voice brooked no argument. "First, if you're going to come to the fairgrounds, you need to do everything. At least twice. And," he shot her a slow, sexy grin. "It's part of my plan to persuade you to be my treasurer."

"By spoiling my son?"

"And you too." He stroked the back of a finger down her cheek. Tingles cascaded straight to her core.

She had to say no. Needed to say no. For both their sakes. But the longer she spent with him, the weaker her resolve became.

"Please, mom?"

She pinched the bridge of her nose. Dax looked so... hopeful. How could she say no to him when he looked at her with those big saucer eyes? She blew out a rough breath and nodded. "Fine. Just this once." She looked between the two and covered a laugh. Travis wore the same excited smile as Dax.

Dax slipped his hand into Travis's and dragged him in the direction of a target game. She could enjoy these few hours. For Dax. How could she deny the boy an evening of rides and too much sugar? He'd be talking about this for weeks.

"Mom, mom, mom," Dax called as she caught up with them. "Lookie! Travis won me a Minion."

She pressed her lips together to stop the grin from crawling across her face. "That didn't take long." Travis gave her a sheepish smile and a shrug as he handed her the big yellow creature. "I don't know who's more excited," she laughed, unable to hold back any longer. "You or Dax."

His eyes gleamed. "It might be a toss-up."

Her heart hiccupped. He didn't smile often. But when he did, it stopped her in her tracks.

Regret replaced the warmth in his eyes. "I have to take off, but meet me behind the scoreboard after the fireworks? You'll see the patrol cars." He squatted down in front of Dax, offering him a fist bump. "Thanks, buddy. I had fun. Now, make sure your mom has some fun?"

"Okey-dokey."

"I'll see you after the fireworks, 'kay?"

But Elaine wasn't sure Dax heard. He was already dragging her away. "Mom, did you see? They have pony rides!"

When she peeked back over her shoulder, her stomach fluttered. He was still watching them.

Hours later, she and Dax made their way through the exiting throng to behind the scoreboard, stuffed with carnival food and pleasantly exhausted. A quick scan of the area showed no Travis. No Weston either. Her pulse quickened. Maybe she should go. She didn't belong here.

"That you, Elaine?" Dottie's daughter, Cassidy, called from her perch next to Parker Hansen on the back of the ambulance. "Travis told me to keep an eye out for you. He and Weston are directing traffic. Pull up a chair."

Parker hopped off the back of the ambulance and pulled over a big folding chair. "You're lucky, it's been pretty slow tonight."

She settled into the deep pocket of the chair and pulled Dax onto her lap. He was almost getting too big for this, but he could barely stand. And tonight, she'd glimpsed more of the boy he was before the tornado. Soft and snuggly. Enthusiastic. Happy.

"I heard he did great the other day." Parker gestured to Dax.

Elaine warmed. It never ceased to surprise her how kind people were about Dax. One of the many things that made Prairie special. People seemed to really care about each other. "He had a great time." She stroked his head as he burrowed into her shoulder, still clutching the Minion.

"Anything we can do to help… we mean it."

She was starting to understand that their offers weren't simply platitudes, but came from a genuine desire to help Dax recover from the trauma of the tornado. She didn't deserve their kindness in the least, but she was grateful for it nonetheless. She dipped her head, letting Dax's hair sweep against her cheek and inhaling his little boy essence. He'd need a bath tomorrow, but right now she didn't care. Her baby was a happy boy. She shut her eyes, breathing in the quiet sweetness of the moment.

"Elaine. Time to go." Travis shook her awake. She came fully alert as he lifted Dax off her lap, suddenly cold in the warm night air. Gone were the crowd noises. All that remained were the sounds and muted conversations of clean-up. She followed Travis to the car and waited while he settled Dax in the back seat before opening the passenger door for her. An easy silence settled between them on the ride back to her trailer, and sleep pulled at her eyelids.

"Wait here," Travis ordered, once he'd pulled up to the trailer.

Before she could open her door, Travis hopped out and stalked up the short walkway mumbling something about 'unlocked doors' before disappearing into the trailer. As she opened the rear door, Travis stepped in to pull Dax from the back seat.

"You really don't have to,"

The look he gave her said otherwise. Without a word, he carried Dax into the trailer. By the time she crossed the threshold, he stood in what passed for a living room, engulfing the entire space. "Thank you for today," she murmured.

Travis stepped out of the shadows and into the pool of

light cast by the lamppost through the open door. Her heart pounded in her ears. Could he hear it? She couldn't hear anything else except the way her breath caught when she tilted her chin to look up at him. The hungry look in his eyes heated her blood, sending a shot of arousal to pool between her legs. She clenched her thighs to steady herself, but the ache only grew. His presence permeated the small space. She'd never look at her living room the same way again. She itched to run her hand across his jaw. Put a finger on the throbbing vein at his temple. Let the day's stubble scratch her. Scrape over any number of tender spots. She'd never wanted a man before. Not like this. Never like this.

"Elaine." His voice was tight. Rough. Like the first time she'd tried whiskey. "Say yes."

How could she say no? She would regret saying yes until her dying day. She'd regret saying no for eternity. Tension radiated off him, like he was holding himself in check the same way she was. And yet he was in her space, so close his heat enveloped her, wound through her, weakening her resolve. His hand settled at her hip, thumb stroking through the thin cotton of her shirt. Her chest grew tight and she couldn't breathe as the air around them electrified with possibility. She opened her mouth but no words came out – her mouth had turned to ash. She licked her lip at the same time a strangled noise came from his throat, and he brushed her mouth in the barest kiss. So light she must have imagined it.

But there was no imagining the electric shock that pulsed through her, hardening her nipples to tight peaks before liquefying her panties in a burst of desire. And she certainly didn't imagine the second time it happened when his arm tightened around her and his breath skated across her cheek.

"Yes," she breathed out on a sigh, leaning into him, her body buzzing as his lips brushed hers a third, then a fourth time.

But just like that it was over. Travis made another strangled noise and stepped back, taking with him the warmth that had so briefly encased her. He coughed and cleared his throat. "Good. Good. I'll… ah… be in touch."

He disappeared like a phantom, vanishing into the darkness. And long after his car pulled away, Elaine stood rooted to the floor, fingers pressed against a mouth still tingling from his touch.

CHAPTER 9

MOONLIGHT STREAMED IN through the open window. Travis rolled to his side, punching his pillow into submission for the fourth time that night, and shut his eyes. But all he saw was Elaine's face, glowing and kissable in the moonlight. What the hell had he been thinking, kissing her? He hadn't. His cock had been the one calling the shots. And it stirred now, taunting him.

She'd looked so sweet and vulnerable in the dark, and once he'd had a taste, he couldn't stop. He couldn't help himself. Her mouth had been softer than a feather. And she tasted like cotton candy. More incredible than he could have possibly imagined. It had taken superhuman effort to back away. His cock stood at full attention now, pressing against the elastic of his shorts as he replayed the scene over and over.

"Goddammit," he groaned.

He rolled over in the other direction. Fuck him for being such a perv. He slipped a hand inside his shorts, fisting his cock and giving a sharp pull. His balls tightened as electricity circled up the back of his legs. He stroked again, imagining that sweet pink tongue lapping him up. He squeezed harder, pulling in short, strong, strokes, visualizing creamy full breasts, dusky pink nipples begging to be nipped and suckled.

What undid him was the vision of her spread open and ready for him, dipping his head to taste her, seeing her writhe in ecstasy before he finally pushed into her slick heat. He'd make it so good for her. Stroking in and out until she cried his name. His hips bucked as he pulled once, twice, three times, and came into his hand with a groan. He stared up at the ceiling, breath coming in harsh rasps, as his brain returned to earth. A bead of sweat trickled from his temple, slowly moving down the contours of his face to drop to the sheet. He was soaked. And still frustrated as hell.

Fuck this shit.

It didn't matter it was before zero-dark-thirty. Sleep would only continue to elude him. He needed to work Elaine out of his system. He slipped off his shorts, and pulled the sheets from the bed, balling everything up and mashing it in the hamper. After a quick shower, he gathered up the sack of laundry and brought it downstairs to the washer. Then he went to the weight bench, which stood in front of the large stone fireplace where a couch had once been.

One of the many advantages of being a bachelor. No woman to tell him to hide his weights in the basement, or the barn. His setup right in the middle of the living room kept him from slacking off. He never missed a day of PT. Even on the coldest, stormiest mornings, he'd work up a sweat, then run the perimeter of the ranch before heading into the office. Being up at the ass-crack of dawn meant he'd get it over with sooner.

He started off with reverse sit-ups, but instead of his usual fifty, he doubled them.

"Ten." Elaine was a Prairie resident.

"Twenty." She was coming to work on his campaign.

"Thirty." She had a kid.

"Forty." She must be at least ten years younger than he was.

"Fifty." She had scars, and probably a past.

"Sixty." So did he for that matter.

His abs started to burn. "Seventy." He'd never met any-one with a stronger work ethic. She must work seven days a week. And she was sweetly strong. *She'd make the perfect rancher's wife.* He grunted. "Eighty. Motherfucker." He wasn't fucking quitting now, even if his abs hated him for a week.

"Ninety." And he didn't need a wife. His mother had dipped a toe in the ranching life pool, decided it wasn't for her, and left them high and dry when Colton was two. Nope, if he started the ranch again someday, it would be without a wife.

"Hundred." He dropped back, abs screaming.

He doubled his pushups to two-hundred.

How many times had he wanted to rub away the tension she carried at her neck? Or do something to ease the tired look in her eyes? She'd laughed yesterday, and his insides had gone all funny seeing her face light up. She was too young to carry all that worry with her. Most kids her age were probably doing keggers at college parties. She had the air of someone much older.

Travis collapsed on the floor, arms aching. Dragging himself up, he pulled on his running shoes. Making sure the door was locked behind him, he jammed the key in his shorts pocket and took off at a steady clip for the fence line. The moon was just setting, but the sun would be up by the time he finished.

Forty-five minutes later, his lungs burned as he forced himself to sprint over the final rise and back to the barnyard, now framed by a riot of pinks and oranges lighting up the morning sky. Weston stood waiting for him, lounging on a porch post, thermos in hand.

"What the hell is this?" he gasped between taking spiky breaths of air and surveying the work crew accompanying Weston.

"Morning to you too, sunshine." Weston tipped his hat and hopped down the stairs, offering him the thermos. "Time to fix this place up. You're running for sheriff. Your property can't look like it hasn't seen the light of day in a decade." He unscrewed the thermos lid and poured hot liquid into it. "Drink up. If people see you neglect your property, they'll think you'll neglect your job."

Travis rolled his eyes. "Oh, Jesus."

"Praying won't help you win," Weston chuckled. "But polishing your image will. And you wanna win, don't you?"

"You sure this isn't about you taking over my job?"

Weston smiled enigmatically and lifted a shoulder.

"What's the trailer for?" Travis gestured at the horse trailer attached to Weston's truck.

"Saw in the back of Rancher's Monthly yesterday that there's an auction next town over. A nice gentle mare and a pony are up. You come from ranch stock, gotta have animals for your flyers."

"But I'm a policeman."

Weston tsked and shook his head. "Doesn't matter. Voters want someone like them."

A knot formed in Travis's stomach. "This is a bad idea, Wes."

"This is the perfect way to scrub up your grumpy bachelor policeman image." Weston cuffed him on the shoulder. "You're a man of the people now."

Travis shook his head. "You should go work for your old man."

Weston made a face. "Nah. I never want to set foot in DC

again. But I'll happily use what I learned as a kid to help a friend in need."

"I don't need anything," he grumbled. What had he gotten himself into, agreeing to run for sheriff?

Weston glared at him. "What you need is a family. But I have to work with what I have, so horses it is. And I know of at least one kid who'd be thrilled to ride a nice gentle pony."

"Shows what you know. Ponies can be ornery. Don't underestimate them because they're small."

"Then stick Dax on the mare. I don't care." Weston turned to the barn. "With the crew here, we can have the barn looking good by the end of the day. You're going to take more work."

There went a chunk of his nest-egg. But the barn desperately needed work. At least this way it would be ready for someday, whenever that was. He took another swig of the coffee. "Let me go change. I'll come help."

Upstairs, he threw on an old pair of jeans, and dug out his old pair of boots from the back of his closet. An uncomfortable ache settled below his throat. Funny how the smell of leather and sweat could tie him up in knots. He'd sold off the last of the cattle the last time he'd worn these. A few months after he'd kicked Colton out of the house, and he'd realized too late he couldn't hack ranching on his own.

But he'd had rules and Colton had crossed the line one too many times. He'd been justified in giving him an ultimatum – clean up or get out. Colton had chosen the path as much as he had. A pang of longing hit him in the stomach. What would Colton say about him running for sheriff? His breath came out in a harsh grunt. It didn't matter. He'd slammed the door on their relationship that awful night, and he'd have to live with that. They both would.

He shoved one foot into the worn leather, then the other. As far as he was concerned, those memories could stay buried in the back of the closet. He grabbed a pair of work gloves and jammed on his straw hat before taking the steps two at a time. Weston was out by the old chicken coop repairing the fencing when Travis joined him.

At first, they worked in silence. Then Weston slid him one of those looks that said they were about to have a "conversation." "Elaine and Dax seemed to have a nice time yesterday."

The knot in his belly grew.

"It was great to see them smiling."

Travis clipped his pliers around a piece of chicken wire embedded in a post and yanked extra hard. He didn't want to talk about Elaine and Dax. Or anything else for that matter.

"I even saw *you* smiling."

Travis shook his head, unable to help the way his mouth curved up. "Shut up. Don't start."

Weston chuckled. "Don't need to. It doesn't take a rocket scientist to tell you're thinking about it, and you're tied up in knots."

He tossed another piece of old chicken wire onto the growing pile. "Doesn't matter. Not happening."

Weston dropped his pliers and leaned on the post, arms crossed. "You haven't been the same since the tornado."

Travis stepped around him, moving on to the next fence post. "You're not gonna let this go, are you?"

"Nope. When was the last time you talked to someone about it?"

The knot in his belly morphed into a ball of barbed wire, and he ground his molars together, as he gave another yank to the chicken wire. "Few years. Before I was promoted to

Chief."

"So why are you still letting it define you?" Weston's voice called out behind him. "One thing I learned up in Montana that's stuck with me is that you can let what happened to us be a part of your story or BE your story. You get to decide."

Travis clenched the pliers like a lifeline. Grief sucked, the way it snuck up on you when you least expected it, slicing through your defenses to stab you at your very core, then disappearing like a thief in the night, leaving you shaken and helpless. "Those guys would all be married with children by now," he gritted out through the ache in his throat.

"Would they? Are you?"

"That's different."

"Bullshit." Weston's voice grew sharp. "You denying yourself what they were denied is sick as fuck. Especially when I've watched you leave ten-dollar tips under your coffee cup every day for the last two years."

Travis whirled, throwing the pliers to the ground. "She's a single mom. She needed it," he roared. "You've seen how she lives."

"Keep telling yourself that," Weston shouted back. "You may be too thickheaded to realize it, but you're in love with her. You have been for ages. And I, for one, was glad to see you looking HAPPY yesterday."

Travis's breath came in huge gulps. He was *not* in love with Elaine. Weston was full of shit.

Shaking his head, Weston dug into his pocket and tossed him a set of keys. "Go take the trailer to the auction. The address is on the seat. Crew will have the stables ready by the time you get back."

Travis trudged down to the truck and pulled out onto the drive. How could you be in love with someone you barely knew? Or barely kissed? Let alone... The image of Elaine's creamy skin glowing in the dark assaulted him. He turned onto the road, head filled with a picture of her naked and waiting for him.

"Motherfucker," he gritted when his mistake became obvious. He'd turned too late and was on a trajectory for the ditch. Pushing thoughts of her aside, he jerked the steering wheel and jammed the truck into reverse. "God*dammit*," he yelled, realizing he'd just made it worse and that the trailer was in danger of jackknifing. Now he was stuck blocking the road. He turned the wheel, not quite so tight this time, and jimmied the truck ahead as he registered the whine of a motorcycle in the distance.

Great.

Now he was holding up traffic. They'd just have to wait until he got himself straightened out. Hopefully it was a stranger and not someone he knew. He'd never hear the end of it if word got out he'd gotten himself parked sideways across the road while pulling a trailer. Total rookie move. The whine of the engine grew louder.

CRASH!

CHAPTER 10

THE TRUCK JERKED as the sickening sound of twisting metal filled Travis's head. Adrenaline surged through him as he unbuckled and hopped out the door, heart pounding in his ears. His stomach reeled at the sight of a red bike embedded underneath the trailer, front fender broken and bent.

Where in the hell was the rider?

Scanning the road, he spotted a black leather-clad rider lying in a heap in the ditch. For a heart-stopping moment, his body seized as he recognized a patch on the shoulder. Oh, God. Not another casualty. Prairie couldn't take another hit. "Cassidy?" he shouted, legs springing to action. He reached her in three steps. She groaned and moved.

His vision hazed. "What. The. Ever. Loving. *FUCK*?" he roared, heating at her carelessness. She was a good rider. She *knew* better than to come careening around a blind turn at breakneck speed. From everything he'd heard, she was a stellar helicopter pilot. Responsible. Smart. And the guys at the station said she was a great firefighter too. God, what if she'd hit the truck and not the trailer? What if Dax had been with him? His stomach flipped as half a dozen catastrophic scenarios flew through his head.

She raised a hand but winced as she gave him a sheepish smile. "Hi, Travis. Nice morning?"

"Are you fucking out of your mind?" How could she be so casual about this? Hadn't they all been through enough? A wave of nausea ripped through him at the thought of telling Dottie something had happened to Cassidy. The woman had already been put through the wringer, losing the diner.

"Nice to see you, too."

He dropped to his knees and started squeezing her legs at her ankles, checking for broken bones.

She pushed him away. "I'm fine, Travis. I can move my fingers and toes. No spinal injury."

"What about the rest of you?"

"I'll be sore. *Ow.*" She winced and squeezed her right knee.

"You'll need to get that checked out."

"I'll be fine. I probably hit a rock when I tumbled. Nothing a few aspirin and some ice won't cure."

He glared at her. "You should go to the doctor."

"And get grounded? No thanks. I'm fine." She tried shrugging him away as he brought his hands up to her neck. "C'mon, Travis. Help me up."

"Not until I know I'm not injuring you further," he growled. "You shouldn't've sat up."

"Right. I should have waited for the ambulance to come tell me I'm okay? Not."

He clenched his jaw. She needed his patience, not his temper. "I should haul your ass to jail for how fast you were going. At the very least, cite you for reckless driving. Take off your helmet, and try not to move your neck."

"I wasn't going that fast. Honest."

Sure. And he was the king of Spain. He held up a finger. "Follow my finger." He moved it left, right, up, and down watching her eyes. It didn't look like she had a concussion.

His heartbeat slowed from a breakneck pace.

"You're overreacting. I've been through worse. You probably have, too." She leaned back on her hands. "Look, I appreciate the drill, but I'm fine. We Soldiers are tough, right?" She flashed him a smile.

"You're incredibly lucky, you know that?"

Her smile broadened. "Of course I am. The gods are with me."

Did she honestly think playing the military card would work? She was worse off than he'd thought. He'd recognized the signs, understood her need for speed. But everyone had to walk their own path through the minefield of memories. So he'd laid off. But no more. Not when her behavior was endangering others, too. "Until they aren't. Then what? Do I get the pleasure of knocking on your parents' door telling them you've flamed out? Or worse, on the door of some hapless victim of your stupidity and selfishness? You're not invincible. Even if you've survived combat."

A flush crept up her face. "I'm a safe rider, Travis. You know that."

"Like hell you are," he bit out. "I've been watching you for weeks. I know exactly what you're doing, and none of it's safe. It's dangerous, and it's gonna get you or somebody else killed."

"How dare you say that?" she fumed. "My safety record is impeccable."

"Not on the ground, and you know it. I see how you zip around on your bike, and how you put yourself in risky situations for the rush of it. I get it. The problem is, out here, you're a danger to yourself and others."

Her mouth thinned to a flat line. "I'm fine," she spit out. "I just need to walk it off. And if it will make you happy, I'll slow down."

His teeth hurt from holding his jaw. God, he wanted to shake her. "I don't think you understand me. You won't slow down. I know that look in your eye. I've seen it before. Speed won't help you find that high you're looking for. Or get back what you've lost."

"I have no idea what you're talking about."

"You can lie to yourself, Cassie, but you're not fooling me. Call it survivor guilt or the need to feel alive like you did downrange, but you're taking larger and larger risks with your life and with the lives of others."

"Help me up. I want to see my bike."

Travis extended his hand, and she winced as he pulled her up. "You're deflecting, Cassie," he said harshly. "Classic tactic."

She took a step and gasped.

Her mask slipped, and he glimpsed the raw pain underneath the facade. Was that what Weston saw in him when he needled him to the point of blowing his stack? He softened toward the woman he'd always considered a sister. "Need help?"

"I'm fine." She shook out her leg, then hobbled over to her bike.

The front tire of the bike was lodged completely under the trailer, the front fender cracked. He had to give her props for her stubbornness. She wouldn't give. But she'd met her match in him. If he could help it, he wouldn't let her flame out. It would destroy Dottie. "Last time, Cass," he bit out. "You need help?"

She studied her boots, her face flickering with emotion. "Yes," she whispered. "It's stuck."

Travis joined her, studying the wreck. She'd ruined her

fancy bike. There would be no repairing it. "Damn, Cass. How fast you reckon it was going when it hit the trailer?" Judging from the skid marks and how firmly it was lodged underneath the trailer, he'd venture about seventy. Cassidy was lucky to be in one piece.

She looked so vulnerable, staring down at the pavement, and it pulled at a spot deep inside him. Hell, maybe Weston was right. Maybe he did need to talk to someone. How could he help her if he couldn't help himself? He had to try. And he'd consider Weston's advice. "Look. Here's the deal. You can keep speeding, and I'll write you up as soon as I get to town, or you can come out with me to the Hansen ranch tomorrow and spend some time with Hope and me working to gentle a new crew of mustangs."

"What will that solve?"

Her voice sounded defeated. Hopeless.

He glared at her, unsure of how to get through to her. "The point is," he punctuated, "you've destroyed a vehicle and damaged a trailer. What next? You? Someone else? Consider this your friendly intervention. I don't think your Guard unit or commander would look kindly on an arrest record."

Her eyes grew wide. "You wouldn't."

So that was her pressure point. Anything to stay in. "Try me. I give no shits about your military record."

Cassie flinched and fisted a hand. "You're an ass, Travis."

"I've been where you are. I know what you're going through. You can run, but your memories run faster."

"You don't know shit about me, Travis," she yelled.

He stepped into her space. Her little temper tantrum had gone on long enough. Did she think she was the only one who'd gone through this? Had nightmares? Flashbacks? Fuck that. "Bullshit. You fly around in your little helicopter playing the hero, extracting assets. Shooting your weapons at faces you can't see because all you have to do is look for a flare, a confirmation and a direction of enemy fire and you can unload your ordnance. Talk to me after you've looked a man in the eyes then slit his throat," he yelled, pacing away from her. He scraped a hand over his face before looking back at her. "You don't have a fucking clue about *me either*, Cassie." He stalked back, pointing a finger at her. "And I may be off-duty, but I can still haul you up on charges."

"Please, Travis. No."

Begging wouldn't work with him. Not now. He was done with her shit. "You have a choice. You can show up tomorrow at the Hansen ranch and help me out, or you can sit your ass in jail for a day and explain this all to your C.O."

She glared at him. "Fine," she ground out. She yanked at her bike again. She'd never get it out by herself. He checked his watch. If he hurried, he could still get to the auction.

But by the time he'd helped Cassidy get her bike stored in her parents' garage and made it down the road to the auction, the horses were long gone. Travis ground his teeth in frustration as he made his way back to the truck, horseless. This day had gone to shit before he'd even gotten out of bed. He jammed the truck into gear and pulled back onto the road, making sure he didn't fuck up the turn this time. He didn't have time to care for horses anyway, so why was he suddenly so pissed off about missing this opportunity? He turned on the radio in a feeble attempt to silence those thoughts, clenching the steering wheel at the sight of a billboard he'd failed to notice on the drive over. An enormous image of Steve Lawson smiled down at him with the words *LAWSON, the REAL Law and Order Sheriff.*

CHAPTER 11

ELAINE DOUBLE CHECKED the coffee carafes, casting about for something to do. It was early yet. They wouldn't have a rush for at least another hour. The first wave of ranchers would show up after their morning chores.

Travis hadn't stopped by the day before. Was it because of her? Maybe he regretted kissing her. She'd never regret it for a second, even though it couldn't happen again. Wouldn't happen again. She winced at the dull ache throbbing in her chest. Men like Travis never went for women like her. Maybe he'd decided not to offer her the job and didn't know how to tell her. She sighed heavily. It was probably for the best.

"We're all set."

She spun at the sound of Travis's gravelly voice, a thousand butterflies taking flight in her stomach. Her nerve endings sizzled at the sight of him. He was out of uniform, dressed like he'd been the day he'd taken her and Dax out to the Hansens. She liked him like this, with his plaid cotton shirt stretched tight from the hard muscles underneath. In uniform, there was so much padding and gear, he was a giant wall. Dressed like a rancher, he was deliciously human. Touchable. She itched to run a hand across his chest.

She must have looked confused, because he spoke again. "I filed. For sheriff."

"*Oh.* Wait. Don't you need anything from me?" Like a

kiss? She couldn't stop staring at his mouth, hungry to feel it on her again.

Stop it, Elaine. He's not for you.

He shook his head. "Nope. I filed at the election office. The rest is all online. And I'll set up a checking account later today."

"Oh." She took a deep breath. "So, what do I do next?"

He widened his stance, crossing his arms. "Apparently I have to have an office, and it can't be the police station. So we're set up out at my ranch."

Her heart sank to her toes, all her plans for new things for Dax and a nest egg for community college evaporating. How was she supposed to work for him if she couldn't get out there? She shook her head, fighting the disappointment that crashed over her. "Travis, I- I don't think this will work. You know my–"

He held up a hand. "I've thought about this, and it's okay. You're here every day until afternoon. I'm at the station every day until about the same time. I'll pick you up after work and we can get in a few hours before I bring you home."

She shook her head again. "But what about Dax? I can't afford–" She faltered. She probably could for what he was paying her, but she couldn't bring herself to leave her son. She didn't have anyone in town she trusted besides Dottie, and the woman had given her so much already, she wouldn't dream of imposing further. And Dax didn't like being away from her either.

Travis gave her a reassuring smile. "Dax too. And if we work late, he can go to sleep on the couch."

"Once school starts, he'll have to go to bed early."

"No problem. You tell me what he needs, and I'll take care of it."

Her insides turned to pudding even as her heart beat out a warning. Falling for him because he was sweet to her son would surely end in heartbreak.

"Pick you up at four?"

"Today?" her voice cracked, stuttering along with her pulse.

Travis handed her a folded piece of paper. "What's this? *Oh.*" Her breath stuck in her throat as her brain registered the amount on the check. More money than she'd ever held in her life. Her hands went cold and clammy in the morning sun. "Travis?" She met his eyes. "Are you sure about this?"

Hunger flared in his eyes, heating her blood. And just as fast, his eyes shuttered and he nodded curtly "Yep. We have an agreement." He ran a hand through his hair. "And about that...the other night..."

Ah, yes.

She swallowed down the ache that blossomed in her throat. The other night had been a mistake. Holding up a hand, she stopped him with a smile that felt just shy of genuine. "Dax and I had a lovely time." Somehow, she managed to keep the catch out of her voice. But she couldn't stop the painful squeezing in her chest. She'd never be good enough for a man like Travis. She was too poor. Too burdened, too... everything.

Her only consolation was the tortured look that flickered briefly across Travis's face. "We're going to be working closely together. So it's probably good we establish some boundaries."

She nodded vigorously, blinking hard at the sudden itch in her nose. "Of course. We've always been professional with each other. Why would that change?"

"Exactly," he answered a little too enthusiastically.

An awkward silence settled between them.

This would not do. If she was going to survive working with him, she not only had to get a grip on her libido, she had to be able to talk to him like he was a normal person, not the super sexy superhero cop she'd imagined him into. She filled a paper cup and held it out. "Coffee?"

His hand brushed hers and remained a second too long. Electricity raced up her arm, swirling around her nipples and settling in an ache between her legs.

"Thanks," he murmured, taking it from her.

She could do this. "Day off today?"

He shook his head, eyes hooded as he stared at her intently. "Nope. Helping Hope Sinclaire break a set of mustangs she's rescued."

"Oh." That seemed to be the only word she could form around him this morning.

"Once I know what I've gotten into, and it's safe, do you think Dax would like to come and watch?"

It would be so much easier to keep her distance if he didn't demonstrate such a soft spot for Dax. "I'm sure he'd love to. He thinks the world of you. And between his visit to the Hansens and the pony rides at the fairgrounds, you've succeeded in making a horse nut out of him."

Travis grinned at her and cocked an eyebrow before taking a sip of his coffee. "Good. Then my plan is succeeding."

"And what plan is that?"

"Someone's gotta teach Dax how to be a proper cowboy. So it's a date then?"

"Sure."

"I'll let you know when. In the meantime, meet you back here at four?"

"I'll be ready."

Travis lifted the cup. "Thanks for the coffee." He turned

and headed down the street.

She couldn't help staring as he walked away, mesmerized by the way the jeans molded to his ass. Until she caught Dottie staring at *her* with a knowing smile tipping up the corners of her mouth.

CHAPTER 12

O F COURSE, SHE'D had to wear the blue shirt today. The one that made him want to drown in her big blue eyes. With a grunt of frustration, Travis crushed the empty paper cup and tossed it in the nearest trash bin as he walked down Main.

Four construction trailers stood in the middle of the street. Reconstruction would begin in earnest today. That would give everyone something positive to focus on for the remainder of the long, hot summer. With luck, some of the buildings would be finished in time for the holidays. He could only hope.

But even the prospect of a brand new Main Street wasn't enough to pull his thoughts from Elaine for more than a second. She'd looked so sweet and uncertain, standing there, staring up at him. The urge to fist his hand in her ponytail and tilt her face up so he could take a taste of that full mouth had been powerful, and had his cock pressing painfully against his zipper.

And what had he done right after he'd insisted they keep strict boundaries? Gone and made a date with her by way of bringing Dax back to the Hansens. Stupid, stupid, stupid.

Another rule broken.

How many rules did he have to break before he got burned? The odds were increasingly against him where Elaine was concerned. He was a former Navy SEAL for chrissakes. The sharpest of the sharp. He could calculate wind drift for a bullet from a thousand yards away. He could kill a man before the man was even aware he was there. Why couldn't he exercise any self-control where Elaine was concerned?

He'd have to do better.

He'd calmed down by the time he joined the Hansens down by their training pen. "Where's Cassidy?"

Parker gave him a look of surprise. "I didn't know she was coming this morning."

"She better," he growled, irritation flashing through him. "We had a deal."

Parker scowled, then turned to Hope. "What do you need us to do?"

She gave each of them a hard look. "These horses are already spooked. We want to gentle them, and that starts with our first interaction. Follow my instructions and we'll be good. Go all cowboy on me, and we're gonna have problems. Understand?"

Parker and Gunnar nodded, and she swung her gaze to him. "Travis?"

He nodded once, not caring that he was glowering. Where in the hell was Cassidy?

An hour later, they were hot and sweaty. The horses were calm in their new environs, and still no sign of Cassidy.

"Travis," Hope called out. "You're up first." She held out a harness and a lead line. "We're starting from scratch here. You're going to have to get the horse to trust you enough that she'll let you put on a halter."

"What do I do?" He could do anything, she just needed to show him once and he'd have the sequence committed to memory.

She chuckled, shaking her head. "It's more being than doing. For now, just walk around the ring."

The big bay snorted at the other end of the pen and eyed him warily. He could do this. How many times had he charmed virtual strangers, gained critical information his unit was able to use to save lives? *Except once,* the voice in his head condemned.

"Get the horse moving," she called quietly. "Pick a direction."

He raised his hands and the horse started, trotting around the fence and stopping on the other side of the ring. He dropped his hands. "Now what?"

"You have to keep it moving. Move in closer."

Focusing on the horse like she was a target, he advanced. She whinnied and hopped, moving around to the other side. After several tries, he succeeded in getting the horse to circle the ring, but even after Hope demonstrated how to build trust and get the horse to let her put on the halter, Travis failed repeatedly, frustration growing with each attempt.

"Okay, back off for a sec. Walk with me," Hope tugged on his sleeve. "What's her name?" Elaine's face shimmered before him. "Flipper," he responded automatically. He hadn't thought of the imaginary mascot Weston had made up during a low point in BUD/S training for years. Flipper the man-eating mermaid had gotten them through the worst moments of their ordeal. But he was on land now, with no threat of having his balls chewed off. Of course, failing in front of the Hansens didn't feel swell.

"What's going on, Travis?" Hope barked at him exasperatedly. "You're confusing the horse. You're sending it all sorts of mixed signals. I don't know what kind of stuff is going on with you, but you either need to let it all out in the ring and get through it, or leave it on the other side. Flipper here deserves better." She crossed her arms, waiting.

Shit. Weston might as well be sitting on his shoulder. He could just see Weston's smug grin as Hope went on. "You might be able to bullshit your friends, but a horse can always tell when you're bullshitting."

Whose story are you living, Man? He could hear Weston asking. Weston was right. He should be living a good life for his fallen comrades. A life of enforced solitude didn't honor the dead. It just made him dead.

"Earth to Travis." Hope waved a hand in front of his face. "You wanna try again? Or are you done?" The challenge in her voice was clear.

"I'm in."

"Good. Let's go again. Follow me."

This time, he settled his thoughts the way he did on a mission. Focusing only on the work in front of him, letting his awareness heighten. He was surprised when he checked his watch forty-five minutes later. He'd completely lost track of time in the pen with Hope. Instead, focusing on Flipper's breathing, and the way she pricked her ears, or licked and chewed. His heart lifted the moment she dropped her head and let him place the halter over her ears. He gave her an appreciative scratch. "Good girl," he murmured. "You're a good girl."

"Good job, Travis. You made good progress with her today."

Excitement buzzed through him. There had been a moment in the pen when Flipper looked at him, and he swore she looked right into him. Right through the shit and into his soul. He wasn't one to get hippy-dippy, but Hope was right. Somehow, Flipper could sense the bullshit. And when he'd let it go, had settled into his breathing, she'd calmed right down. He had to tell someone. There was too much energy ricocheting through his body to keep it all to himself. He pulled out his phone, then deflated.

Who was he going to call? Weston?

Elaine.

His chest grew tight, and he slowly replaced the phone, excitement draining from him.

Parker cleared his throat. "So I heard you're running for sheriff?"

Shit – how long did that take? He wasn't ready to go public, even if he'd pretty much slapped Steve Lawson's face with a glove the other day. He didn't even have a website up yet. "I see the rumor mill is fast at work," he answered a little too brusquely.

"No one would be better."

Travis snorted as he fisted his hands on his hips, toeing the dirt. "Thanks. Not a done deal. Not sure I want the job." He'd do the job. Hell, he'd be a great county sheriff, and people would be safer because of it. But given the billboards popping up, it might not be easy to beat Lawson. Weston had mentioned the day before that Lawson had the ear of the governor and other elected officials in the county, along with a hefty bank account.

Travis could match it with his own funds, but every dollar he spent now took him a step farther from his dream of someday restarting the ranch. At least the barn was done and looking great. Too bad it would go unused except for a few as-yet-to-be-acquired horses.

As soon as he could politely make his excuses, he took his leave, promising to return as often as his schedule would allow. He'd intended to go straight home, to shower and change before returning for Elaine and Dax. But instead, fifteen minutes later, he found himself staring at the new front door of Millie's Organic Grocery.

What in the hell was he doing? He didn't cook. He didn't know the first thing about cooking. Not real cooking.

The kid would need dinner. And something better than the microwave burritos he usually grabbed from the gas station. Travis's hand hovered over the handle. It wasn't too late for him to turn around. No one would be the wiser.

"Travis?" Millie Prescott yanked open the door just as he reached for the handle. Adrenaline shot into his legs, making them twitch. He should go. This was a bad idea.

She stared at him quizzically. "Are you lost? Dottie's is two blocks over." She smiled up at him hopefully, her yellow hair a fuzzy halo, and he glanced behind her at her stocked shelves, taking in the markdowns.

Shit.

Even though she'd come through the storm relatively unscathed – her building had been narrowly missed – she was still struggling. He made a note to remind the force at their next morning staff meeting to make sure and stop by. It wouldn't hurt him to stop by either. Maybe learn to cook, even though he'd never stop eating at Dottie's or Gino's Trattoria, or ordering tamales from Luci Cruz. He cleared his throat, unsure of what to say. "I need help," he finally blurted out.

Millie's face lit with a huge smile. "You've come to the right place."

CHAPTER 13

A T FOUR O'CLOCK sharp, Travis pulled up in Weston's truck. Elaine had barely managed to get Dax showered and into a clean pair of shorts – he'd positively squirmed with excitement when he heard they were going to be visiting Travis's ranch.

"Does he have horses, too?"

"I don't know, kiddo. You'll have to ask him."

Dax bounded over and waited impatiently as Travis hopped out of the truck looking positively yummy. Heat pooled between her legs. He'd showered and changed into a crisp white shirt with the sleeves rolled up. Now she could secretly drool over the corded muscles and veins in his forearm as he drove.

She couldn't hear what Dax asked as he bent to give the boy a fist bump, but her pulse skittered at the smile he gave her son. Even Dax's father, when he'd been alive, hadn't shown this much interest in him. Travis seemed to genuinely like Dax, and it made her throat go all itchy.

Travis stood, turning the weight of his gaze to her, heating her like a hot poker. "Shall we get started?"

Business. This is just business, she reminded herself sternly. But she couldn't help answering his smile with one of her own. His hand burned a hole in the small of her back as he followed her around the truck and opened the door for her.

"Wait here while I get Dax settled."

He turned to help Dax into the back seat, and she caught a whiff of his spicy cologne. But it was the view of his shoulders stretching his shirt tight across his back as he bent to secure the seatbelt that had her squeezing the door handle to steady herself.

Travis straightened and turned, towering over her in the small space the open door created. Her mouth went dry and she focused on the line of buttons going down his front, grateful for once that she couldn't see his eyes through his aviators. He extended his hand. "Need a hand?" His voice scraped over her, sending a delicious shiver down her spine.

All he'd have to do to win the election was say that to every woman in the county. How could anyone resist a voice with the burr of Elvis, but none of the drawl? Packaged in a hard body with a million-dollar smile? Lawson didn't stand a chance. At least she hoped so. She shuddered to think what would happen to her if he won.

Dax kept a running commentary from the backseat the entire drive from town. It was better this way, wasn't it? No pressure to fill the silence with small talk. No opportunity for a misstep. But when the truck pulled over a little rise and she laid eyes on the big red barn and the two-story farmhouse with the wrap-around porch across the yard, she gasped. Her hand flew to her throat. "This is lovely, Travis. You have a lovely home."

A far cry from the dingy two room walk-up she'd lived in as a child before she'd finally run away. Or the abandoned house she'd squatted in the first time she took a knife to her arm. The scene in front reminded her of a picture book she'd seen once as a little girl. So pretty. So… normal. Longing pressed on her chest. She'd never be able to give Dax anything as nice as this.

"I wouldn't exactly call it a home. At least right now. But it's been in my family for generations."

"It looks like a storybook."

"Not what it used to be. Don't have time for the upkeep."

"Will you have more time if you're elected?"

Travis grimaced and shook his head. "Probably not." He sighed heavily.

Open mouth, insert foot. She hadn't even left the truck and already she'd misspoken. "Do you miss it?"

Travis glanced over as he brought the truck to a stop. "Ranching? Sometimes. It's a tough job. Seven day a week job. No vacation."

"Kind of like being a police chief. Or a Navy SEAL."

He let out a little laugh, nodding his head. "Yeah. I guess you could say that."

It spoke volumes to her that he'd chosen careers that demanded a high work ethic. Admiration filled her. She'd never met anyone who worked as tirelessly as he did.

"As a rancher, you call your own shots. And you live close to the land. Both of which I like."

He looked unsettled. His finger tapped relentlessly on the steering wheel. He seemed like he wanted to say more. "But?"

He shot her a look full of consideration. "I'm good at what I do. Crime's down. People know each other better. We have a strong community, and I like to think I'm part of why that is."

"I think that's why you'll make a great sheriff." He *had* to win.

He shot her another grin that made her weak in the knees. "First, I have to win."

"Let's get to it, then."

She slid down off the seat, and was struggling with the seat latch when she felt his hand at her back again, solid and warm. His breath skated across her neck, setting her pulse racing. "Need help?"

"I've got it." More than anything, she wanted to turn into him, bury her face in his neck and drink in his strong, masculine scent.

"Here, let me. I noticed it can stick."

His hand covered hers, firmly moving the latch into place and pushing the seat forward. But there was no way she could unbuckle Dax without climbing back into the truck. She was simply too short. Travis must have come to the same conclusion because he stepped around her and easily released the seatbelt. But what made her throat catch was the smile on Dax's face when his arms went around Travis's neck. Travis held Dax like he weighed nothing. Even though Dax was on the small side for a seven-year-old, he was still too big for Elaine to pick up. He'd grown out of that before they'd moved to Prairie. Seeing him in Travis's arms did something funny to her insides.

Dax clambered down and made a beeline for the oak tree that stood off the corner of the house. "Mom, mom, mom. Can I, can I, can I?"

"Not right now," she called across the yard. "I don't want you to fall and get hurt. I brought your favorite toys for you to play with inside."

Travis snorted. "That tree has seen three generations of Kincaids. No one's fallen out yet."

Elaine reached for the bag she'd filled for Dax and slung it over her shoulder. "And until this spring, a tornado had never touched down in Prairie, either."

Travis unlocked the front door and paused, hand on the

knob. "He'll be fine."

She started to say more, but the words died in her mouth as she stepped inside and took in the giant open space. A thick rug lay in front of an enormous stone fireplace. A long leather couch stood opposite the rug, and behind it a long sturdy table. Beyond the table was an open kitchen with two bags of groceries and a bottle of wine on the counter.

Dax darted around her and pounced on a box of toys waiting on the floor by the couch, activity bag forgotten.

"Advantages of having a family attic." Travis gave her a sheepish smile before shutting the door and turning the bolt.

She froze at the sound, heart pounding in her throat.

"Something wrong?" His eyes filled with concern.

This was Travis. He'd never hurt her. She swallowed, finding it hard to breathe. "Would you mind leaving the door open?"

Travis's face pulled taut as they locked gazes. For a long moment, neither of them moved. Then releasing a heavy breath, Travis nodded once. "Sure." He turned the bolt and pulled the door halfway open.

The easy connection that had been there on the drive over disappeared. All business, Travis strode to the table, gesturing for her to follow. "Travis?"

"Here." He handed her a cell phone.

"What's this?"

"Moving forward, you're a key member of this campaign. I'm going to need to reach you. You're going to need to make phone calls."

A flush raced up her spine, and she shook her head vehemently. "Oh, no. I couldn't possibly. You're already paying me too much." She couldn't let herself become indebted to him like this.

He went on as if she hadn't spoken. "I've loaded it with key numbers. The election office. My cell, the police station and fire station. Dottie's number, and Weston's. You can add whatever you need." He pressed it into her hands.

Didn't he understand she had to do things on her own? "Travis, I can't. This is too much."

His mouth firmed into a line. "It's not too much. But if it bothers you that much, you can return it after the campaign. The laptop too." He tilted his chin to the brand new laptop at the end of the table.

"You got a laptop too?" Her voice sounded unnaturally high to her ears.

Travis raised a hand. "Before you trot all the excuses why you can't, hear me out. We're both going to need to use a computer at the same time. And once we get your house wired for internet, you can do extra work after Dax goes to bed. Or watch Netflix."

Her body went briefly numb. Clearly, her brain had overloaded. Travis had called her pathetic little trailer a house. *She* didn't even call it a house. She knew better. But he was right, with her salary, she'd finally be able to afford internet. Which meant instead of watching Netflix like he assumed, she could finish studying for her GED.

Travis's voice went gravelly. "Say yes, Elaine."

The way he said it took her right back to the other night and his barely-there kiss. The heat in his eyes told her he'd gone there, too. But he'd made it clear kissing was off the table, so she'd ignore the riot of butterflies in her stomach. Not trusting herself to speak, she cleared her throat and nodded.

A knock sounded at the door, and Elaine dragged her gaze away. Weston stood in the entryway, a funny expression on his face. "Am I interrupting something?"

CHAPTER 14

THE SHOCKED LOOK on Weston's face was priceless. "Am I interrupting something?"

Hell yes, Travis wanted to shout, irritated by more than the unlocked door. Why did Elaine have to fight him at every turn? He was just trying to help. And then her face had gone all soft. Her lips had parted and her tongue had darted out to wet the bottom one, and he'd been transfixed by her pulse rapidly fluttering at the base of her throat.

But interrupting them wasn't what had put the look of surprise on Weston's face, and they both knew it. It was a one-time deal, leaving the door open and unlocked. But he'd seen the panic ripple through Elaine's body when he'd bolted the door, and as uncomfortable as he felt with an open door, he wouldn't do that to her. He could suck it up for a few hours.

Weston strolled into the room, and arched a brow. "Re-decorating too, I see."

Travis scowled at him and shook his head. Elaine didn't need to know that he'd spent most of yesterday hauling his weights up to his old bedroom. It was only for the campaign. And Dax. He didn't want Dax climbing all over his weight set and possibly hurting himself. And he had to admit, the room *did* look nice with the big leather couch he'd hauled back from Manhattan.

He cleared his throat. "I was just briefing Elaine on the campaign equipment."

Again, Weston's knowing smile. "Ah, yes." He turned to Elaine. "Travis is right, you know. You can't work a campaign in this day and age without equipment."

She gave them a nervous smile. "I'll do my best to earn it, then."

"You don't have to earn it," Travis snapped, done with her resisting. "Maybe you deserve a few nice things."

"Whoa there, Tex," Weston interjected and turned to Elaine. "You'll have more than earned these by the time the campaign is over, so don't worry about it."

"It's just—"

Elaine looked distraught, and the thought that he'd put that look on her face, cut.

Weston raised his hand. "We're a team. The only way we'll win is if we work together, and that means you need the necessary tools." He cocked his chin at the kitchen. "And it looks like Travis grabbed the tools for a good meal. Is that a loaf of French bread I see? Are we celebrating?"

Heat licked at the back of his neck. He'd wanted to have real food on hand for Elaine and Dax. He hadn't wanted anyone, especially Weston, to make a big deal about it.

Elaine's eyes widened and filled with admiration. "You cook, too?"

Her look warmed him. What he wouldn't give to receive that appreciative look from her every day. It buzzed his insides. And thanks to her gorgeous blue eyes staring up at him, he wasn't about to let on that this was his first time in the kitchen. He snuck a glance at Weston, who rolled his eyes and shook his head. He'd buy the man a beer next time they were out if he didn't bust his chops.

"Can I help?" She offered shyly.

"Not this time." She worked so hard, he'd wanted to do something nice for her, and in the heat of the moment standing in Millie's grocery store, cooking seemed like something simple. Something with no strings attached. But then Millie'd had him believing he could give Mario Batali a run for his money when he was done making what she'd called "the world's best spaghetti recipe." What a sucker. "But maybe Dax would like to help? What do you say, Dax?" he called. "Wanna help me cook dinner?"

"What are we eating?" he asked, rolling a dump truck across the rug.

"Spaghetti with meat sauce, salad, and garlic bread."

"Can I butter the bread?"

"Sure thing." It never ceased to surprise him what interested little kids. Especially someone like Dax.

Dax picked up the dump truck and brought it with him, placing it on the counter.

Travis reached for a cutting board and the bread. "Can you grab the butter?" Too late, he realized his mistake.

Truck in hand, Dax opened the fridge and looked in. "You have a lot of burritos in here."

Busted by a seven-year-old.

Across the room, Weston snorted. "We call that bachelor food."

"I want bachelor food. Mom, can I have bachelor food?"

"Only if you eat all your salad," Elaine shot back. Two pink spots stained her cheeks. "So I take it spaghetti is a special occasion food?"

And busted by the mom.

What a clusterfuck.

Weston came to the rescue. "Hell yes. It's campaign kickoff night. And everyone knows that on campaign kickoff night, the candidate cooks for the staff.

Elaine made a disbelieving noise in the back of her throat. But a smile pulled up the corner of her mouth. "This I have to see."

"You doubt my prowess in the kitchen."

"Given you eat two meals a day at Dottie's, yes," she shot back.

He threw his head back, laughing. He liked it when she showed her fire. "Prepare to be amazed."

For the most part, dinner was a success. Weston only had to step in once, right as the spaghetti was about to boil over. And Dax had made the salad almost all by himself.

Elaine tossed her napkin on the table. "I'm impressed. This was delicious." She craned her neck at the couch where Dax had stretched out, then turned back, delight in her eyes. "And you've tired him right out."

He warmed under her appreciative gaze.

"Now we can include on your introductory mailer that you're an excellent cook," Weston teased. "That's sure to garner you a couple dozen votes."

Travis rolled his eyes.

Weston grew serious. "Given the hour, I'm gonna suggest we strategize tomorrow. Be prepared to put in long nights from here on out. There's lots to do and not much time."

"But the election's two and a half months away" Elaine said, looking surprised.

"That's about a day in campaign time. Remember, most campaigns start a year or more before election day. This is a special election, so we have to scramble." Weston stood. "I'll let myself out." At the door, he turned. "Goodnight, kids. Don't do anything I wouldn't." He gave them a salute and left, shutting the door behind him.

Silence settled between them, punctuated by Dax's soft snores on the couch.

"Why don't I do the dishes?" Elaine pushed up from the table and moved to the sink, turning on the water.

"I'll help." Why wouldn't he? He knew where things went.

It had absolutely nothing to do with the fact that he could stand next to her, legs flush, brushing her hand as she handed him dish after dish.

It had nothing to do with the fact that she smelled like spring and roses.

And it had absolutely nothing to do with the way his heart tap-danced at the delight on her face when she'd first seen the ranch, or when she'd reluctantly accepted the electronics. Nothing at all.

"Thanks for bringing the toys out. Dax was thrilled." She rinsed a plate and held it out. "He's in love with the dump truck."

Travis took the plate, letting his fingers brush hers simply to enjoy the snap of awareness that twined up his arm.

"Yeah, my brother loved the dump truck too." For a moment, he saw his brother at Dax's age. Long before the troubles had started.

"You're not an only?"

He was surprised she hadn't heard that through the town gossip mill. Surely someone would have let it slip that he'd turned in his own brother, and kicked him out of the house. His stomach slowly sank to his toes. Worst night of his life. And that was saying something. He shook his head, pressing his mouth closed. "We're not... close." That was a polite way of putting it. "We disagreed on the path his life should take.

He rodeos now." Travis was sure she was curious. He'd be, if the roles were reversed. But he made sure his tone of voice conveyed the subject wasn't open for discussion. That chapter of his life was closed, and there was no sense drudging it up.

"Oh." Her voice was small. Wistful. "I always wished for a sibling."

He didn't know how to answer that. So he fixated on her soapy hand circling the inside of the spaghetti pot, watching as the bubbles slid off to reveal her tiny, strong hand.

"Do you miss him?"

Her words slid under his carefully constructed armor, stabbing him in the underbelly. Bringing up all sorts of emotions he wasn't prepared to unpack. Not now, maybe not ever. His body went tight, pain winding through him and squeezing his throat closed. He took the pot from her, hiding behind its bulk and moving it to the stove, as much to avoid her question as to give it space to dry.

But her eyes still lifted in question when he returned. He nodded, barely. "Yeah. I do." His answer came out just above a whisper. The farther he got from the incident, the more he questioned his action. But it was too late to change anything. And after the words they'd exchanged... a simple apology wouldn't cut it.

With a sympathetic noise, she turned, reaching a soapy hand to squeeze his arm. "I'm so sorry, Travis," she said sincerely. "I'm sure he misses you too. I hope... I hope that someday you can mend fences."

It was possible he loved her right then. Her belief in him shining on her face, so sweet and earnest. He didn't deserve it. In spite of it, hell, maybe because of it, he couldn't resist tucking a strand of hair that had fallen out of her ponytail behind her ear. Her eyes went dark and she gasped, her perfectly kissable mouth dropping open a fraction. Where in the hell was his willpower? Lost. Drowning in the dark pools of her eyes.

"I shouldn't do this," he whispered. "It's improper."

"I don't want you to be proper, Travis," she whispered back, eyes hazy with desire.

"I'm too old." He swiped a thumb across her lower lip, unable to help himself. He had to see if it was as soft as the day before. It might have been softer.

"Age is a frame of mind."

"Too hardened."

"You have a soft heart."

"You're my employee now." He traced a finger across her delicate cheekbone.

"I haven't cashed the check."

"You live in town." He dropped his fingers to the top of her ear, brushing it in the barest of caresses.

She let out a little moan, a sound that went straight to his cock. "You don't."

"You leave the doors unlocked."

She smiled faintly. "Always."

That alone should have been reason enough to stop him. But he was too far gone. She drew him like a moth to flame, and she would burn him up. Cupping her neck, he dipped his head, sealing his mouth over her cotton candy lips. She sighed, a sweet sound coming from the back of her throat, as he teased his tongue over the inside of her full lower lip, and yielded. The feel of her tongue against his set off a chain reaction, starting at the top of his head and racing down his spine to settle in his belly in a molten ball of need. Groaning and pulling her close, he plundered her mouth, stunned as she came alive in his embrace, her tongue thrusting and stroking with a fire that matched his own.

He slid a hand down her back to cup her ass, high and firm from being constantly on her feet. The curve fit his palm perfectly, and she canted her hips against him. But this wouldn't do. The angle was wrong. Not breaking their kiss, he clasped her hips and lifted, setting her on the counter and stepping between her legs so he could press his cock where it belonged against her sweet spot. She hooked a leg around his waist and molded herself to him, breasts pushing against his chest in a form of glorious torture.

Slipping a hand under the hem of her thin cotton shirt, he skated fingers up her satiny skin, stopping only when he encountered the lace of her bra. Brushing a thumb up the swell, he found her nipple, stroking back and forth through the material until she groaned into his mouth and arched into him.

Pulling back, he peppered her jaw with nipping kisses, tongue drawing a line down the creamy column of her neck, tasting a different kind of floral sweetness that made his cock jerk against his jeans, begging to be set free.

"Intoxicating," he murmured into the space between her neck and collarbone, giving a little nip.

"Oh, yes, Travis," she moaned quietly, running her fingers through his hair. "So good."

God, she was gorgeous like this. Hair mussed, lips swollen and eyes drunk and heavy-lidded from his kisses. If they were alone, he'd ravish her right here on the kitchen counter.

If they were alone, the sober recesses of his brain reminded him.

Dax.

The thought acted like a bucket of ice. The kid would be traumatized for life if he woke up and saw him pounding

Elaine. All the reasons why kissing her was the worst idea in the world came slamming back with a vengeance.

He pushed away, immediately missing her heat. "We can't do this," he said harshly.

"What?" Her eyes were still fuzzy and unfocused.

Every cell in his body argued against him, but he had to do it before he did something he'd truly regret. For both their sakes.

"This was a mistake."

Her eyes focused to sharp points as understanding dawned and her face shuttered.

Jesus, what kind of an ass was he?

Might as well go for broke. She could hate him the way Colton did. He turned, making it to the door in half a dozen steps, pausing when the door swung open. "And in my house," he said roughly, hand on the knob. "We lock the door. Always."

He stalked into the darkness, feet carrying him across the yard and around the paddock.

What in Zeus's butthole had he been thinking?

CHAPTER 15

WHAT IN THE hell had just happened? One minute she'd been convinced he was going to take her to bed. The next, he'd pushed her away and yelled about the damned door being unlocked. Elaine let her head fall back to rest on the cabinet, thoughts whirling, body still buzzing from the high of his touch.

Never in her twenty-four years had she been kissed like that.

Ever.

And for the first time in her life, she wanted more. She couldn't help it, she wanted all of Travis Kincaid. Was it possible to be half in love with someone you'd only kissed once? She'd felt a world of possibility in that kiss, a future spinning out before her filled with happiness. Stability.

Pressing her fingers to the bridge of her nose, she inhaled a deep stuttering breath and slowly let it out. "Think, Elaine. Think."

But she couldn't. Not just yet, anyway. Travis's kiss had detonated a bomb inside her. It was going to take a few minutes to collect herself. Her throat grew itchy and hot. She would not give into tears. She was stronger than that. Had endured too much. She'd made the mistake of allowing herself to hope. Something she wouldn't be doing again.

Sliding off the counter, her gaze landed on the open bottle

of wine. The temptation to pour herself a glass to steady her nerves was powerful. But she couldn't risk it. Only one more year and then she could live like a normal human being. Blowing out a long sigh of frustration, she turned to the few remaining dishes still soaking in the sink. Turning on the faucet, she ran more hot water and soaped the sponge. At least her hands could stay busy while her thoughts raced.

Dax was asleep on the couch and Travis had stomped out. Who knew when he'd be back? Did he expect her to curl up on the couch next to Dax and wait for him to finish his little tantrum? Anger flashed through her. Should she call Weston? Or Dottie?

She shook her head, putting the soapy dishes on the other side of the sink to rinse. No, she was figuring this out on her own. But as soon as she took her GED she'd ask Dottie to teach her how to drive. For now she was stuck. But she wouldn't be forever.

She rinsed the remaining dishes and grabbed a towel, slowly drying and putting them away, becoming acquainted with Travis's kitchen layout. It had been a nice meal. Weston and Travis one-upping each other in an effort to make Dax laugh. And she'd been excited about the first project Weston had given her – identifying potential supporters based on analytics. She'd had no idea that voting software could be so sophisticated.

In spite of the way Travis made her feel, she wasn't going to walk away from this job. The money alone was a game changer for her. And she'd endured far worse conditions for far less money. She'd have to keep reminding herself this was a business opportunity and nothing more. She pushed down the hard knot of disappointment that had lodged itself in her chest. Love just wasn't in the cards for her.

With the kitchen set to rights, there was only one thing left to do. Squaring her shoulders, she headed for the door, stopping to brush her fingers through Dax's light hair and give him a kiss on the forehead. His round pudgy face, angelic and sweet when he slept, pulled on her heartstrings. Everything for him. He would have the opportunities she never even knew existed.

Giving Dax a last kiss, she stood and marched out of the house. The night air was heavy and still. Not even a hint of a breeze. Her trailer would be an oven tonight, even with the tiny window AC unit running full blast. She had no idea where to look for Travis. She didn't even know how big the property was.

Stepping off the porch, she wandered across the yard, scanning for anything out of the ordinary. Her ears filled with the sounds of crickets and frogs. Whoever said the country was quiet didn't know what they were talking about. A coyote yipped in the distance.

As she came around the barn, a glorious sight stopped her in her tracks. A three-quarter moon hung low on the horizon, pouring light over the hills in its yellow majesty. Peaceful. Serene. A stark contrast to the man who leaned on the fence on the far side of the paddock, also gazing skyward.

The urge to go to him, to soothe the tension that held his shoulders tight, zipped down her legs, pushing her feet to move. But she held steady. She approached slowly and stopped within calling distance. The draw of his shoulders told her he'd heard her soft approach. Taking a deep breath, she braced for the words she knew she had to get out. "I'm not going to let you blow hot and cold with me, Travis." She kept her voice low, but strong. "I deserve better."

He dipped his head, arms tightening on the rail, but

didn't turn around.

Taking another fortifying breath, she continued. "I loved kissing you. But I can see you're not ready for…" She cast about for the right word, but how could you describe anticipation and desire all rolled up into one? "Whatever it is that's between us. Tomorrow I will cash your check, and when you pick me up I'll be nothing more than your campaign person."

She hated saying those words. They ripped through her with the intensity of a Band-Aid coming off. But it was for the best. At some point, if they became truly intimate, he would expect her to share things. Talk about her past. And then it would be over for good. Better a little pain now than total heartbreak later. "Please take me and Dax home."

He swung around, his face stark and tight in the moon-light. "I'm sorry," he rasped, scraping a hand across his jaw and shaking his head. "I shouldn't have… I never meant to…" His eyes raked over her, wild and raw with turmoil. "You're so beautiful. And soft. I would ruin you."

God, that hurt. Hearing him say she was beautiful and that he'd ruin her in the same breath. As if she hadn't already sunk so low. Hot tears poked at her eyelids. No one had ever called her beautiful. Or looked at her with the kindness that Travis had. But she had to think straight for her son. "We're both adults," her voice came out clipped and rehearsed. "You've given me a great job opportunity and we both can be professional."

Travis sagged against the fence and nodded his head. "You're right." He pushed off and passed, giving her a wide berth.

That hurt too.

You've been through worse, she reminded herself as she

followed at a distance. She waited below the porch while he checked the house, and returned with Dax folded over his shoulder, her new phone in hand.

After he locked the door, he stopped in front of her and stretched out the phone. "Take this with you," he said roughly. "You never know when you or Dax will need anything. And teach Dax how to call 911."

She nodded mutely and followed him to the truck, touching him as little as possible when he helped her up. The drive back seemed endless, silence pressing in on them from all sides.

"Wait here," he said when he pulled up in front of her little trailer. He proceeded up the short walkway and let himself in, turning on a light. She jumped down and waited at the end of the truck while he pulled Dax out and marched ahead of her into the trailer. She hovered by the door while he put Dax to bed, unsure of where to stand so she could avoid his physical presence. But the place was so tiny, there was no avoiding him. He paused in front of her, stony-faced. For a long moment she held his gaze, unable to look away. He raised a hand and gently cupped her cheek, thumb sliding across her cheekbone. The ache in her chest was so intense, tears sprang to her eyes. Before she could blink them back, he'd stepped away and disappeared through the door.

CHAPTER 16

*I*T WAS HOTTER *than fuck. And dry. All he wanted was a glass of ice water. But if he moved, if he twitched, he'd give away their position to the enemy and they'd all get blown to bits. He still didn't understand how they'd ended up using the same rendezvous point as the insurgents. Focused on the neck of the target in front of him, the hilt of his knife loosely grasped between his fingers, he was ready to let fly the second recognition hit the guy's eyes. He would not compromise the mission. The figure turned and the knife clattered from his hand.*

What the fuck? Dax?

Travis sat bolt up, body covered in sweat, breathing in great gasps.

Motherfucker.

He covered his eyes, still breathing in huge gulps, heart slamming in his ears.

"Oh God, oh God," he gasped, hand shaking as he reached for his phone. "Oh fuck, pick up, pick up, pick up." His stomach churned as the phone rang once, twice, three... four times.

"Tell me you're calling in the middle of the night because you finally got laid." Weston's voice came through the speaker like a lifeline.

If only.

"No. I need the name of your shrink. The dreams keep

getting worse."

Weston's voice became instantly alert. "How bad?"

He couldn't tell him. No one could know how bad this dream was. He wanted to puke from it. "Killing people I know. Confusing them with former ops."

"I'll text you the number right off. Anything happen tonight to trigger it?"

"I kissed Elaine."

"'Bout damn time."

He might laugh if the dream hadn't been so horrifying. "You know I can't do that."

Weston sighed into the phone. "Don't sell me that truckload of manure. Not interested. You need to kiss her and keep kissing her until it's okay. Or until she tells you to get lost for good."

"Oh, *that's* brilliant advice." His voice dripped with sarcasm.

"All it is, is sensitization. Just like the horses. If kissing Elaine triggers you – kiss her more. If storms trigger you, go do a Goddamned rain dance until you can do it naked and laughing. But if you don't believe me – talk to Doc Munger about it. All I can say is it helped me."

His heart rate had slowed but was still racing. As long as he lived he'd never get that vision of Dax blotted from his head. "I think I'm gonna go take a walk."

"That's a good place to start. And Travis? This campaign is gonna be stressful. It's good you're dealing with this at the start."

If this was the start, God help him when the going got tough as Weston had warned the other day it would. Still, if this was a wake-up call, maybe it was a good one. He didn't ever want another dream like that one.

He grabbed his shirt from earlier, draped over the chair by his desk. Threw it on over his pajama bottoms and took the stairs two at a time. He had to get out of the house before the walls closed in on him. The tightness in his chest eased once he'd stepped off the porch. The moon cast everything in a pale silvery glow. Plenty of light for navigating through the pasture. He avoided his path this time, needing to focus his thoughts on where he stepped. Focusing on the unfamiliar always seemed to help drive the thoughts from his brain. He counted two rises before he saw the figure standing on the other side of the fence line.

Cassie.

Good. He needed to have a conversation with her anyway.

Judging from the way she held her body and the fact she was wearing pajama bottoms like he was, she'd had a rough night, too. "It's the same moon over Kandahar," he called out softly. "But the stars are brighter there."

Cassie yelped, spinning around. "Jesus, Travis, you scared the shit out of me." Her horse nickered in agreement and flicked her ears. "You scared Winny too. How in the hell do you do that?"

"Walk silently? How do you think?" The hard edge had returned to his voice.

She cocked her head studying him. "You okay?"

"If I was, I wouldn't be out here. And neither would you."

"Humor me, Navy boy."

He laughed harshly at her jab. She had enough problems of her own, he wasn't about to burden her with his. And she was the closest thing he had to a kid sister. He was supposed to be helping her. "Let's just say it's nothing that a moonlit walk won't cure."

"Why'd you rat me out to my mom?"

Travis cocked his head. "Who says I ratted?"

"Mom said she'd talked to you. Said you'd told her to tell me not to be late tomorrow."

This time, he chuckled in earnest. "Your ma's no dummy. But I didn't rat you out." He'd never betray her near miss, but he wasn't above using her healthy fear of her mother to get her to show up to the Hansens'. "I might have applied a little tactical pressure though."

"Hmph."

His voice turned steely. "You blew me off today." Had that really been today? So much had happened since then that his morning workout with Flipper seemed like ages ago.

"About that…" A cow lowed in the distance.

Travis placed his hands on his hips and studied the stars. "I'm waiting," he muttered after a long silence.

"I had a nightmare after I fell asleep while on call the other night. I thought Parker was a Taliban fighter when he tried to wake me up." She spoke so softly he barely heard her. But it registered, and when it did, he couldn't help the sharp gasp as Dax flashed before his eyes again.

"That sucks."

"Yeah." She leaned her forehead into Winny, stroking the mare's shoulder. "Surprised Parker, too. He landed on the floor. Woke up the whole unit." She let out an embarrassed chuckle.

"You know, he may not have said it, but it doesn't take an genius to see that Parker's crazy about you."

The pain in her voice echoed his own. "I don't see why. I'm a fucked-up hot mess who can't make it through the day without freaking out."

So was she going to throw in the towel? Just give into it?

"You don't have to be," he yelled in frustration, more at

himself than her, as Weston's words fell out of his mouth. "You get to decide if your combat experiences are just a part of your story, or if they're your only story."

Fuck.

Weston was right. He had to get over this latest round of shit for himself. And for the sake of the town he loved. After a long while, he spoke softly. "No one ever goes on a mission solo. You're part of a team, Cassie. And a smart warrior knows when to ask for help."

"You know as well as I do, they'll think I can't hack it anymore, or they'll try and medicate me." Her voice was thick with worry and unshed tears. "I don't know who I am when I'm not in the thick of it."

And I don't know who I am when I'm just Travis.

The awful truth of it hit him like a freight train. He might not have the addiction to adrenaline that she did, but he was no better off, hiding in his daily routine, keeping a rigid schedule. Protecting himself with rules and regulations so he didn't have to think about who the real Travis was, outside of his chosen role as community protector. Hearing her was like holding up a mirror. Could he do the same for her? Be her mirror?

Travis pulled his gaze from the sky and focused on her. "So when you come home, you get a job as a firefighter and take unnecessary risks on the back of your bike. And you keep searching for that adrenaline high because that's what you know."

"But I love what I do," she answered softly.

He nodded. "I know, I *know*." He fisted his hands at his hips and looked up at the sky again. Maybe they could help each other. "Look at me. I'm no better. I went from killing machine to community protector."

"At least you keep people safe."

"Do I?" he asked harshly as names and faces flashed through his head. "Ask Parker's uncle Warren or the others who died in the tornado how well I did that." *Ask my unit how well I protected them.* Guilt hit him, fresh and hot as the hours after they'd died.

Did you ever get over it? Maybe that was a question for Dr. Munger. Could you ever go back to a normal, happy life? And if there was no going back, how did you move forward?

She scraped a hand over her face, nodding. "I was a coward today for blowing you off. I'm sorry. I'll be there this afternoon."

He grinned at her. He'd find a way. For himself and her too. "Admission is the first step to recovery. And this time, I'll bring you myself."

"Screw you, Travis."

"I think the correct answer is hooya."

"That's hooah, Navy boy."

CHAPTER 17

"DON'T GO FAR, Dax," Elaine called. "Travis will be here any second to pick us up." She grabbed a very full trash bag from the bin, tied it and hauled it out. She'd have just enough time to run it to the dumpster before Travis arrived promptly at four. He was never late.

The late July heat beat on her neck as she walked the distance to the dumpster. She simultaneously loved and dreaded every afternoon. She'd been surprised to discover she enjoyed the analytics of voter identification. Because of her work, Travis's first piece of mail was about to be sent out to targeted residents across the county. It felt good, knowing she was making a difference. But it didn't quite make up for the ache at the base of her throat that sprang up when she occasionally snuck a glance his direction.

It was for the best, their enforced distance, even if it felt awkward when they were alone. She could tell that Weston was doing his best to act as a buffer, staying for dinner every night. Even going so far as to offer to run her and Dax home. But one thunderous look from Travis and he'd backed off, allowing Travis to continue making the nightly trip.

An SUV she didn't recognize pulled up, and Travis leaned an elbow out the window.

"What's this? Did something happen to Weston's truck?"

Travis shook his head and grinned. Her stomach tap

112

danced right up to her heart. He didn't smile nearly enough. But when he did, she couldn't help but smile back. The hard planes of his face softened, and even though they were obscured by his aviators, she could tell his eyes sparkled. "Nope. Thought it might be time to retire my beat-up Chevy. Drive something more sheriff-like." He hopped out of the car and opened the passenger door. "And check this out." He gestured for her to look in the back seat. "Built-in booster seats."

She leaned in, enveloped by new car scent. Sure enough, the middle of the back seat was folded down, and she could see how the seatbelt had been adjusted. "Sweet. Dax will love this. I don't think he's ever ridden in a new car." Neither had she for that matter.

"Do you like it?"

She backed out of the door and shut it, turning to study him. There was something in his tone of voice that pulled at her. Was he looking for her approval? "Sure. I think it's great."

He seemed to relax. "Good, good." Putting his hands on his hips he scanned the picnic area. "Where's Dax?"

"He was here a second ago. Let me go find him."

"No need." Travis took off before she could stop him, calling back over his shoulder. "He's probably on the swings."

Elaine bit back a sigh. The view was just as gorgeous from behind as it was from the front. His worn Wranglers molded to his ass and cut into the back of his thigh. The man filled out a pair of jeans perfectly. She could keep her libido in check, but it was the sight of Travis and Dax returning together, hand in hand, that made her go gooey on the inside and had her fighting to find air. Dax was grinning from ear to ear and bouncing when he walked. The last time he'd bounced was the afternoon the tornado hit, when she'd given him a few dollars to get candy at the Five 'n Dime, and he'd bounced out of Dottie's without a care in the world. Thanks to Travis, she was seeing a glimpse of her little boy again.

Not trusting herself to talk, she hurried around the front end and settled in, awed by the electronics and buttons on the dashboard. She'd relaxed into the very comfortable seat by the time they pulled to a stop at the end of the drive. Dax launched himself out of the back seat and made a beeline for the porch, shouting as he ran.

She hurried to catch up. "What's this?" she asked when Travis reached her. Propped up against the porch was a brand-new bicycle. It was obviously for Dax, but she couldn't understand why.

Travis shrugged, avoiding looking at her, instead watching Dax with a small smile. "He seemed bored inside. I thought he might like to learn."

Elaine shook her head vigorously, staving off the panic that fluttered at the edge of her consciousness. She couldn't be indebted to Travis like this. He'd done so much for them. Too much. "That's so kind of you. But we really can't–"

"Of course you can." The tightness returned to his mouth. "Every kid needs to learn how to ride a bike."

"But what if he falls? Gets hurt?" If anything happened to him, she'd never forgive herself.

"Elaine." Travis turned, clasping her shoulders. "You've got to stop treating him like he's porcelain. You have to let him be a kid."

His touch warmed and comforted her. But not enough to let it go. Her throat caught. "But Warren died keeping him safe." She shut her eyes, fighting the tears that sprang up at the thought of Warren's sacrifice. She still couldn't think of him without crying.

Travis pulled her into an embrace. She sagged against him, letting herself lean into his solid strength. Maybe it made her weak, that she needed his reassurance. But she couldn't help it. She'd nearly lost her son. She couldn't risk losing him again.

His hand came to her head, fingers massaging her scalp. "Warren did die protecting your son. And that is as wonderful as it is awful. But you have to let Dax be a little boy. If you teach him to stay afraid, he'll go through his whole life that way. You can't do that to him. I know you don't want that for him."

She nodded against his shirt, eyes wet.

"He'll be okay. Even if he falls and scrapes a knee."

She nodded again, taking a big shuddering breath, his masculine scent setting her head buzzing. Travis's arms tightened around her and the air between them shifted. Became tense with sexual energy. Heat surged through her, setting her skin tingling and dropping with an ache to her core. Squeezing her eyes shut, she fought the butterflies that had taken flight in her stomach. With a small sigh of defeat, she pushed on his chest and stepped out of his embrace. But not before the lust in his eyes licked through her in another surge of awareness. She wanted that look. Wanted what came after a look like that. The kisses and caresses. And God help her, she wanted his cock. In her hand, in her mouth, pushing into her and filling her up six ways to Sunday, putting a glorious end to the tension that strung her out like a junkie.

Tearing her gaze away, she turned to the bike. "You have a helmet?" Her voice didn't sound like her own.

"On the porch." Neither did his. His words came out strangled. Tight.

She could do this. Act like there was nothing there. Be professional. Forcing a smile to her mouth, she called to Dax. "Let's get your helmet on, kiddo."

Dax grabbed the helmet hanging on the lintel and put it on his head. "I know how this works."

"Let me help you snap it under your chin." Travis moved to the bike and bent, securing the helmet. "Okay buddy, you can use the bike and go anywhere in the yard, but don't use the pedals yet, got it?"

"Why not?"

"You've got to learn to balance first." He gave Dax a fist bump.

Elaine cocked her head in wonder. "That's very clever."

"It's how I learned. It doesn't take long at all. Sometimes just a few hours. Did you learn with training wheels?"

She shook her head, shame prickling up the back of her neck. Yet another example of her pathetic childhood. "Never learned," she said with an offhand shrug, hoping it came off like she didn't care. There'd barely been food in the cupboards, let alone money for something as extravagant as a bike.

A muscle ticked in Travis's jaw as he shook his head and he stalked around the corner of the house. Her insides burned as she watched him disappear. Was it that bad? That she'd never learned to ride a bike? She bit the inside of her cheek, focusing on the sharp pain instead of the dull ache in her chest. At least Dax had opportunities.

"Here, have a try." Travis returned with an adult sized bike.

"Are you kidding?"

That hint of a smile was back, doing funny things to her insides. "Does it look like it? Never too late to learn."

She crossed her arms. "Oh, no. I'm too old."

"C'mon. I promise I won't let you fall."

Of course he wouldn't. He'd stand right next to her, a protective tower of testosterone. And she'd fall over, not because she couldn't balance, but because all she could think about was rubbing herself against him. A nervous giggle escaped. "But you don't have a helmet."

"Didn't wear one when I learned. And you'll be fine here in the yard."

There was no getting out of this. She could tell by his determined stance. Opening her hands, she gave in. "Fine. Teach me how to ride a bike."

The smile he gave her pulled at something deep inside her. He looked as excited as Dax. "Okay, same rules as Dax. Hop on and I'll adjust the seat." He held onto the handlebar and stood aside so she could swing a leg over the seat.

She covered his hand with hers, just for balance, of course. And stood still while he squatted down and ran a hand up the side of her leg. She was pretty sure touching her thigh had nothing to do with adjusting the seat, but she wasn't about to complain. Not with the waves of electricity shooting up to rest at her apex. She clenched her thighs, but that did nothing to stave off the sweet ache. Only one thing would do that, and it wasn't in the cards for them.

Travis's voice was husky in her ear. "There. That should be better. Sit back."

She settled on the seat and discovered she could easily keep her feet flat on the ground.

He nodded his approval. "Great, now walk the bike around in a big circle. Get a feel for how it moves."

It was awkward going, at first. The backs of her legs hit the pedals. But she widened her stance and the bike moved more easily.

"Travis," Dax called. "Chase me."

His grin returned. "Duty calls. Will you be okay?"

"Of course."

He jogged to where Dax was scooting across the yard, waving his arms and making monster sounds. She laughed out loud. If her camera hadn't been in her purse, she'd have taken a video. She'd gone crazy over the last few weeks, taking pictures and videos of Dax, entertaining them both. She didn't have any baby pictures of him, so she wanted to make up for lost time.

Elaine continued scooting around the yard, keeping half an eye on the pair. What would happen if she gave a hard push? Sticking one leg out, she pushed with the other. The bike wheeled forward with a little wobble. She tried it on the other side. Still a wobble. Stopping, she made sure her weight was evenly divided and pushed again. This time the bike went a little further with no wobble. Confidence surged through her. She could do this. Giving a harder push, she tried a little turn. The bike tipped. Down came her foot. Okay, not ready for turns. But balancing was coming.

"Mommy, *look*!" Dax called from across the yard. Travis gave the boy a push and he rolled across the yard, feet sticking out to the side before the bike wobbled. He'd gone about three feet, but it was a start. "Good for you, honey," she cheered.

The proud smile on his face spoke volumes. "Your turn, Mommy."

She gave a push, imitating Dax, and getting almost as far before the bike wobbled.

"Good job, Mom."

She couldn't help the happy laugh that bubbled out of

her. "I'm getting there."

"Here," Travis's gravelly voice slid over her. "Let me give you a push. On three." He counted off and sent the bike flying, feet crunching close behind. Elaine kept her feet out as long as she dared, laughing at the pure joy of it. He was right there, wrapping an arm around her shoulder once she'd rolled to a stop. "I knew you could do it."

She warmed at the pride in his voice. Wanted to wrap it around her like a blanket. Letting out a sigh of pure contentment, she leaned her head against him. "Thank you, Travis. This means so much to me."

He stiffened, dropping his arm. Clearing his throat, he stepped back, a scowl on his face and all business again. "Time to head in." He turned and marched back to the house without a backward glance.

CHAPTER 18

TRAVIS PULLED TO a stop in front of Elaine's trailer and reached for the box on the front seat. He seemed to have a soft spot for Dax he couldn't shake. Last week it had been the bike, and this week when he'd returned to the police station from Manhattan, package in hand, Weston had cocked an eyebrow and shaken his head.

"What?" he'd growled. If the kid was gonna learn to ride horses, he needed a real pair of boots. And what kid didn't want a cowboy hat?

"When you gonna wake up and smell the coffee?" Weston had asked.

There was no coffee to smell. Dax was a good kid. And he enjoyed having Dax at the house. Why wouldn't he want to do things that put a smile on the kid's face? He hadn't exactly had the easiest life to date.

And the SUV had made good sense. Granted, it dug into his nest egg a little more than he'd wanted. Okay, a lot more. But he was tired of borrowing Weston's truck to bring Elaine and Dax back and forth. The built-in car seat in the back was just unexpected bonus. Nothing more. Grabbing the box, he opened the door and jogged up the short walk.

It was only seven in the morning, but already the air was thick and heavy. The heat and humidity had been building for days, and one of these afternoons it would storm. Thankfully tornado season was over, although technically, with the right conditions another one could spin up. Unease prickled up his spine. No one looked at the skies the same way anymore. Not even him.

Elaine's door stood open but he still knocked twice, pushing away the flash of irritation at her insistence on leaving her home unsecure. That was a battle he wasn't going to win.

"Come in," she called from inside. "Dax is finishing breakfast."

Stepping in, he tucked the box behind his back. Not that it got past the eagle eyes of a seven-year-old.

"What's that?" Dax pointed to the box.

"Something you need for today."

Elaine gave him a look of exasperated pleasure that had his cock jerking in his shorts. By the time the special election rolled around, he'd be immune to her, right? *Ha. Tell yourself another lie, asshole.*

Ignoring the voice in his head, he laid the box on the table. "Go ahead. Open it."

Dax dug into the box with the enthusiasm of a kid on Christmas morning. He couldn't wait to see the boy's reaction to the boots. His chest pulled tight, then relaxed at the delight on Dax's face. It felt so good he almost wanted to bring him something every day. Just to feel that warmth spreading across his chest again.

"Travis," Elaine reprimanded, but unable to keep a smile off her face. "You really don't have to do this."

"Nonsense. Every boy around here needs a hat and boots." He glanced back over at Dax, who'd immediately put on the cowboy hat, and was sitting on the floor, pulling on the boots. His heart twisted. For a split second, he'd flashed to a memory of Colton yanking on a pair of boots, excited to ride with their dad. He ignored the tickle in his throat and kept talking. "If he's going to spend a day helping us with the horses, it's a requirement."

Elaine reached for her wallet. "At least let me pay you, then."

He widened his stance, crossing his arms. "Nope." He hadn't intended to buy anything on his weekly trip up to Manhattan, but he'd found himself in front of the western wear shop on Poyntz, and he couldn't resist taking a look.

"Travis." Her face softened and the faintest whisper of pink crossed her cheeks. Maybe her plain white shirt was his favorite. It set off her pale skin and brought out the color in her cheeks, as well as the blue of her eyes. She opened her mouth to speak, but Dax interrupted.

"Mom, mom, *mom.* Look."

She swung her gaze to her son, her face lighting. Her reaction was even better than Dax's. He'd definitely bring them something every day to be the recipient of *that* look.

"Every inch the cowboy." She turned back to Travis, eyes full of concern. "You'll make sure he stays safe?"

He nodded. "Of course." There was no way he'd let anything happen to Dax. "Remind me where you're off to?"

Dottie crowded into the living room. "I'm driving Elaine to Manhattan to take her GED today. You ready, sweetie pie?"

"What?" His stomach sank. He should be the one to take her. "Why didn't you tell me? I could have–"

A flush rose up Elaine's neck. "I wanted to do this on my own. You've done so much already."

God, he wanted to hold her. Reassure her and kiss away her worry. He hated seeing her face pinched with anxiety. It made his chest hurt. He would do anything to see her smile.

He cleared his throat. "I'm sure you'll knock it out of the park."

And there was the smile that warmed his belly. "Thanks. Dottie's been a great tutor. I'm prepared." And her quiet confidence. "Are you sure you'll be okay with Dax?"

"Don't you worry about Dax, sweetie pie," Dottie reassured her. "Between Travis and the Hansens, someone will have eyes on him at all times."

Elaine bent and gave Dax a hug. "You be good, 'kay? Listen to Travis?"

He squirmed out of her hug. "I'll be *fine,* Mom."

She stood and took a deep breath, turning her focus to him. "Thanks again. Call if you need anything."

The urge to take her in his arms and press away the wrinkle above her nose had his hands twitching. But he stepped aside to let her pass, fisting a hand at his side so he didn't reach out.

"All set, kiddo?" Travis asked, dropping a hand to the boy's shoulder.

Dax grinned up at him. "I'm having a man's day, huh?"

"You bet, buddy. But let's go get some grub first. How does special breakfast at the food truck sound like?"

Travis fought to keep from laughing as Dax's eyes narrowed shrewdly. "Can I have chocolate milk?"

"Does your mom let you have chocolate milk?"

He looked a little guilty. "Sometimes, but not at breakfast."

This kid. He should say no. "Well, I bet once won't hurt. Chocolate milk it is." Warmth spread across his chest as he was rewarded with another toothy grin.

Hours later, Dax stood on the rungs of the pen, arms draped over the top as he watched Hope coach Cassidy through a pattern with a big gelding. Travis slung an arm over his narrow shoulders as Cassidy left the ring. "What do you think, buddy? Would you like to do that someday?"

Dax nodded eagerly. "And I want to ride a bucking bronco too."

Again the pang. Colton had become obsessed with bucking broncos at roughly the same age. "First, let's get you riding tame horses. How does that sound?"

Hope returned to the paddock with a small palomino mare. "This is Sunny. She's half Arabian. I picked her up in Oklahoma about a week ago. She's real gentle and on the small side. Does she fit the bill?"

Travis nodded. Pleased. She'd be the perfect first horse for a new rider. He tilted his head and eyed Dax. "What do you say? You want to ride her?"

"*Yeah*," he shouted, hopping off the fence.

"First rule of horseback riding," he said as he caught up to Dax. "No yelling around the horses. It scares 'em, right? And what do you think would happen if a horse got scared?"

Dax thought for a minute. "Would it buck you off?"

"It might. And we promised your mom safety first, right?"

Dax nodded.

Hope bent. "Okay, Dax. I'm going to teach you how to join up with Sunny here. You know what that is?"

Dax's eyes were saucers. He shook his head. "It's when the horse and rider get to be friends. Would you like to be friends with Sunny?"

He nodded rapidly.

She handed him a looped lead line. "Okay, I'm going to be right here next to you the whole time."

Travis hung back by the gate, watching with a combination of excitement and pride as Hope took the boy through the same process she'd taken the adults.

Cassidy came to stand next to him, her eyes fixed on the pair in the ring. After a minute, she spoke. "You were right, you know. About the horses helping. Thanks."

"I know someone you can talk to if you decide to take the plunge. It's been… helpful." He wouldn't admit that to many people, that his sessions in Manhattan with Dr. Munger had helped him. But maybe by being the example, she'd see that talking to someone wasn't as scary as being afraid to go to sleep.

Cassie narrowed her eyes. "Does this bend toward self-improvement have to do with running for sheriff or with a certain lady?"

He shrugged, avoiding her gaze. "We all have shit to deal with. Maybe I just got tired of hauling mine around for so long."

"Hhmph."

"Hey Travis, look!" Dax called enthusiastically from atop Sunny. "I'm riding all by myself."

The warm spot in his chest grew. "Lookin' good there, kiddo." He pulled out his phone. "Let me take a picture and send it to your mom. She'll be so proud of you." Dax gave him a huge smile and he snapped a picture, sending it off in a quick text to Elaine.

Cassidy nudged him. "Your grin is about as big as his. What gives?"

His smile froze. "Nothing. He's a good kid, that's all."

She cocked an eyebrow. "I always knew the Navy was filled with bullshitters." Pushing off the fence, she gave him a finger wave as she headed for her old Yamaha motorcycle. "See you 'round."

Cassidy was wrong. He'd be proud of any kid who had

begun to turn around the way Dax had. It was his job to be kind to all the children in Prairie. Teach them that police were friendly, safe. Sure, he liked Dax. Dax was a great kid. But it wasn't like he was related to the boy.

The breeze shifted, bringing with it the scent of rain. Travis turned and studied the sky. Clouds were building to the southwest. They probably had another ten, maybe fifteen minutes before the rain came. Thunder rolled in the distance. Travis glanced over to the pen. Dax had stiffened in the saddle, face scrunched up.

Poor guy. He didn't like storms much either since the tornado.

"Hope, let's wrap things up. Storm's a comin'"

She gave him a thumb up.

Travis circled the pen and came around to where Hope's mustang, Buttercup, stood. "Come on, girl. Time to get you back to the barn." He took the reins, and began leading the horse around to the barn. By the time Buttercup had been put in the stall and the tack put away, the sky had gone dark and big fat raindrops were splatting on the ground.

When he reached the pen, he could see Dax with his hands full of rope, eyes wide with fear. "It's just a storm, Dax. No one's going to get hurt. Take the rope to the tack room, and then head up to the house, will you?"

Hope handed Travis the reins to Sunny. "Take Sunny to the barn and tie her to the post. We can unsaddle her once we've put the rest of the stuff away." She gestured to the remaining obstacles and tack at the far end of the arena.

He hurried to the barn with Sunny, looping her reins around a post halfway down the aisle, and turned just as a bright flash of lightning and an instant clap of thunder ripped across the sky. The heavens opened up, and the rain came down in curtains. Hunching his shoulders, he jogged to the pen, instantly soaked through. "I'll take the rest. You head up to the house," he shouted over the din. Hope handed him the last of the tack, and he raced for the barn.

The storm was a doozie. The rain came in sheets as black sky glowed where lightning popped around him. He hurried through the rest of the chores, glad that Hope was around to reassure Dax.

When he arrived on the back porch several minutes later, Hope handed him a towel. "I hope Cassie made it home before the rain hit," she said breathlessly. "I haven't been caught in a downpour like that in ages."

"Me either." Shaking out his Stetson, he scanned the porch, then went cold. "Where's Dax?"

Hope gave him a funny look. "I thought he was following after you?"

He shook his head, icy fingers of dread clutching at his heart. "I sent him to the tack room with the ropes and told him to head up here."

"I'll check inside."

Wind screamed through the trees as the rain pelted down furiously. But the sky didn't have any of the sick green color that indicated tornadoes were close. This was just a big summer thunderstorm. Totally normal for Kansas in August. Travis tried to calm the rising panic in his chest. He was probably hiding somewhere inside, scared of the storm.

Hope returned, shaking her head. Travis was off the porch in a flash, running through the mud to the barn. Dax had to be in the barn. Goddammit. Why hadn't he thought to check the weather today? Or ask Elaine how Dax had reacted to storms since the tornado? "Dax?" he called out as soon as he'd pushed open the barn door. "I'm here, Dax. Everything is okay."

Nothing but the deafening sound of rain and thunder shaking the timbers. The storm was louder out here than in the house. Much louder. "Dax," he yelled. Dread gnawed at him. He was a cop for chrissakes. Elaine had relied on him to keep her son safe, and he'd gone and lost the boy.

Travis searched the empty stalls. No Dax. A sick ache fisted in his chest as he checked the tack room. He paced the aisle. Where in the hell was he? Maybe in the loft? "Dax?" he shouted as he climbed. He would *not* give into panic. "Panic is not productive," he chanted in time to his climbing. He squinted through the dim, looking for anything unusual or out of place. Nothing. And the storm was even louder up here. No place for a scared kid. Surely he couldn't be out in the storm? Travis slid open the second-story door to look out, just in case, but he couldn't see for shit. The heavy rain had reduced visibility to a few feet. Another bang of thunder shook the barn.

The ache in his chest grew, squeezing on his throat. "Think, Travis. Think. If you were scared, you'd try to make yourself as small as possible." The boy *had* to be somewhere in the barn. He must have missed it in his panic. He climbed down the ladder and looked again in the stalls, giving extra care to the dark corners.

"*Dax.* Come out, buddy," he choked out. "I'm here, kiddo." He'd never forgive himself if anything happened to the boy. He stepped inside the tack room, flipping on the light this time. He passed over a pile of blankets, then paused, looking closer. "Dax?" He crossed the room in two steps, sinking to his knees. He pulled back the blanket and sagged with relief, hands shaking as the adrenaline released.

The sight of Dax curled into a tiny rigid ball, eyes

squinched shut, a grimace on his face and fingers stuffed in his ears, shredded him to his core. His throat grew tight with emotion and his eyelids prickled. "I'm here, son. It's okay. You're safe. I'm here." He hauled Dax into his lap and leaned back against the wall, rocking him and stroking the boy's back, repeating the words over and over. He tightened his embrace, aware that Dax was shaking like a leaf.

Travis had never been so afraid in his life, nor so relieved. Not even when his unit had been ambushed. The realization slammed into him with the force of a freight train, momentarily stealing his air. He loved this little guy. More than anything. Travis dropped his head back to the wall, blowing out a breath. Fucking hell. What was he supposed to do now?

CHAPTER 19

TRAVIS PACED THE kitchen like a caged lion, alternately checking on the burgers he was prepping for dinner and on Elaine, who sat at the table with her back to him. How many times in the past month had he wanted to quit their stupid charade and kiss her? She belonged with him. They just *fit*. He couldn't explain it any other way. The house felt like a home with her here at the table and Dax running around in the yard. He no longer felt uncomfortable with the way the front door stood open, so they could keep an eye on Dax. The election would be over in three weeks' time. Then what? He couldn't go back to the way things were. Wouldn't.

"What do you think of this ad?" Elaine called from the table.

Travis stopped behind her and braced an arm on the table beside her. Heat licked up his spine as he caught a whiff of her shampoo. He shut his eyes against the zing of awareness that had his cock doing a happy dance.

He slid a glance her way. She sat perfectly still, jaw tight. He itched to trace a finger down the line of her jaw, melt her cool facade. See her drop her head and expose the creamy curve of her neck. His cock jerked against his jeans as he stared hungrily at the pout of her mouth. How many restless nights had he endured over the last month? How many of his dreams had she haunted? He'd lost count. What he longed for, hell, *needed*, was to feel what they'd felt that first night in the kitchen at the beginning of the summer. A world of possibility had opened up for him in that moment, and he'd been too much of a chickenshit to seize it. This distance was his fault.

She glanced over, her eyes widening, mouth parting. Could she hear his heart pounding? "Elaine," he rasped, dipping his head.

Weston burst in the door. "Did I interrupt something?" he asked with a smirk.

Asshole.

Travis stepped back with a growl. "Yes," he snarled, done with the bullshit.

"No," Elaine answered at the same time.

"You two will have to work out whatever's going on between you another time. Right now we have to talk about the First Responder's Ball in two weeks."

"Not going," he gritted out, crossing his arms. He hated those damned events. He'd happily give them his money, but he wasn't going to stuff himself into a suit and stand around making small talk with a bunch of young responders who only wanted to get drunk and dirty dance with their girlfriends.

"Not going to what?" Dottie poked her head in the door behind Weston.

Jesus Christ on a pogo stick. Were they all conspiring against him today? "First Responder's Ball."

Dottie stepped around Weston, holding an envelope and skewering him with a pointed look. "Considering the funds raised this year are going to defray my future son-in-law's medical bills, I hope that's not the case."

Shit. Parker had recently been injured in a burnover out in Colorado and had barely escaped with his life. "I'll write a check. Double it. But I'm not going to that thing. You know how I hate them."

Weston crossed his arms. "I know you've refused in years past, but this time, *Mr. Candidate*, you're going. Half the town is going this year. First responders are your people. You need to go shake hands. I guarandamntee you that Lawson will be there, so you're going, too." He narrowed his gaze, eyes snapping. "Unless this candidacy is pure BS. In which case, quit wasting Elaine's and my time." Weston's tone brooked no argument.

Elaine stood. "Maybe I should check on Dax?"

Dottie shook her head. "He's riding his bike in the yard. And I need to talk to you." She waved the envelope and held it out. "This came in the mail."

Travis didn't miss the way Elaine's shoulders tightened. She pushed her chair back. "Do you think?"

Dottie nodded expectantly. "Open it."

She shook her head. "I can't. I'm too nervous."

"Don't be, sweetie pie. You were ready for that test." Dottie pressed the envelope into Elaine's hands.

Even from across the room, Travis could see how her hands shook, pulling apart the paper. But her smile had him crossing the room before she squeaked, "I passed."

With a shout, he pulled her into a hug and spun her around, kissing her forehead. "I knew you could do it! I'm so proud of you."

She laughed, eyes shiny with unshed tears, and hugged him back. He knew the exact moment when she caught herself because she stiffened in his arms. Biting back a groan of frustration, he let her slide down his body, not releasing her until her feet touched the floor.

"We all knew you could do it, sweetie pie," Dottie

stepped over and wrapped her in another hug.

Weston caught his eye and arched a brow. God, he wanted to fucking punch something. Why shouldn't it be the most natural thing in the world for him to swing her around? He loved her. The realization pulled him up short. Weston was right, maybe he'd loved her from the start. There was no denying she'd crawled under his skin day one and taken up residence. But the transformation had been so subtle. Like he'd been walking north without a compass and ended up facing south. And everyone had seen it but him. It shouldn't surprise him, he loved Dax. Would do anything for the boy. And how could you love one without the other?

The problem was, what to do about it? This changed everything. For starters, their self-imposed distance needed to end, pronto. They could figure out the rest later.

"I only popped in for a minute," Dottie said as she moved to the door. "And Travis, I better see you at the First Responder's Ball." She gave him a no-nonsense glare that had him squirming down to his toes.

"Yes ma'am." He never could say no to Dottie. She'd been like a second mother to him.

As soon as the screen door clicked shut behind her, Weston tossed a thick manila envelope down on the table. "Elaine, you'll need to go with Travis. He'll need someone to help him remember everything in this dossier. It's a list of names and photos of all the police chiefs, assistant chiefs, fire marshals and fire chiefs in the county, as well as any pertinent cases from the last five years."

Elaine's eyes grew wide and she backed up, shaking her head. "Oh no. That's a bad idea. I'm no good at that sort of thing. An-an-and I don't have a dress."

Weston crossed his arms, mouth drawing down. "You

have time to get one. It's a week away. Besides..." His mouth twitched. "That's why Travis pays you the big bucks."

"I need to check with Dottie, too. You're not the only person I work for."

"Don't you think she'd have said something just now, if it was going to be a problem? Besides, it always looks better when the candidate has a date. Voters want to see Travis as settled and capable. And Lawson is the kind of guy who'd show up with... someone less classy than yourself. It's an opportunity to point out the difference between the two without saying a word."

She was grasping at straws. And he knew why she was doing it. Would she change her mind once they'd talked? He didn't want to put on a penguin suit and parade around shaking hands any more than she did, but he could manage it with her by his side. Hell, it might even be fun.

Weston continued. "There will be other dignitaries there as well, and likely a few people from the unions and the governor's office. They've rented out the ballroom at the Bison & Bull Inn. I've already reserved adjoining suites for the two of you. Elaine, you'll have to find someplace for Dax to spend the night."

"Oh no. I'm not spending the night away from him. What if he needs me?" The fear radiating off Elaine was palpable, but it wasn't like Dax was a baby.

"He'll be fine with Dottie and Teddy," said Travis. "And we can head back early the next day."

"Travis never sleeps past zero dark thirty," added Weston.

"But if Dottie is going who would stay with Dax?"

Damn, the woman was stubborn when she made up her mind. He admired it, even as her refusal to join him irritated the heck out of him. "Dottie won't be spending the night, she's got to open up the food truck. My guess is he'd stay with Teddy. Teddy hates these things as much as I do."

She shook her head firmly. "No. I'm sorry. You can go, but I'm going to stay here."

"Dax will be fine, and if he's not at first, he'll learn to be fine."

Elaine bristled, voice rising. "Don't you tell me how to parent my child. I know him better than anyone."

That got his hackles up. Didn't she see what she was doing? "You suffocate him," he countered, voice tight. "You hardly let him be a kid. He needs to fall down. He needs to be scared and know he's going to come out of it okay."

"What do you know about parenting?" she yelled. "You just come around like a jolly uncle. All fun and games. None of the worry, none of the anxiety."

That stung. Especially after his experience with Dax in the storm. "I know I was raised by a single dad and it wasn't easy, and I turned out fine," he yelled back. Except Colton hadn't turned out so fine. And when their dad had died not long after he'd passed his SEAL Tactical Training, Colton had been pretty much left to fend for himself. No wonder he'd made bad choices.

Elaine's eyes sparked with anger and hurt. "You don't know what he's been through. He's had enough fear to last a lifetime."

"Then he damn well better learn how to handle it," he roared. "All you're teaching him is to be afraid of everything."

"Stop it, stop it," cried Dax from the door. "Stop yelling at my mommy." He stood just inside the door, a look of worry and fear on his face, covering his ears.

Fuck. The fight drained out of him. He was an asshole. How many times had he pleaded with his parents to stop the yelling before his mother had finally abandoned them? How many times had he hidden on the stairs, half covering his ears, terrified of what he'd hear but unable to block it out completely? His stomach churned.

"I should go," Elaine said quietly. She looked over to Weston. "Can you bring us home, please?"

No. Nononono. Shit. He had to make this right. He crossed the room and squatted down to get eye level with Dax. "I'm sorry you heard me yelling, buddy. I didn't mean to scare you. Sometimes adults have disagreements. Even–" *Even adults who love each other.* Voicing that thought scared the shit out of him. "Even adults who are... good friends," he finished lamely. God, he was making a clusterfuck out of this.

He turned back to Elaine. The look on her face cut him to the core. He had to make this right. *Had to.* He stood and closed the distance between them, taking her hand between his. "Please don't go? I'm sorry I lost my temper." A knot formed at the base of his throat. "I was out of line. But I want you to know..." he swallowed, the words sticking in his mouth. "I-I want you to know how much I care about Dax." She looked like she was about to cry. Because of him. What an ass. "Please say you'll stay?"

CHAPTER 20

WESTON'S VOICE CUT in. "All right kids, time to get back on track. I've got to get back to the station." He strode to the door, stopping to ruffle Dax's hair. "You two need to put this aside and remember the election is in twenty-one days. The work only gets more intense from here on out. I'll see you two tomorrow." He gave them a little salute and shut the door behind him with a click.

The sound echoed through the room.

Elaine inhaled deeply, trying to steady the riot of emotions swirling through her. The urge to run, embarrassment at the realization that Travis was right. She *did* hover over Dax. She couldn't help it. Sitting in Dottie's basement in the dark, wind screaming around them – her life had flashed before her eyes. More importantly, her life without her son had flashed before her eyes.

She covered her face, momentarily overwhelmed. "You're right. I helicopter. And I don't mean to. I'm just. *So.* Scared," she said thickly. Hot tears rose up, and try as she might, she couldn't stop them this time. "I couldn't live if anything happened to him."

Travis's arms came around her, pulling her into his chest. His strength, the steadiness of him, was her undoing. The tears came freely. "You have no idea how terrifying it was. Sitting there, in the dark, not knowing if he was okay. If I'd ever see my baby again."

"Hush, now," he soothed, rubbing her back. "You're both okay now. And I promise I'll do my best to keep you both safe."

The conviction in his voice drove right to her heart, twisting in the most bittersweet way. She loved him. And it hurt that this was the most she could hope for – a gentle hug and words of encouragement when she needed it. It could be worse. He could hate her. She sniffled, dragging in a rough breath. Her job with him would be over in three weeks. Maybe it was time to think about moving on. Travis would be elected sheriff. He'd have to move to Marion. And someday, he'd find some nice, respectable lady to settle down with. Someone without an embarrassing past who'd make a nice sheriff's wife. And she wasn't sure she could handle watching that. She had limits.

She stepped out of Travis's embrace, instantly missing it. But it was for the best. She couldn't torture herself this way. Wiping a finger beneath her eyes, she nodded. "Weston was right. We need to get to work."

Travis gave her a hard look, then nodded slowly. "Right. I smell the burgers. C'mon Dax. Why don't you help me put dinner out?"

The burgers were delicious, but did nothing to cut the tension between them. Even Dax remained subdued. Elaine studied Travis, sneaking glances at him throughout the meal. His face was alternately thunderous, then soft. The lines of his mouth would grow deep at turns, then soften. As if he was wrestling with some kind of inner beast.

After dinner was no better. Travis was distracted, missing every question she directed at him, and when he finally heard them, only answering in one-word grunts. "Enough," she said sharply, pushing back from the table. "Please take us home. We're not getting any work done here."

He gazed at her intently, eyes inscrutable. "Weston was right."

"About what?" Why did her heart pound when he stared at her like that?

"All of it. About needing to go with a classy date."

"I'm not classy." The words were out of her mouth before she realized it.

"Of course you are," Travis objected flatly.

Fine. He wanted to go there? "I'm a high school dropout, Travis."

"Who just earned her GED."

"I had Dax when I was *seventeen*." She shuddered at the memory. "You know what they called me in school? Slut. Whore." She held out her scarred arms, unable to stop the barrage now that she'd let go. She was like a bubbling pot of shame and humiliation. "And I know you've seen these. I see the questions in your eyes when you look at them." Her chest flamed. "Classy, isn't it? A girl who slept around and cut herself? Who has a track record of shitty choices?" She stopped short of telling him the worst. The words were right there. But she couldn't bear to see the disappointment that would surely cover his face. It would break her.

She brushed her eye and took a shuddering breath, diving back in to press her point home. "You know who's classy? Emmaline Andersson. She makes beautiful dresses that everyone oohs and ahhs over." She couldn't stop. It was like he'd unscrewed a faucet. "Millie Prescott is classy. Look how she opened up her store after the tornado and gave everyone food. I'm just a single mom who works two jobs to barely get by. I don't even know how to drive." Her neck was on fire.

Her cheeks too, from the feel of it. How pathetic was that? Twenty-four and she didn't even know how to drive. She shook her head, lowering her gaze so Travis wouldn't see the tears threatening to spill over again.

The silence weighed heavy between them. "All that shows is that you've done what it takes to support your son. You've never said an unkind word to anyone or about anyone as long as I've known you. And Dottie sings your praises. She doesn't do that for just anyone."

She glanced up at him through wet lashes, surprised by the gentleness in his voice. His expression took her breath away. His eyes lit with earnestness, his face a mixture of frustration and admiration. "You're plenty classy, Elaine."

Well, color her stunned.

First, he called her beautiful, now this? That he thought she was classy? She opened her mouth to object, but the fire went out of her. She snapped it shut. "Fine. I'll consider going."

The car ride home was quiet. Nobody felt like talking, and that was fine with her. She was all out of words anyway. Dax's quiet snores filled the interior. Travis shut off the car. "Wait here."

She laid a restraining hand on his arm. "You really don't have to do this."

"Of course I do," he growled, and slipped out the driver's side door.

Of course he did. He'd never let her enter a space that he didn't know for certain had been secured. Not in a million years. Sighing, she stepped out of the SUV and leaned against the side, studying the stars. They were just enough on the edge of town, the sky was littered with stars. Not as many as on the ranch, where it was truly dark. But more than in town.

She traced the few constellations she knew while she waited for Travis to complete his nightly ritual.

The first time he'd done it, she'd been mortified. She'd left a pile of laundry on the bed, including her underthings waiting to be folded. Now she didn't leave the house until her room looked tidy. She turned toward the sound of Travis's boots crunching on the gravel, heart thudding extra hard at the smoldering look he sent her way as he opened the rear passenger door to grab Dax. Her son still looked small, draped over his shoulders, snuggling into his neck. She shut the door behind Travis and followed them into the house, casting about for someplace to stand while Travis put Dax to bed, and finally settling for perching against the banquette where she and Dax usually ate.

Travis covered the few feet between Dax's bunk and where she stood in three steps. He stopped in front of her, his bulk dominating the space. Something was different this time. Energy radiated off him and she couldn't look anywhere but into his intense eyes. He brought a palm to her face, thumb caressing her cheek, before sliding his hand around to cup the base of her head. Her hand landed on his chest, drawn there as if by a magnet. His rough voice, skated over her skin, drawing it tight. "We need to talk. But first…"

She registered his intent a millisecond before his head dipped and his mouth came crashing down on hers, hot and possessive. Fireworks exploded in her head with the force of a Fourth of July grand finale. She softened and melted as his arm came around her, pulling her against his hardness. With a sigh of homecoming, she opened to his tongue, thrusting and licking against him in a timeless dance. Heat burst through her nerve endings, turning her skin to a sensitized, tingling mass. His mouth was at her throat, her ear. Every place he

TESSA LAYNE

touched drove the flames higher.

Somewhere, in the recesses of her brain, a saner voice cut through the haze. "Travis, we can't," she gasped, fighting for some kind of control. "We agreed."

"Mmmm," he rumbled, peppering her face with kisses and sliding his hand over the curve of her hip. "Now who's worried about the rules?"

She pressed on his chest, and he lifted his head, eyes hazy and unfocused with lust. "It's not good for Dax. I won't be *that* kind of single mom – where there's a revolving door of men."

The heat in his eyes scorched her before he took her mouth again, this time softer. Sweeter. "Has there ever been a revolving door of men?" he murmured against her lips.

"Not since... No," she whispered, shaking her head.

"I'm not going anywhere."

His mouth was on hers again, hot and insistent, and she surrendered to the sensations ripping through her, tearing down her carefully constructed defenses. Sweeping her up into his arms, he settled them on the couch.

Nestled in his embrace, engulfed in his masculine scent, her resistance melted away. How could she deny this when it felt so right? She twined an arm around his shoulder, fingers skating through the hair at his neckline, and slipped her tongue across the inside of his lower lip. His answering growl set her core throbbing, and he slid his tongue against hers, thrusting then teasing until her breath came in harsh puffs.

Travis lifted his head, running a hand down her arm. "I don't know what to do with you, Elaine. You break all my rules and yet I can't get enough of you. I think about you when I'm not with you. I've tried staying away and made myself crazy in the process. I'm all in, Elaine. And we can take things as fast or as slow as you like."

He kissed her forehead with so much tenderness, her heart squeezed painfully. "I mean it when I say I'm not going anywhere. I think I fell for you the first day I saw you at the diner."

She gasped, her heart taking off at a gallop, as she tried to wrap her mind around his words. He drew a finger down the bridge of her nose, giving her a funny little grin. "You looked scared, but determined. You made mistakes, but you kept going and didn't break down. And you've raised a great kid who I happen to adore."

It was too much to process. Her brain was going to overload from it all. "What are you saying, Travis?" she whispered.

He smiled all the way up to his eyes, and kissed her again. "That I love you."

"I don't understand."

"I'm crazy about you, Elaine. I want to be with you, and I want the world to know it."

Was she hearing right? "But you said…" She cocked her head, half afraid at what he'd say next. "Are you sure about this?"

"That I love you? Yes."

He angled his head to place a kiss in the hollow below her ear. The tingles went zinging straight to her nipples, hardening them into expectant peaks. At this rate, she'd lose what little rational thought remained, oh… in about six more kisses.

She leaned back, eyeing him. "But I leave the doors unlocked."

He nipped her earlobe, breath skating across her neck. "We can figure it out."

"What about the fact you think I'm too young?"

He kissed down the column of her neck, sending cascades of shivers straight to her toes. "Over it."

"Or that I'm working for you?"

"Don't care." He kissed along the edge of her shirt.

"Or that I live in town?"

"So?" His hand slipped under her tee, finger pads skating across her bare skin.

She was so close to giving in. Heck, her body already had. But she owed it to him to try and explain. "Travis... I- I'm not perfect." She took a shuddering breath, mustering her courage. "I-I did things when I was younger that I'm not proud of."

He raised his head, eyes serious and intense. "We all have a past, sweetheart. And I'm not interested in swapping war stories right now." He took her mouth, punctuating his words with a kiss that made it very clear what he was interested in right now. But his hands stayed planted on her hips, playing with the skin just underneath her shirt, as if he was waiting for a signal from her to move.

She loved him for that. And she'd give him that signal. Loud and clear.

CHAPTER 21

E LAINE SCRAMBLED OFF his lap and stood, bright-eyed and pink-cheeked, lips swollen from his kisses. She held out her hand and tilted her head toward the sliding screen that comprised a bedroom door in the tiny trailer. "C'mon."

His cock jerked in anticipation. He'd made up his mind somewhere between dinner and the drive over that he was done hiding from what was between them and had stuffed a handful of condoms in his front pocket on the off chance he'd need them. But he wasn't going to pressure her into moving faster than she wanted. "Are you sure?" He placed his hand in hers, lacing their fingers, and stood.

She grabbed the front of his shirt and pulled as she raised on tiptoe to reach his mouth. He swallowed a groan when her tongue slipped into his mouth again, hot and sweet. But he held himself in check, letting her take the lead. His breathing was ragged when she broke away. "Absolutely." She tilted her head back, eyeing him. "But we have to be quiet, and you can't be here when Dax wakes up."

Fair enough. He nodded and followed her into her room, eyes on the sway of her hips. He pulled the screen shut and latched it with a click as she bent to turn on a small lamp on the side table, casting the room in a yellow glow. "Light stays on," he rasped. He wanted to see all of her.

Her eyes lit at his command, and her hands hovered at the

hem of her shirt. A teasing little smile played at the corner of her mouth. She pulled it up a few inches, exposing the creamy soft skin at her midsection. If it was any time other than their first, he'd devour her right now. Instead, he clamped down on his tongue and watched, rapt. Her eyes snapped to his, gauging his reaction. He crossed his arms and leaned against the wall, waiting to see what she'd do next. She dropped her shirt, hands fluttering to the button on her jeans.

"Elaine," he said, voice strangled. He took a step toward her, and she scrambled onto the bed, rising to her knees. "Are you trying to kill me?"

Her breathy laugh filled the room. "Yes? No... Maybe?" She laughed uncertainly, eyes darting back to his. "Is this okay?"

"Perfectly." His cock could wait all night if need be.

"Take off your shirt?"

He reached a hand behind his neck and pulled off his tee in one move, dropping it to the floor. She studied his chest hungrily, tongue darting out to lick her lips. *Yeah. Lick me, baby.* He might have puffed his chest out under her heated gaze. The back of his neck burned, and it suddenly felt fifteen degrees hotter in the cozy room.

She inched up her top, stopping at her bra line. Maybe she *was* trying to kill him. Then she snaked her body sideways as she shimmied her shirt over her head. Damn, that was hot. Where had she learned *that?* It didn't matter, because he was riveted by her rosy nipples peeping through the mostly mesh bra. His cock pressed painfully against his zipper. He sure as hell hadn't expected that.

Her breasts thrust upward as she rolled her shoulders down. That teasing little smile had returned, and damn if he didn't want to lick the corner of her mouth. She did that snaky shimmy again, hand behind her back, and in a blink her bra was gone and he was staring at her gorgeous tits. Perky and high, the hard rosy peaks an island in an expanse of glowing skin.

An ache built in his balls. He jammed his hands in his pockets to keep from reaching for her. Or himself. He swallowed hard and cleared his throat when she cupped her breasts, thumbs flicking against her nipples. His mouth watered at the thought of finally taking a peak with his tongue. He was dying. He fucking loved it.

"Pants off," she said breathlessly, a sharp edge to her request. His ears perked up. She was as turned on by this as he was.

"You ready for that?"

Her eyes lit in anticipation, and she nodded slowly. "Very."

He pulled the condoms from his pocket, tossing them before her. Keeping his eyes on her face so he could see the exact second she reacted to his nakedness, he toed off his shoes then slowly unbuttoned his pants. Her eyes flamed. But he wasn't going to give it to her just yet, not after her little tease show. He waited, thumb hooked under the waistband of his shorts. And when her tongue darted out again to slick her lower lip, he pushed down, letting his cock spring free.

Her sharp intake of breath acted like a match on tinder. His skin flamed as desire roiled through him. He kicked out of the legs and stepped to the edge of the bed. Immediately, she reached for him, drawing a finger up the underside of his cock and circling the head, slicked with pre-come. It took all his self-control to hold still while she explored, the ache for release growing more intense as she moved her finger down his hard length.

"You're driving me wild," he groaned.

"You're... huge," she breathed out.

His chest puffed at her pronouncement. "All for you."

But two could play this game, and he drew the back of his finger up from her waist, slowly circling one breast, then the other. Her skin pebbled as he circled closer and closer to her nipple, finally brushing back and forth against the hard peak. She dropped her head with a sigh, and he bent, taking the bud in his mouth and sucking as he swirled his tongue over and around it until she cried out and clutched his head. "Yes," she hissed. "So good."

"You have the most perfect tits," he muttered as he moved to worship the other breast in the same fashion. He slipped a finger inside her waistband, and her hands joined his, helping him push down her pants. Lying her back, he pulled them off her legs and tossed them aside, heart sticking in his throat at the vision of her naked before him.

How many nights had he dreamed of this?

"Open for me, Elaine. I want to taste you."

Her eyes went hooded as her knees dropped open, exposing her glistening pussy, partially hidden by pale curls. He was going to take this slow. Even if it killed him. He'd waited so long, what was a bit more agony if it blew her mind?

Settling himself between her knees, he stroked up her silky soft thighs, lightly drawing a thumb through her wet slit. A shudder wracked her body, and she gave a little moan. His mouth traced the same path until he came to the juncture of her leg. He could sense the trembling just underneath her heated skin. Her hand came to his head, fingers threading through and clutching his hair. The pull sent a jolt of electricity straight down his spine.

He inhaled, letting her heady scent fill his senses, before

sinking into her sweetness. She tasted like everything he'd dreamed of. Spring after a rain, late summer heat, and cool autumn mist all rolled into one. Of laughter and sunshine and everything that is good in the world. Drawing his tongue slowly through her essence, he brought the flat of his tongue to her hardened clit, caressing and teasing it. Her sharp hiss and increased grip on his hair told him he was on the right path. Hell, he'd let her pull his hair out if that helped her have the orgasm of a lifetime. He wanted to make sure she never forgot this moment between them for as long as she lived.

He licked and sucked until her body shook from head to toe, and she whimpered when he pulled away, reaching for a condom. Sheathing himself, he paused at her entrance, the head of his cock teasing through her folds.

She tilted her hips, making a humming noise in the back of her throat. "Yes, Travis."

Her words hit a place deep inside him, and he slowly entered, heart slamming. His whole body tensed as he sank into her glorious pussy, so tight and hot. Need spiraled low and hard, pushing him closer and closer to the edge. But he refused to give in and let go. Dropping his head to her neck, he grazed her collarbone, nipping and sucking along it while he moved slowly within her.

She fit him so perfectly and moved her hips against his, writhing and panting as she chased her orgasm. "That's right," he whispered in her ear. "Do what makes you feel good. I want you to feel so good." Her thighs squeezed against his hips as he continued his slow thrusts, fully entering her before pulling partially out. He found her mouth again, taking it in the same slow way, tongue thrusting languidly into her recesses as her breathing intensified. Her hands were everywhere across his back, grabbing, clawing, seeking release that only he could give her. It wouldn't be long now.

With a cry, she came apart, her orgasm wracking her body, her pussy spasming around him. And he let go, climaxing with her, vision hazing from the intensity of it. He continued to move within her as they rode the waves of ecstasy back down to earth.

He brushed a tendril of hair from her face. "You're amazing." Never in his life had he come so hard he'd seen spots.

She smiled up at him, sated and soft. "Can we do that again?"

CHAPTER 22

"DAX," ELAINE CALLED, leaning her head out the front door. "Come eat your breakfast. Dottie's coming to pick us up and take you to school."

Dax came galloping around the corner of the trailer on an imaginary horse, shooting an imaginary gun. "When am I going to help Travis with the horses again?" He clambered up the steps and slid into the banquette where she'd laid out a bowl of cereal.

"You like the horses?" She polished off the last of her coffee and placed the dish in the sink.

"Yeah. And I like Travis too."

Warmth spread across her chest. Travis had definitely made a positive impact on Dax.

"Is he your boyfriend?"

Her breath caught in her throat. It had only been a few days. And while they'd tried to stay low key, especially around Dax, they hadn't exactly hidden their relationship. And better that he hear from her than through the rumor mill. She nodded. "Yeah. I guess you could say that. Is that okay?"

Dax gave her a big smile, nodding vigorously. "I think it's *great.*" He lifted his spoon for emphasis. "I love Travis."

Her heart squeezed so hard it hurt to breathe. "I do too, bud. I do too." *Then tell him.*

"Are you gonna marry him?"

Shit. She hadn't prepared for this line of questioning. "I don't know, kiddo. Grown-up relationships are complicated. Not like the fairy tales I read you."

"Well I think you should live happily ever after." He brought his dishes to the sink.

Elaine wrapped him in a hug, marveling again at how much he'd grown over the summer. "I think you should too, sweetie pea." A car pulled up outside. "Dottie's here. Grab your backpack?" Pride surged through her as he ran for his bunk and came back a second later with a backpack slung over his shoulder.

This was the first year she hadn't had to rely on the kindness of others to provide for Dax's school supplies. Travis had taken the two of them into Manhattan and helped Dax pick out a backpack and lunch box. And when her back was turned, he'd purchased a few new Transformers for Dax as well, much to the boy's delight. She'd purchased him brand new clothes and shoes, and grabbed some additional items in bigger sizes, because at the rate he was growing, halfway through the year, he'd need the next size up.

Once she got past today, she'd begin to feel like she really had made it through the tough times. Dax leaped down the steps, clearing all three in one jump, and ran for the car giving Dottie a quick hug where she stood by the rear passenger door. Dottie beamed up at her. "Ready?"

"Let me grab my papers and I'll be right out." She grabbed her purse from the bedroom, double-checked her manila envelope and ran down the steps to join Dottie. As soon as they'd dropped off Dax and made it out of town, Dottie glanced over, giving her a critical stare.

"I like your outfit. It's new, isn't it?"

Elaine nodded. "Travis insisted I get something for myself

when we went to Manhattan to do Dax's school shopping." After collecting Dax's school supplies, he'd ushered her into Yee-Haw and refused to budge until she'd purchased something for herself. While she'd never be more than a jeans and t-shirt kind of gal, she'd fallen in love with the skinny jeans, white tunic top and thigh length tailored brown suede jacket on a mannequin. She'd splurged and purchased a pair of tall brown riding boots to go with the ensemble.

"Good man." She nodded her approval emphatically. "I'd have done it if he hadn't. It's high time you did something nice for yourself."

She felt different in the outfit. More confident. More... respectable. Someone to be proud of.

Dottie looked over again. "Reach into my purse, hon. There's an envelope for you."

"What's this?" she asked when she'd pulled it from Dottie's giant sack.

"I think you need to apply to get your probation reduced. You've earned your GED, you've been the steadiest employee I've had in a decade, and you've really turned your life around. You've grown up a ton since coming to Prairie, and I'm real proud of you. You've made a good life here, and I hope you'll stick around once you're released." She smirked a little and raised an eyebrow. "I think Travis would like that real much."

She couldn't speak from the tightness in her chest. Gratitude for this woman who'd become like a mother to her overwhelmed her. "I don't know what to say."

Dottie reached across the console and patted her knee. "No need to say anything, sweetie pie. I love you like you were one of my own. Give your officer that letter, it outlines all the important stuff. There's no reason why they should say no."

The thought she could finally be free of her past, the

darkness and pain, in a matter of weeks or months, instead of another year, made her stomach dance with hopefulness. "I don't know how I can possibly thank you enough for giving me a second chance at life. I'm forever grateful."

Dottie waved a hand. "Hush, now. You're not the first one I've done this for, and you won't be the last. I know there'd be many in town scandalized by the notion that I hire folks who need a leg up, but all I'm doin' is paying it forward. Once upon a time, someone I loved didn't get the second chance they deserved, and that didn't set right with me. So I made sure I could do somethin' about it when the opportunity came callin'." She tapped the steering wheel. "Now, have you mentioned any of this business to Travis?"

The knot in her stomach tightened and she shook her head. "I've hinted at it. But the opportunity hasn't really presented itself. And until recently, it didn't seem important."

Dottie gave her a stern look. "And now?"

She understood the older woman's meaning. Loud and clear. "I want to, I really do. But not until I've put it all behind me and I can show him I'm standing on my own two feet. That I'm more than a record."

"You're doing that. You've *been* doing that for two years."

"What if I hurt his chances to become sheriff? If people knew, he might be guilty by association." She frowned, worry consuming her. "You know how people are. And I would hate to reflect badly on him in any way. I've made a fresh start, Dottie, thanks to you. I don't want to ruin things for you or him. I just want to leave that awful chapter of my life behind." She would have to tell him soon. It wouldn't be right to pretend it had never happened. Especially since they'd become intimate. But telling him now? At the most stressful point of the election? Surely waiting a few more weeks wouldn't hurt?

The crease at the corner of Dottie's mouth deepened. "I don't see how he could think badly of you when he…" She pursed her lips and shook her head. "Travis is no saint either. But you're right. It's probably best not to stress him out any more than he already is. Just promise me you'll tell him as soon as the election's over."

"I promise." Anxiety churned her stomach. Dottie was right, as soon as the election was over, she'd share everything. She blew out a nervous breath casting about for something to say.

"You have a dress picked out for the First Responder's Ball?" Dottie asked, keeping her eyes on the road.

She nodded, relieved the silence was over for the moment. "Emmaline is working on something for me."

"You'll look like a princess when she gets done with you. That gal can make magic from potato sacks."

"Dottie, I have a favor to ask. I–"

"Is this about Dax?" Dottie waved her hand again. "Weston mentioned you might need some help. Teddy's staying home. Won't go near those things with a ten-foot pole. And I'll be back before midnight. Do you feel okay about that?"

The tension in her shoulders released as relief washed through her. "Thank you so much. Weston says it's really important Travis has a date."

"And you deserve to go have a nice time, sweetie pie. Besides, it'll be ages before I have grandchildren. Cassie and Park might never want them. And right now, they're just focused on Park's recovery."

Dottie launched into a lengthy explanation of Cassie and Parker's upcoming wedding details, and before she knew it, Dottie had pulled into the parking lot at the Shawnee County Courthouse.

Dottie shut off the engine and swiveled in her seat. "You gonna be okay, hon? Do you want me to come with you?"

Feeling a newfound shot of confidence, Elaine shook her head. "I'm good. Time for me to stand on my own two feet."

Dottie reached over and gave her an encouraging squeeze. "I'm right here if you need anything."

Clutching the manila envelope and Dottie's letter, Elaine marched into the courthouse. Maybe it was the new clothes, maybe it was her improved confidence, but the building didn't look as scary as before. Didn't seem so intimidating. She pushed the elevator button and studied a swirl in the polished floor while she waited. Her phone buzzed, and she pulled it out, seeing a text from Weston.

> **W:** I need you to prep call sheets for the south county precincts tonight.

She typed back a quick response as she stepped into the elevator.

> **E:** They'll be waiting for you when you arrive :)
>
> **W:** thx

"Well, well, well." She froze at the sound of Steve Lawson's voice, the phone slipping through her fingers and clattering to the floor. "Look what the cat drug in... *Ellie May.*"

Backing up a step, she fought the panic that rose through her at light speed. The sound of her heart beating wildly filled her ears. "What are you doing here?" Her voice came out shaky and small.

Lawson advanced, casually bringing a hand up to the bank of buttons and stopped the elevator between floors.

Warning bells, both real and imagined, filled the space as he smiled coldly. "None of your business, sweetheart. But it sure looks like luck was on my side today."

"W-wh-what do you mean?"

"Took a little digging, but I knew you looked familiar. What would Prairie's police chief say when he finds his treasurer is nothing more than a common criminal?"

"That was–"

He cut her off, expression smug. "And once I'm sheriff, you better watch out, because I'll have you in my sights."

In spite of her terror, his threat triggered something deep inside of her and she pulled herself up as tall as she could. "I haven't done anything wrong. That part of my life is over."

"Is it ever? *Ellie?*"

"Stop calling me that."

He took a step closer, voice silky. "How badly do you want me to keep your dirty little secret?" His eyes went hungry, sending a chill up her spine.

Her throat went dry and she swallowed. "You wouldn't."

"I think you know I would," he said with an edge of menace. He stood so close she could reach out and touch him. "Think about it. All the good folks in town double-checking their change. Clutching their purses a little tighter. Eyes filled with suspicion when you walk in their store. Knowing you'd taken their beloved police chief for a ride."

Nononono. Not after all she'd worked for. To rebuild. "Don't. Please," she whispered, panic darkening her vision.

"You know what I want… Ellie Mae. What I've always wanted from you. It would be so easy to make all this go away."

Rage blasted through her. "You're a disgusting pig. I wouldn't give into your demands then, and I won't now," she reached past him and slammed the elevator button, shutting off the dinging alarm. The silence was just as loud.

"Play it your way then, bitch," he snarled, as the elevator came to a stop. "I made you pay the price once, I have no problem doing it again."

Her blood turned to ice, but something inside her snapped. "Don't forget, I know what you tried to do."

His eyes narrowed. "And who do you think the public will believe? A lawman? Or a girl with a rap sheet? Go up against me, little lady, and you will lose. And so will that cop of yours. Big time." He turned on his heel and stalked out of the elevator as it opened, leaving her trembling in the corner.

She let out a half sob. He'd do it too. Lawson was too big and powerful. There was no doubt in her mind. He'd hurt Travis if she said anything. Her hands turned to ice. No matter what, she couldn't let him hurt Travis. And he was right, too. In the court of public opinion, no one would believe her. They'd never believe that a cop would try what he had. Her stomach flopped at the memory. She'd been lucky to escape with only bruises on her arm.

Hurrying to exit before the doors shut again, she sniffed and rolled her shoulders. It took the entire walk to the probation officer's door to still her shaking hands. Her confidence shattered, she could barely make eye contact with the secretary, and she stood quietly in front of the woman waiting for the pee cup while she tried to collect herself. The secretary offered up a cup without even glancing up. "You know what to do," she said in a monotone.

Biting back a snarky comment, she grabbed the cup and headed for the private stall. She wasn't even a person to these people. Just an unfortunate cog in the wheels of justice. A moment later, she returned and set the sample down on the edge of the desk and took a seat.

Ten long, silent minutes dragged by. It didn't matter that she was expected to show up promptly. Once she was here, she was on their time. She was convinced they did it on purpose, to keep them off-balance.

"Elaine?" Officer Marshall asked. "Come on back."

She forced a smile onto her face as she followed the man back to his office. Down past the permanent stain in the carpet, past the photo of wildflowers and the broken ceiling light, turning the corner to the second door on the left. Forty-two steps closer to never coming back. He held the door open and shut it behind them.

While the door didn't lock, her pulse still ratcheted up. Every time. She perched on the edge of the chair, hands folded in her lap, spine like a steel rod. Her defense attorney had taught her well, and somehow, over the course of two years, it had given her a small measure of confidence – that she could be scared to death and not cringe.

Officer Marshall took a seat behind the desk that took up most of the office. "Have you used drugs since I saw you last?"

The same questions every time. *Of course not. Have I ever peed positive?* "No."

"Alcohol?"

"No."

He looked at her sharply. She met his gaze head-on. He never believed her when she answered no.

"Are you driving?"

He already knew the answer to that. "No."

"Still employed?"

"Yes."

"Same place?"

He knew the answer to that too. She tamped down the

irritation that flared to life inside her. She didn't have the right to be offended by his questions. Her future was in his hands. "Yes."

"Still living in the FEMA park?"

"Yes."

"Son in school?"

"Yes."

"How's he doing?"

His tone of voice belied his interest. "Fine. He likes school."

"Anything else you'd like to tell me?"

She hated the open-ended questions. Say too much, or the wrong thing, and it could hurt you. Don't say enough, and that could hurt you too. This time, she had an answer prepared. She laid the manila envelope on his desk. "You'll see here that I earned my GED."

His eyebrows shot up in two perfect arches. "Good for you."

She swallowed hard, gathering her courage, and laid Dottie's envelope on the desk. "I-I would also like to request that my probation be shortened." Her heart galloped a mile a minute. Taking a belly breath, she continued. "I've been a model citizen over the last two years. I've held the same job, and this letter is from my boss. I've completed my GED per the terms of my probation, never been late to or missed a meeting, never had a positive drug screening, and my son has thrived in his new environment."

Officer Marshall sat back, hands clasped behind his head. "You understand you'll have to petition the court?"

She nodded.

"There's a lot of paperwork to fill out, and it needs to be signed by both the prosecuting attorney and the defense attorney. Are you sure you want to do that?"

"Yes." So that she could get her life back and never step foot in this building again? Hell, yes.

Officer Marshal leaned forward and stood. "I'll bring it to the judge as soon as you have it on my desk. You can probably get a hearing in ten days' time after that." He narrowed his gaze, studying her. "I have to say I'm surprised. Most of you never make it out of the system."

She didn't miss the dig, and it raised her hackles. "What do you mean?"

He shrugged, pulling the envelopes across the desk. "You know, women like you."

Asshole. She stood, clamping down on her temper just enough to ensure she didn't say something that would ruin her chances. But there was no way in hell she was going to let that dig slide. "You mean women who've had a tough break? Who weren't lucky enough to have a stable home life? Who did everything they could to make sure their children eat?" She glared at him for a long second. "Tell me exactly, and in small words so I understand. What does 'women like you' mean?"

Officer Marshall's mouth thinned to a line and a flush pinked the skin on his neck, right above his collar.

"I will get you your paperwork as soon as possible. Thank you." Shaking, she turned and marched out of his office clenching her jaw the forty-two steps to the secretary's desk. All the way back to the elevator where she punched the button and a tear squeezed out of her eye.

CHAPTER 23

TRAVIS GAVE A low whistle as Elaine turned once for him, silk chiffon swirling around her legs. Dottie was right, the dress Emmaline created made her feel like a princess. "You look incredible." He pushed off the bed and came to stand before her, skimming his hands down her arms. "I want to peel this back off you."

She shivered the sexy burr in his voice, offering her mouth for a kiss. "We'll miss dinner if we start again." They were already running late, but they'd had to take advantage of being alone in the suite.

"Fine with me," he growled into her neck, tongue darting across her collarbone. "We can order room service."

She giggled pushing at his chest. "Weston is going to have a heart attack if we're any later."

Travis shrugged into his jacket while she fixed her lipstick. She hated the stuff, but Emmaline had insisted it made the outfit. Not that the outfit needed anything additional. The soft pink material felt like a cloud, the design somewhere between a Greek goddess outfit and a 50's cocktail dress. The woman was a genius, and she'd never felt sexier.

"Showtime," Travis said as he held out his arm.

Too bad the dress did nothing to ease the knot of worry filling her chest. Lawson would be here tonight, but surely he wouldn't make a scene? She hoped so. A wave of nausea roiled her stomach, making her hands clammy. She wanted nothing more than to hide in the room and wrap herself in the soft sheets. But that wouldn't help Travis, and she wanted this night to go well for him.

Focusing on the floor lights above the elevator, she tried to quell the nervous energy zipping through her. Two orgasms hadn't done a thing to relax her. She bit down on her lip, rolling it between her teeth, then stopped. Her lipstick would come right off if she persisted.

"Hey." Travis tipped her chin, voice gentle and sweet. "You're gonna be great. We're in this together, remember?"

She nodded, giving him a half-hearted smile.

"All we have to do is get through dinner." He ushered her into the elevator and took her hand. "One step at a time. First we find Weston."

Weston was waiting for them when they arrived in the lobby. "Lighten up you two. You're not going to a funeral." He flashed them a grin. "Elaine, you look stunning."

Travis tightened his grip on her hand and leaned in. "He's right, you know."

Weston continued. "Cocktail hour is in full swing. All you need to do is circulate. I'll be with you, and running interference if necessary. Lawson's already in there. He's too smart to be an asshole tonight. If you run into each other, just smile politely. Don't say a word. Got it?"

They both nodded.

"And another thing. No booze tonight. I want you two to be the sharpest tacks in the room. Booze loosens people's tongues and inhibitions, especially in a stressful situation. Got it?"

They nodded again. Apprehension settled in her bones, drawing her shoulders tight. She prayed Weston was right about Lawson. In eleven days it would all be over, and she could tell Travis everything.

"Once you sit for dinner, you're home free," Weston reminded them. "No one expects you to stay for the dancing. Ready?"

"Let's get this over with," Travis grumbled.

"Keep smiling. No matter what. I don't care if the mayor's wife jabs you with her stilettos, take it with a smile on your face."

Elaine gave Travis an encouraging squeeze. "Got it, boss."

They followed Weston into the crowd, and first thing, he introduced them to the fire marshal from Marion. They were off and running. The remainder of the hour passed in a blur of handshakes, platitudes, and so many smiles Elaine's face hurt when she finally sat down in the chair Travis pulled out for her.

Weston had ensured their table was filled with their circle of friends and close colleagues. Dottie and Jeanine from dispatch sat across the large table. Weston to Travis's right, Parker's mother, Peggy Hansen, and Zack Forte to her left. On the other side of Zack sat Chief Castro and his wife, whose name she couldn't remember. And lastly, Mason Carter. Mason and Zack, both gazillionaires, had set up a foundation to promote rebuilding and new businesses in Prairie, and had both been named to the future Warren G. Hansen Memorial Clinic board of directors. For billionaires, they were surprisingly down to earth. Zack always made a point of bringing Dax puzzle books when he came to town.

Chief Castro stood and struck the side of his glass with a spoon, quieting the tables. "Thank you all for coming this evening. Tonight, we honor one of our own. Parker Hansen, who many of you know is one of the finest firefighters and medics we have in the region. What you may not know is that he also runs a Forest Service hand crew, protecting a wider community from out of control wildfires. If you've read the pamphlet left on each plate, then you know he was injured in a burnover in Colorado. And while he's projected to make a full recovery, the bills as you can imagine, are crippling." Chief Castro paused and took a sip of his water. "I want you to look around this room. All of us act as safety nets for our individual communities. But we're also part of a wider community. And tonight, it's up to us to be that safety net for Parker. Give back to him in his time of need. Now, I don't doubt that we'd do that for any one of us. But tonight, it's Parker's turn. None of us is a silo. We live and work in community, and it's an honor to be a safety net for someone who has been that so selflessly for others on a daily basis."

Sitting there, contemplating the smiling faces at the table, listening to Chief Castro, she was struck. She'd only ever considered her net to be Dottie, and recently, Travis and Weston. But she was wrong. Everyone at the table cared about Dax, went out of their way to say hi to him in town, do nice things for him. And not because he was a charity case. But just... because. How many others in Prairie had she overlooked? Jamey Sinclaire for sure. The Hansens. Gratitude for this community of people filled her.

Travis nudged her and leaned in close. "Hey. You okay?"

Blinking hard, she turned to him. So close, she could kiss him if she leaned in a little further. "Yeah." She nodded. "Yeah. Just... happy." It hit her like a load of bricks. She didn't need a perfect life to be happy. Right here, with Travis at her side, surrounded by people she loved and cared for, she was happy. It bubbled up inside of her, like a spring that had just been uncapped.

She smiled at him without worry or reservation.

"I hope I have a little bit to do with that?"

"A lot, actually." The words caught in the back of her throat, and she hesitated. *Say it. Tell him.* Letting out a shaky breath, she stepped out into what felt like thin air. "I love you," she murmured so only he could hear.

Surprise registered in his eyes followed by delight, then fire. He reached an arm across the back of her chair and leaned in close, placing a soft kiss above her ear. "Can we leave yet?"

She huffed out a little laugh, warming at his innuendo. "Not soon enough."

The remainder of dinner felt like the most exquisite torture. Every look, every hidden brush of their thighs or hands under the table designed to make the other squirm. After coffee had been served, the bar reopened and couples began to drift out to the dance floor. Travis pushed back from the table and stood, offering his hand. "Dance with me?"

Her body buzzed with anticipation, and her mouth curved in a slow smile. "Love to."

Electricity snapped up her arm when he took her hand and her heart thudded a little faster. When they reached the parquet flooring, he spun her and pulled her flush against his body. "No it's not a cucumber. Yes, I'm happy to see you," he murmured into her ear.

She giggled breathlessly, even as her nipples pulled tight, aching for his touch. "We can go now, if you want."

"Oh no." He moved them in a slow circle. "I like feeling you like this."

The music changed but their rhythm didn't, and he sang the lyrics to *Despacito* soft and slow into her ear.

She tilted her head back, impressed. "I didn't know you

spoke Spanish."

"Comes with the territory."

"You mean when you were with the SEALs?" He nodded and pulled her closer. "Shall I translate?"

She flicked her gaze up to him as he serenaded her in Spanish. She didn't have to know Spanish to understand what he was singing. The heat in his lively hazel eyes told her everything she needed to know. His hand settled at the base of her spine and pulled her closer as he gave a twist of his hips. The movement made his intentions loud and clear and sent her heart beating up somewhere around the hollow of her throat. A rush of heat pooled in the lace between her thighs. Her skin drew tight, goosebumps erupting everywhere.

He ducked his head, breath warm against the shell of her ear. "I want to see your hair dance. I want to be your rhythm. I want you to teach my mouth… your favorite places. Let me pass over your danger zones until you cry out and you forget your name."

His words about did her in right there. Fire raced up her limbs setting her insides ablaze. The man's voice was like liquid sex. Her mouth went dry at the thought of his mouth on her. Licking and sucking until she floated with the stars.

Her desire must have shown on her face, because he gave a low chuckle as he skated his fingers up and down her spine. "Remind me to play this song when we're alone, and I'll take you through it phrase by phrase."

"I might combust if you do that."

His eyebrows swept up and he gave her a smile full of sexy promise. "I hope so."

Elaine glanced around, scanning the crowd. Bodies of the younger attendees writhed together on the dance floor and most of the older guests had drifted out to the bar in the lobby. "Travis?"

"Mmmhmm?" his chest rumbled.

"How about now?" she offered breathlessly.

He met her gaze, eyes hooded and heavy. Threading his fingers through hers, he navigated them out of the room and to the elevator. His body was taut, tight, as they stood at the back of the crowd. The elevator opened, but the crowd hardly moved and it was full again. Letting out a growl of frustration, he gave her hand a tug and led them to a side hall. He pulled open the door to the staircase, led her through, then spun her against the wall, caging her with his arms. "I haven't been able to take my eyes off your tits all evening. They're so perfect." He slipped a finger under the deep vee of her neckline, grazing the swell, before taking her mouth in a searing kiss.

There was something so right about his mouth on hers. It settled her nerves while it lit up others. His tongue flicked at her lips, teasing until she opened with a little sigh, letting him claim her, giving back with her own licks and thrusts until her chest burst into flames.

"Someone will walk in on us here."

"I don't care," he growled, nipping at her earlobe.

"Not exactly the image you want to convey as future county sheriff."

Letting out a frustrated sigh, he pressed his forehead to hers. "Tell me why I'm doing this again?"

Before she could form an answer, he swept her up into his arms as if she weighed nothing and turned for the stairs, taking them two at a time.

"Travis," she squealed, a giggle bursting from her. "I can walk." Her protest was half-hearted. She had to admit, she liked it when he got bossy and took over.

"Not fast enough," he muttered.

In no time they were on the top floor. The man wasn't even winded. He pushed open the door and stepped into the hall, striding the short distance to their suite. He kissed her again before letting her slide along his length as he returned her to the floor. So. Hot.

He whipped out the key card and tossed it on the credenza as he pulled her into the room and locked the door. This time, there was no hitch of fear, no niggle of worry. Only naked anticipation of what was to come next.

"Now," he said, voice sliding over her like hot caramel. "Where were we?"

CHAPTER 24

E LAINE SLOWLY BACKED into the room, pulse racing. "I think you were about to very gently, without ripping my pretty dress, remove my clothes." She turned around, and peeked back over her shoulder. "You might want to start with the zipper?"

Travis closed the distance between them, eyes hungry. She lifted her hair off her neck and his hand came to her waist. The sound of the zipper broke the silence and cool air hit her back as the dress split open.

"No bra?" he asked as the zipper paused.

No other things either. But he'd discover that soon enough. The zipper tugged again continuing down the curve of her back and exposing the skin all the way to her bare bottom. Travis hissed out a breath as his hand slipped through the opening and caressed a cheek. "Naughty."

She loved the effect her little surprise had on him. And the way her body responded to the husky burr in his voice. Her clit pulsed expectantly and a needy ache blossomed between her thighs.

Travis slipped the dress down her arms and the dress pooled at her feet, a sea of pink chiffon. "Like Venus rising from the sea," he murmured as he drew a finger along the bottom curve of her ass. "Widen your stance," he said thickly. "And hold onto the chair."

Grabbing the back of the chair, she opened her legs and gasped as his finger dove into her slippery recesses, rubbing over her clit. She leaned into his fingers, wanting more, and relishing the electric shocks moving through her. His hand came to her breast, and his breath was hot on her ear as he teased her nipple. "You're so hot in nothing but a pair of heels. I want to fuck you hard and fast tonight." His words incinerated her, and when he gently squeezed her clit she came undone with a cry.

He chuckled low and kissed the back of her neck. "We've just begun." His tongue blazed a trail down her spine, starting another fire in her belly. Dropping to his knees, he slipped his fingers from her, replacing them with his mouth.

She threw her head back, moaning. He licked through her slit, flicking his tongue across her sensitized clit before sliding back and thrusting into her entrance. Her head swirled deliriously as the sensations ripped through her body.

"You taste so good, smell so sweet," he groaned, starting his pattern of licking and flicking again.

"That feels so good, Travis," she gritted out between gasps.

He squeezed her thighs, pulling her legs wider. "Come for me, sweetheart. Come on my tongue."

She canted her hips into him pursuing the building ache, riding his tongue to a crashing release. Her knees buckled and he caught her, gently lowering her to the floor. Through a blissed-out fog, she heard his jacket hit the floor, followed by the jingle of his belt. Propping herself up on her elbows, she watched avidly as he stepped out of his pants, erection springing free. Her mouth watered at the thought of taking him into her mouth, tasting him. She flipped to her knees, drawing her palms up his thighs.

"Grab hold of the chair," she said, turning his words on him.

He braced his hands on it and gazed down at her through hooded eyes which turned molten when she cupped his balls. His cock bobbed, hard and heavy in front of her. The scent of his arousal hit her, spicy and hot. She leaned in and sucked the top of his thigh where it met his torso, washing her tongue over his heated skin. Reaching up, she ringed the base of his cock with finger and thumb not quite touching and stroked up. He groaned and thrust into her hand. Delight at his reaction surged through her, stoking her own fire.

Then she dipped her head and drew her tongue from his balls to the base of his cock, then slowly up the underside of his thick shaft. He let out a feral growl and dropped his head. When she reached the engorged head, she flicked her tongue across the slit where a drop of pre-come sat. He tasted salty and sharp, and she loved it. Her body buzzed with anticipation.

Slowly, she licked around the head before drawing it into her mouth and sucking. "God, Elaine, you're killing me." His hand dropped to her head, fingers tangling in her hair. She swirled and sucked on him, her hips beginning to move in time with his. Then she opened wide and drew as much of him as she could into her mouth. His breath was coming in harsh pants now, muscles on his legs bulging with tension. When his cock hit the back of her mouth, she swallowed. "Enough," he grunted, and pulled out. "I want your sweet pussy," he said roughly, hauling her up and walking her back to the bed.

When the back of her knees hit the edge, she scrambled to the center while he rolled on a condom. "Shoes stay on." His eyes were wild with lust as he climbed over her and pushed her back. "Remember, hard and fast."

A thrill rippled through her as she dropped her knees. With a possessive growl he thrust home, mouth crashing to hers in a claiming kiss. He filled her completely and she nearly wept with the joy of it. She lifted her hips, meeting him stroke for stroke as their sweat-slicked bodies raced for oblivion. Travis's ass clenched and he let out a long, low moan as he thrust deeply into her, his climax wracking his body. Two more thrusts and she chased him over the cliff, bright lights exploding behind her eyes.

He collapsed on top of her, and she welcomed his weight pressing her into the mattress. "I love you, Elaine," he said softly, almost reverently. "It's like we were made for each other."

A fire glowed brightly in her chest, expanding to encompass her whole body. She brought a hand to his cheek. "I love you." She lifted her head to kiss the corner of his mouth.

After a moment, he rose and disappeared into the bathroom, returning with a warm washcloth and curling her into his arms once he'd finished ministering to her. He kissed her temple and took a deep breath, chest expanding into her back. "About seven years ago, I was in charge of an op that went wrong. We ran into a teenager while we were in transit between locations. We should have taken him out. But the look in his eye..." He sighed heavily. "It was too much like my brother. I couldn't pull the trigger. He must have alerted the insurgents in the area we were there and they must have tracked us to the next town, because in the middle of the night, the building we were sheltering in was compromised. We lost half our team."

Her stomach dropped at his confession. She turned in his embrace and her heart broke for him. His face was tortured, eyes lost in the memory. "Oh, Travis. I'm so sorry."

"I've never talked about it outside of the survivors, and when I made the report." His voice was heavy, resigned. "But after the tornado I started having nightmares about that op again. Only this time, there were people from town in my dreams."

Pain for him needled her. She didn't know what to say. What could she say? It explained so much.

"I'd gone through counseling right after I got out, but Weston suggested I talk to this guy up here."

"Did it help?"

He took a deep breath, nodding. "Yeah, it has."

"What do you talk about? He's helped me get a better perspective. Figure some things out."

"Like what?"

"Like I want to return to ranching once I retire from law enforcement." His eyes searched hers, and she met his gaze steadily. "I've learned a lot, working with Hope and Flipper. The physical labor is good for me. For my mind. It settles me."

"Then shouldn't you do it now?"

"Hard to be a rancher of one. And I'm a good police chief." He stroked along her side, hand coming to rest on her hip. "A lot of small towns have crippling issues with substance abuse, and we don't. I like to think it's because I'm doing something right here. That *we're* doing something right. And if I'm sheriff, maybe I can help other communities in the county."

This man had her whole heart. She cupped his face. "I love you, Travis. I love your passion and your commitment to this community. I love the way you're gentle with Dax and how every choice you make is driven by care for people."

His eyes warmed. "I love that kid. You too." He kissed her nose. "If no one's told you this, you need to hear that you're a great mom, and you're raising a great son."

"I haven't always… Prairie gave us a fresh start."

He pulled on her wrist, exposing her arm, and brushed tiny kisses along her scars. "Whatever caused you to do this," he murmured against her skin. "I'm so sorry. If you ever want to talk about it." He raised his head, eyes glowing intensely. "Whenever you feel ready. I'm always here for you."

She shut her eyes against the hot sweep of emotion pricking her eyelids. "Thank you."

He kissed her gently, brushing his hand through her hair, then settling it at her hip. "Tell me your dreams Elaine. You must have dreams."

His voice wrapped around her, settling heavy in her bones. Calming her. "I was too concerned with survival to have dreams."

"What about now?" He pressed a kiss to her forehead, thumb making lazy circles at her waist. "There must be something?"

Heat crawled up her chest. She'd never told a soul because saying the words would surely mean it would never come to pass. But she could share this much with him. "I always wanted to go to college."

He tightened his embrace. "It's not too late. The community college takes rolling admissions. You could start in January."

She lifted her head and met his gaze. His hazel eyes sparked with excitement. With belief in her. Her heart constricted. She didn't deserve this man. She tucked her head under his chin and burrowed into him. "I'll think about it after the election."

CHAPTER 25

"YOU KNOW YOU should be out talking to voters, right?" Weston said, full of disappointment. "The election is nine days."

"Help me unload the horses," Travis answered, stepping out of his old beat up truck.

"How many phone calls did you make last week?" Weston called after him as he walked around to the back of the trailer.

"Hundred and fifty," Travis grunted as he slipped the bolt and swung open the door.

Weston caught the gate, frowning. "This is a close election, dammit. You could win this thing, but not if you don't ask for votes."

Travis stepped into the trailer and grabbed Flipper's halter, turning the mare and guiding her out, tying her to a corral post. "Isn't that what my mail is doing for me?"

"Of course. But a personal ask is always more powerful."

Travis pulled back the interior gate, and reached for Sunny's halter, leading the mare out of the trailer and setting her next to Flipper. Hope had introduced the two horses and over the last few weeks, gotten them to accept each other. Excitement fluttered in his chest. Dax's eyes would be saucers when he saw Sunny here. "I never should have let you talk me into this."

"A little late for regrets now that you're neck deep in it,"

Weston snapped. "Polling shows the tide turning in our favor if we hit him hard. But we have to take the punch."

Travis bent over the trailer hitch, releasing the electric cord first. "I've already told you, I'm not gonna run DC politics in Prairie. I don't care what you or your family know about campaigns. Not gonna run my campaign that way. Period." He flicked the safety chains to the ground, where they landed with a clatter.

Weston placed his hands on his hips, gazing skyward. "That's the problem. You're not running a campaign at all. I've done all the op research you need, and Lawson ain't clean. You need to go for the throat this final week and knock him out. Don't be naive and think he's not researching you. He's going to hit you where you're most vulnerable. I've left a dossier on your desk at work sent to me from one of our friends. You might want to spend a little time researching."

He knew exactly which friends. Weston had maintained deep connections with several units of SEALs in the years since he'd retired. Many had ended up in private security, or in shadow ops. He presumed that some of the collecting methods were... not quite above board. He'd never risk his reputation as a lawman by using the information. However useful it might be. "Never. You know that bends the rules."

"Not like you haven't bent the rules."

"Not at the office. *Never* at the office."

"C'mon," Weston pleaded, a note of desperation in his voice. "Aren't you the least bit curious? About him? Lawson's as greasy as they come."

"Course I am." His fingers itched to research Elaine too. Dig into the past she guarded so closely. Only he never did it out of a sense of propriety. And the hope she'd share her secrets with him the way he'd shared some of his. He sighed heavily, chest tight. "Look, I do it for one person, what's to stop me from spying on anyone else? No way, man."

Weston's brow drew tight. "What are you going to do if you lose?"

Travis stared at him for a long moment, then threw his head back, laughing. "You really do want my job, don't you?"

The corner of Weston's mouth twitched.

"Ha. I knew it." Travis slapped his thigh, still shaking with laughter. "If I lose, you'll have to wait a little longer for my job." He shrugged. "And maybe I'll become a dilettante rancher, now that I've got horses to tend to. Help me get them settled. Storm's a comin' and I want to check on Elaine and Dax."

The clouds were piling up to the west, tall and imposing. The air felt sticky and heavy, the kind that produced ugly storms. A shiver slithered down Travis's spine. It wasn't tornado season, but that didn't amount to a hill of beans in Kansas. Hell, he'd heard the sirens pop in November. They could just as easily sound in September, especially with the weather so topsy-turvy lately. Given Dax's reaction to a simple summer storm, he wanted to be there with them, or bring them back home if the weather was going to turn dangerous.

The realization hit him like a two-by-four to the head. Home. The thought had slipped out as naturally as breathing. Elaine and Dax belonged here. Belonged home. Would she consider moving in after the election? He'd make a nice dinner and ask her as soon as everything was over.

The sky rumbled ominously by the time he turned his SUV toward town. It was only four, but the sky had gone black. The sirens began their eerie whine as he pulled up to the sole light in Prairie. "Dammit," he spat, hitting the accelerator. Two minutes later he skidded to a stop in front of

Elaine's trailer, glowing in the eerie dark. Worry thrummed in his veins. Prairie couldn't survive another direct hit. Crossing the walk in two leaps, he burst in the door, grateful for once that she always left the door unlocked.

His heart wrenched at the sight. Elaine sat huddled on the floor looking up at him through terrified eyes, a very scared Dax cowering in her lap. Crossing and dropping to the floor next to Elaine, he pulled Dax into his lap and draped an arm around her, pulling her close. "It's okay. We're safe. I'm here. Everything's gonna be okay."

"But the sirens," Elaine answered tightly just as a clap of thunder opened up the heavens. Rain pounded on the roof of the trailer, turning the tiny space into an echo chamber.

Keeping his voice calm, he raised his voice enough it could be heard over the noise. "Check the weather app I installed on your phone. It should pull up the satellite image."

Dax buried his head into his shoulder, trembling. Travis rubbed his back and kissed his head. "It's okay, kiddo. I'm here now. We're gonna be just fine."

He was damned well gonna make sure of it. This trailer was a fucking death trap. Anger at himself rising with each flash of lightning. He couldn't believe how many storms they'd endured over the summer in this din, and she'd never said anything. His brave, sweet Elaine. Soldiering on, an army of one. No more.

She handed him the phone. Relief melted some of the tension in his neck. The worst of it was to the north. They were in for a doozy of a storm though. As if on cue, the lights flickered and went out, casting them into shadow. Dax whimpered and Travis automatically patted his back.

Then a clunk hit the roof, followed by another. And another.

"Hail," Elaine murmured.

The pinging and clunking increased in speed until the trailer sounded like they were underneath the bleachers at a stadium when fans stomped their feet like crazy.

Elaine turned to him, eyes wide. "Travis. Your car."

He shook his head. "Will be fine. What's important is that we're safe." He tightened his embrace on the two. At that moment, nothing else mattered. They were together. They were safe. Fuck the election. It wasn't important. At least not as important as Elaine and Dax. They were his life. His family, his home. Nothing mattered more than having them in the center of his world. "That's it," he growled when the hail had passed. "You're not staying here a second longer. You're coming home."

CHAPTER 26

I T WAS STILL raining heavily, but the worst of the storm had passed as Travis turned onto the drive. He lifted his chin, talking into the rearview. "Once the storm has passed and you're settled, I'll take you out to the barn. I have something to show you."

Elaine's mind reeled. The whole way over she'd been in a quandary. If Travis was asking them to move in, she would have to notify Officer Marshall, even though her final probation hearing was scheduled for the day after the special election. On the other hand, if she was just 'staying over'... but Travis had made his intent very clear. And strangely, it felt right. They already spent so much time together over here that Dax had a toothbrush and a spare set of pajamas for the nights they worked late. How would Dax feel about her sleeping in the same bed as Travis?

Only one way to find out.

Travis brought the SUV to a stop and turned to her. "Wait here." He hopped out and sprinted to the porch, returning a moment later underneath an umbrella, with a second in his hand. He opened her door and handed her the folded one. "I'll bring in Dax."

She opened the umbrella and hopped through the puddles, jumping up the porch steps. Dax clung to Travis, arms wrapped tightly around the big man's neck, as he carried the boy from the vehicle. The tenderness he demonstrated to Dax hit her smack in the center of her chest. Travis set Dax down next to her and unlocked the door. "Welcome home." He turned to her with an eager smile and extended his hand.

She'd have to get used to carrying a key. Taking a big breath, she smiled back, and slipped her hand in his.

He pulled her across the threshold and led them upstairs. He opened the first door on the right. "This is my old room. Now it's my weight room. Dax, you can come in here anytime, as long as there's an adult with you. Got it?"

Dax's nodded solemnly, eyes like saucers.

Then Travis opened the next door on the left. "This is your room, buddy. It used to belong to my brother, Colton. Come on in. Take a look."

Dax stepped into the room, taking in the rodeo posters plastered on the walls. "Is your brother a cowboy?" he asked, voice full of awe.

Travis's face pulled tight and a muscle ticked in his jaw. Dax didn't notice, he was too busy staring at the posters of cowboys on bucking bulls and broncos. But she could tell it pained Travis to be in here. His shoulders tensed and he kept drumming his fingers on his thigh. If they stayed, maybe they could paint the room for Dax, make it new for both of them.

"He is," Travis answered warily.

"Can he show me how to do that?" Dax pointed to a picture of a cowboy on the back of a bucking bronco, feet airborne, head tossed back, hand in the air.

Travis huffed out a wry laugh. "He rodeos and isn't here." He reached down and ruffled Dax's hair. "But, you get good at riding Sunny and we can discuss the rodeo later."

Dax stared up at him critically. "Promise?"

Elaine smothered a laugh. There was something totally

endearing about the way Dax negotiated concessions from Travis.

Travis stuck out his hand. "Promise."

They shook, and Travis pulled him into a hug. "C'mere. I want to show you something." He straightened and led them across the hall to another shut door.

Elaine stared uneasily at the enormous lock protruding above the handle. It looked like a deadbolt. There was no way she was staying in a room with a lock that big on it. She'd rather camp out on the couch.

The door fell open silently with a turn of the handle. Travis gestured into the large master room, dominated by a king-sized bed. "I thought your mom and I could sleep in here, so we're right across the hall from each other."

Elaine's throat clutched. This was all happening too fast. She should have thought to prepare Dax. Suss out his feelings beforehand. She gave Travis an apologetic grimace but he shook his head just barely.

Dax looked at the bed and back to Travis, a serious expression on his tiny face. "Like you're my dad?"

All the air squeezed out of her lungs. The longing in his voice was palpable. Travis would make a great dad, but she couldn't ask him to be that to Dax. This was too much. She never should have agreed to come. She'd talk to Travis as soon as Dax went to bed and set things straight.

Travis bent and placed his hands on his knees, gazing steadily at Dax. "Well, I was hoping we could discuss that, man to man. See, your mom and I love each other. What do you think about that?"

Dax lifted his eyes to the ceiling, thinking. After a moment he nodded. "I think that's okay."

"Now, I've never been a dad before, but if I was a dad, I'd

want a kid like you."

Dax puffed up, a smile spreading across his face.

Her heart had to still be beating – she was still standing. Her insides felt tossed around like an upside-down salt shaker. She bit down on her lip unsure of what to expect next.

Dax toed the fringe of the rug. "I've never had a dad."

"Would you like one?" Elaine perked up at the husky note in Travis's voice. She wasn't the only one with her heart in her throat.

Dax shrugged and nodded. Of all the things she'd never been able to give her son, raising him without a father hurt her the most. But raising him with a revolving door of bad examples would have been far worse.

"Do you think we can try it for a bit?" Travis asked. "See how it's like?"

Dax nodded slowly. "Does that mean you love me?"

Her hand flew to her mouth, too late to cover the astonished squeak that escaped.

Travis's face was a study of emotion, but he nodded and pulled Dax in for a hug. "Yeah," he said throatily. "It does. I love you kiddo."

Hot tears pierced her eyelids as Dax snuggled into Travis's embrace. She caught a muffled *I love you too* as Dax spoke into Travis's midsection. When their gazes locked, Travis's eyes were shiny and soft. *Thank you,* she mouthed silently. He shrugged, an expression of wonder on his face. "I mean it," he said gruffly. "All of it."

Once Dax had run off to play downstairs, Travis pulled her into an embrace. "You think he'll like it here?" he asked gruffly.

"I think he'll do just fine." She swiveled her head eyeing the door. "But you can't lock this door."

His body tensed. "Why not?"

"I can't sleep in a room with a locked door."

"The door locks for your safety."

"But we're safe here, Travis. I can understand and agree to locking the front door at night. This is a big house. But not the bedroom." Heat prickled over her scalp. "Besides, if Dax is across the hall, I want him to know he can come in if he needs me."

"And I don't want him to barge in on us accidentally," Travis growled back.

Elaine pushed against him, stepping back. "I don't see why you're so obsessed with keeping everyone in."

"It's keeping people *out* that I'm worried about, and you know why," he ground out. "And I'm slowly getting better, you know that." He crossed his arms. "But what I don't know and you've refused to say is why *you're* obsessed with keeping things unlocked." He stared pointedly at her, raising his eyebrows in expectation. "Start talkin' darlin'."

Fear raced down her spine, chilling her all the way to her fingertips. She'd never confessed this to anyone. Not that she'd ever been close enough to anyone to confide something this personal, this... mortifying. She snuck a peek at him through her lowered lashes. Immovable.

"When I was small, younger than Dax, I-I..." Heat exploded on her face. She squeezed her eyes shut tamping down the ugly memory, the terror. "I was locked in a closet as a form of discipline." Even now, she could feel the darkness pressing in on her. The stuffy, hot air choking her.

Travis made an awful noise and her eyes jerked up. Every muscle in his body clenched, poised to pounce or mete out justice. Fear snaked through her. How would he react when she disclosed the rest? "There's more," she murmured thickly, struggling to push out the words through a constricted throat. Keeping her eyes pinned to a square on the rug, she forced out the rest. "A few years ago… before we moved here, there was an incident." She swallowed down the bile that rose up her throat. Lawson had made it clear what would happen to her or to Travis if she ever spoke of the incident. "I… a person locked me in a room and tried to hurt me," she blurted, fighting the wave of nausea that swarmed her belly. "I-I got away before anything significant happened, but I promised myself I'd always have an escape route after that." Her heart pounded ferociously.

"Who?" Travis's voice was lethal. Hard.

"I-it doesn't matter."

"Like hell it doesn't," he bit out. "I'll deal with him."

She'd never seen him like this. Unyielding. Deadly. This was Travis the warrior. For a terrifying moment, she imagined seeing his face on the other end of a rifle. Or worse. A shiver skittered across her shoulders.

"Did you ever report it?"

She shook her head once. "It wouldn't have made a difference."

"Why not?"

She let out a bitter laugh. "Who would I have told? He had all the power. And no one saw us. He made sure no one saw him. It would have been my word against his, and who would believe a–" she caught herself. Who would believe a girl with a record accusing a cop who'd positioned himself as unassailable? No one. "Someone like me?" she finished sadly.

Travis scrubbed a hand across his jaw and shook his head. When he looked at her, his eyes were bright with anger. She cringed, bracing herself for his unleashed fury. She couldn't help it, and hated herself when she saw the hurt look in his eyes. "I will *never* hurt you." His voice came out full of gravel. "Never. And I will deal handily with anyone who does." He swooped down and gave her a hard kiss. "The lock will come off tomorrow." He stalked out of the room before she thought to stop him.

She wanted so badly to lay everything out. To explain herself. But she couldn't do that to him right before the election. Not only would it add to his stress and pull his focus from the campaign, but the backlash over her record would ruin his chances. Cause such a big blow up. Not to mention cost Dottie precious business. People in this town weren't ready for a known criminal in their midst. She couldn't do that to either of them. Once her hearing was over and she'd been released, and it was all in the past, then maybe she and Dottie could talk to Travis together. Explain everything. Just nine days.

CHAPTER 27

"TRAVIS, YOU'RE NOT thinking like a winner," Weston banged his hand on the table.

"Like hell I'm not," Travis countered, voice rising.

Tension had been building all week and had finally spilled over at dinner.

"Guys, Dax is asleep upstairs," Elaine scolded.

She was on pins and needles too, expecting the worst every day when she rushed to the mailbox. So far Lawson hadn't gone on the offensive, but their conversation kept ringing in her ears. They just had to get through the next four days in one piece, but everyone was exhausted and on edge.

"You need to sew this up, Travis, and to do it you've got to go negative."

Travis crossed his arms, triceps bulging under his shirt. "I won't. I have a reputation to uphold in the community. I won't resort to mudslinging."

"All it would be doing is raising questions about your opponent. Legitimate questions." Weston paced the length of the table. "Look. I can call my dad's designer and have something put together by midnight. There's a printer in Wichita we can pay for an expedited run. They'll be finished by mid-afternoon tomorrow and I will personally deliver them to the post office. We'll have to pay first class postage, but they'll arrive in some boxes Saturday and the rest, Monday."

"You've thought this through completely, haven't you?" You could cut the tension in Travis's voice with a knife.

Weston rolled his eyes. "This ain't my first rodeo."

"It would cost $14,097.44," she said more to herself than to anyone else.

The men swung to stare at her.

"How do you know?" Travis asked.

Weston smacked his shoulder. "I told you she was lightning fast with numbers. Break it down?"

Elaine sighed, cheeks flaming under their stares. "10,623 voters, times point seven-nine for a six by eight mailer. $8,392.17 in printing costs. Multiply the voters by a first-class stamp and that's an additional $5,205.27. Add five hundred for expedited printing." She shrugged. Not that hard.

Travis grinned at her. "I knew there was a reason why I loved you." He turned to Weston, frowning. "I'm not spending fifteen thousand more of my nest-egg just to hit Lawson in the balls."

Weston's jaw flexed. "How bad do you want to win?"

"I guess not fifteen-thousand more bad. I could use that to get the tractor running again. Or buy a half-dozen calf-cow pairs."

"Thinking like a rancher already?"

"Just trying to keep my perspective."

"Try this perspective. You lose, Lawson becomes your boss. And mine," Weston added. "The guy's bad news, Travis. Is it worth fifteen grand to make sure an asshole doesn't ruin the county?"

Travis's face pulled tight. "You can't put that all on me, and you know it."

Weston paced away again. "At least there's nothing negative Lawson can use on you. Maybe we'll squeak this out, but mark my words. If he wins, it will be harder to unseat him as an incumbent."

Elaine's stomach somersaulted at Weston's words, and she nearly missed what Travis said.

"Elaine? What do you think?"

Both sets of eyes trained on her. She froze. What was she supposed to say? Lawson's threat rang in her ears. Lawson would lash out if he felt backed into a corner. She looked back and forth between the two men. Weston's eyes flaming with intensity and the desire to win. Travis's guarded. Exhausted. What would Lawson do if he lost? Would he still find a way to ruin everything she'd rebuilt? It was too risky. "I-I think we should give him a wide berth."

Triumph flashed in Travis's eyes. Weston looked crestfallen. "I'm sorry Weston."

Weston threw up his hand. "What the candidate wants…" He grabbed his jacket draped over the end chair. "As long as you have no regrets, man. I don't want you coming back in a year or two when Lawson is running the county like a mob boss and telling me you wished you'd spent the money."

Travis's mouth flattened. "Not a chance."

"My work here is done, then. You know what you need to do over the weekend. I'll show myself out." Weston let himself out, quietly shutting the door with a click.

Travis's shoulders sagged, and after locking the door, he flopped on the couch cradling his head in his hands. The poor man was exhausted. Heck, they all were, but the stress of it was finally evident on his face and in his body.

Going to him, she curled herself up next to him on the couch, laying her head on his shoulder and draping an arm across his back. "Hey. You okay?"

Tension radiated off him in waves. She drew her hand up, working the knots at the base of his neck. After a long moment, a shudder wracked his body and he let out a heavy sigh. "Weston warned me this would be stressful."

"Do you regret running?"

He flicked a glance at her, eyes tired but glowing. "Not for a second. I just want it to be over. And I want to know the outcome so I can move on."

Her heart sank a little. So he could move on? What about her? Or them? Or Dax? Maybe it was just a slip of the tongue because he was stressed. But what if it wasn't? And what would he say when she finally told him about her record? Would he still want her then? Even if she was about to be released from probation? She didn't know what to say, so she kept working the knots on his backside. "Yeah, me too," she finally answered quietly.

"MORE COFFEE?" ELAINE smiled down at Anders, one of her morning regulars as she started to refill his cup. "I can run and get your cream." Anders always put three creams in his coffees.

He scowled at her yanking his cup away. "I didn't ask for more, and I'll get my own cream."

"I'm so sorry," she responded automatically, reeling.

Anders wasn't naturally crusty like some of the other old-timers. He usually greeted her with a warm smile and a question about Dax. Maybe he was worried about the reconstruction efforts for the Feed 'n Seed? Builders had broken ground on the new building last week. A shiver snaked down her spine. But what if it wasn't? Her stomach filled with dread.

She shook herself. According to Weston, anything bad

would have hit by now. She only had to get through two more days. She was just anxious about the election. About talking to Travis after. That was all it was. Nothing more than a few jitters. She replaced the coffee pot and grabbed a washcloth from the bleach bucket.

Dottie stepped out of the food truck. "You okay, sweetie pie? You look like you're carryin' the world on your shoulders."

Elaine put on a smile. "Yeah. Just worried about the election tomorrow." She lowered her voice. "And Wednesday."

Dottie wrapped her in a hug. Dottie might be squishy on the outside, but she was steel on the inside. Elaine sagged against the older woman, absorbing her resolve. "I'm going to be fine," she said thickly. "This will pass."

"Damn straight you're gonna be fine. Your man's gonna win tomorrow, and then we can talk to him about Wednesday. I'll stay with you every step."

She squeezed her eyes against the hot swell of emotion that stuck in her throat. "I love you, Dottie. I couldn't have done this without you." She sniffed, blinking hard.

Dottie gave her a squeeze. "I love you too, sweetie pie." Her voice grew husky. "I'm so proud of you. Now get back out there and finish up so you're ready when Travis comes to pick you up. You have an election to help win."

Brushing her eyes, she stepped back and took a big breath. This time, her smile felt genuine. Dipping the washcloth in the bleach water, she wrung it out and headed for the tables. As she rounded the corner of the truck, she recognized Travis's brawny figure moving through the tables. "Hey there," she called out, thrilled to see him in the middle of the day. Her smile froze in place when he turned, a thunderous expression pulling on his features.

He stalked to her, holding out a large, glossy piece of paper. A mailer, from the looks of it. His eyes glittered hard and cold. "What in the hell is this?"

She took the piece, hands shaking. Facing up at her was a photo she'd never seen before, but one she would remember for the rest of her life. She hardly recognized the scared eyed, pink-haired girl from more than two years ago staring up at her. But there was no doubt it was her. The red *GUILTY* stamp through her name just made it worse. Her world tilted sideways, sending her stomach with it as she went hot and cold all at once. But what made her want to have the earth swallow her up were the big words "*Campaign Treasurer – CRIMINAL*".

Over her picture, big dark words grabbed the reader's attention.

If TRAVIS KINCAID hires criminals for his campaign, WHO will he hire as County Sheriff?

The blood rushed from her face. She'd ruined everything for Travis.

CHAPTER 28

THE WIDE SCARED eyes staring up at him matched the eyes of the girl in the picture. He didn't want to believe it. Couldn't believe it. *Say something.* But she didn't. She just stared at him, a pained expression on her face, eyes deep dark pools of sorrow.

"What is this?" he gritted out. "Is this you?" Dammit, he wanted to hear her admit it. Own up to the extent of her betrayal.

He'd been shocked when Jeanine had placed the mailer on his desk not twenty minutes earlier. There was no way the woman in the picture could be his sweet, strong Elaine. And yet he'd recognized her instantly.

"I-It's not what you think," she finally uttered, barely above a whisper.

"Then you damn well better start explaining."

She barely tilted her head, scanning the area. "Can we go someplace private?"

"Your mug shot is in the mailbox of every resident in the county and you want to go someplace private?" he barked. "Everyone's gonna know your story before dinner hits the table tonight darlin'."

She winced, pink flushing her cheeks.

Maybe that was too harsh, but at the moment he was too angry to care. She'd singlehandedly destroyed months of effort. Not to mention the thousands of dollars down the drain. His stomach churned at that. It would take him years to recoup his losses. He crossed his arms and glowered at her. "Well?"

Her eyes darted up, spearing him with a look of such pain that his gut twisted. But she would not play him again, and he tamped down the urge to soften. She'd slid under his defenses and it had made him weak. Compromised his judgment. God, it was Kandahar all over again. When would he fucking learn?

She looked down at the space between them and spoke so low he had to lean in to hear her. "Three years ago, Dax and I lived in Topeka." Her voice came out in a monotone, devoid of emotion. "As you know, I was a high-school dropout. There weren't a lot of employment options available to me, especially with a four-year-old. I ended up with a cocktailing job at a gentleman's club called Naughty Nellie's."

Gentleman's club, his ass. "You worked at a strip club," he said flatly. A hot flash of jealous rage drove through him. The thought that creeps and criminals had seen her tits or worse, and had undoubtedly attempted to put their hands all over her had his vision spotting. The law enforcement community was very aware of Naughty Nellie's. It had a well-earned reputation for being the favorite booty call joint for some of the slipperiest criminals in Kansas. Even drawing some of the rougher elements from Kansas City.

"I swear I never took off my clothes," she rushed, a note of panic sounding in her voice.

"Let me guess," he said sarcastically. "You just made introductions for the ladies who did?"

Her eyes flashed. "I had a child to feed. The DJ lived in my building and hooked me up with a job."

"Interesting choice of words."

TESSA LAYNE

She gasped, cheeks going from pink to red.

That was a low blow. One he might regret later when he was drowning his sorrows in a bottle of whiskey, but at the moment, he didn't care.

She took a step closer to him, eyes flashing angry hurt. "I *never* did anything to be ashamed of. The only thing I'm ashamed of is—"

"The fact you got caught," he finished for her.

"No." She shook her head, voice vibrating in anger. "That I was too scared to level with you early on. But I… I couldn't."

"*Bullshit*," he ground out. "I'm the goddamned police chief. You damn well should have leveled with me."

"I wanted to put the past behind me. Coming to Prairie was a chance at a fresh start. The chance to be the person I wanted to be."

"And it was all built on a lie."

"I swear, Travis it wasn't."

"How'd it happen?" Maybe he was an ass for pushing this way, but she was in the wrong. "You accept a proposition in a sting?" The thought made him sick, and he hated himself for asking, but he had to know.

"*No.*" Her eyes glittered with unshed tears. "Why are you assuming the worst?"

"Maybe it's because your mugshot is plastered all over the county with the words 'guilty' and 'criminal'. You tell me. What the hell was it?"

She glowered at him. "There was a sweep. Hard drugs were found in my purse. But I didn't put them there. I've never used. Not once. Not the hard stuff," she amended. "Pot a few times before I got pregnant, but nothing since."

"That's what they all say," he snarled. God, she was just

196

like Colton. What a sucker.

A tear oozed from the corner of her eye and slid down her cheek. He would not soften. Could not. "Don't do this, Travis. *Please.*" He barely recognized her voice through the tears. "I've worked hard to straighten out my life. I haven't been anything but honest with you."

"Except for this," he snapped, gesturing to the mailer. "I broke all my rules for you. Every. Damned. One. How could you not tell me?"

"I should have told you," she shot back angrily. "But I was afraid if anyone knew, that something like this," she shook the mailer, "would happen and hurt your campaign. I didn't want to bring you down." She brushed at her eyes.

"How can you say you love me and keep secrets?"

"You keep secrets too," she raised her voice.

"That's different." No one needed to know what really happened between him and Colton. He'd bear that burden alone.

She crosses her arms. "How so?"

"I shared my deepest secrets with you. Told you about my team. And this is how you repay me?" He might be deflecting, but he didn't care. She'd wormed her way past his defenses. He'd let her see his soft underbelly, and then she'd stabbed him where he was most vulnerable. He couldn't forgive that.

"This isn't about repayment," she countered, voice rising. "It was never a transaction. I did what I felt I had to do to feed and care for my son."

"So you're saying the only reason you took the job was for the money?" Pain knifed through his chest.

She shook her head, eyes dull. "You don't get it, do you?" Her voice caught. "I thought you had more faith in me than this. More faith in *us*." She narrowed her eyes, a muscle in her jaw ticking. "I see I was mistaken. Well you can take my resignation on the spot, Chief Kincaid. And don't bother paying me the rest of my salary." She started to rip the mailer. "In fact, I will bring you a check tomorrow for all of it, minus Dax's school things and the clothes I bought. I will pay you back for those out of my tip money. Consider it a campaign donation."

She tossed the pieces of the mailer to the ground and spun away.

The burning in his chest grew as he watched her disappear behind the food truck, shoulders slumped. He made the walk back to the police station in record time. "Weston," he roared as soon as the door had shut behind him. "Weston."

Weston came around the corner, another mailer in hand, jaw set. "You know you're well and truly fucked."

"Yep." All that time, all that money, gone in a mailer. Judging from the size alone, one that cost significantly more than fifteen grand.

"Did you talk to Elaine?"

He nodded curtly.

"Did you tell her we'll do what we can to shield her from the fallout?"

Travis stilled, a finger of guilt needling him.

Weston groaned. "Jesus. Don't tell me you were an asshat."

"She lied to me."

"By keeping deeply personal information personal?"

"We're LIVING together, for fucks sake. She should have told me." He had to hold onto his anger. It was all he had left, now. He was right, dammit.

"It's not exactly the kind of embarrassing information you volunteer to someone you're crazy about. To someone you're afraid might judge you." Weston folded his arms. "You could have vetted her." His voice became hard. Clipped. "Are you pissed at her or yourself?"

Travis scowled at the wall.

"Could you or could you not have run a background check on her?" Weston asked harshly, raising his voice.

"Not without her consent and you know it," he bit out.

"You know there are other ways."

"Yes, and I also said I'd never use them."

Weston got in his face, eyes blazing. "You realize that Lawson did? To get at you? That guy's a sick sonofabitch. You want to be pissed at someone? Be pissed at him. He's not only ruined your campaign, he's ruined *her* life."

Weston turned and paced the length of the hall, before stalking back and jabbing him in the chest. "Did you think about that even once in your righteous indignation?"

He opened his mouth but Weston held up a hand. "Save me your sob story. I've known you for years, man. I know what pushes your buttons and you need to get the fuck over yourself. What kind of man are you that you're in here sucking your thumb while you're letting a single mom with not much safety net, *and who you love,* spin in the wind?"

There was that finger of guilt again, poking at him. "But I broke the rules for her."

"Fuck your goddamned rules, Kincaid," Weston shouted, mouth tight. "Haven't you learned anything from seeing Dr. Munger? Your rigid rules are a fucked-up coping mechanism that are destroying you and any opportunity you have at happiness."

"*TRAVIS KINCAID*," roared Dottie from the other end of the hall.

He couldn't win today. Why had Jeanine let her in?

"What on God's good green earth did you do to that poor woman? She's beside herself."

Travis snatched the flyer from Weston and handed it over. Maybe now she'd climb down off her high horse. "Maybe you've seen this."

Dottie's eyes widened then narrowed as she shifted her gaze to him. "Tell me you were gentle with her." She raked her gaze over him with a mother's ferocity. The finger of guilt turned into a fist. How was it she could reduce him to about twelve-years old with a scathing glance?

She crossed her arms, mouth pinched into a line. "I see you haven't learned a damned thing, have you?"

His chest burst into flame, crawling up his neck.

"You've judged that sweet thing by the same harsh standards you judged your brother, Colton. I always disagreed with you kicking him out of the house when he was seventeen, but I wasn't there when it happened and figured you'd ask for help from Teddy if you needed it."

Why was she dredging up the past now? And in front of Weston?

Dottie barged ahead. "But you never did. And now it's you all alone at that ranch. Your daddy would be rolling in his grave to see how you've let the Kincaid legacy dwindle to nothing. I had high hopes when Elaine finally moved in with you that you'd made a step in the right direction."

He had to make her understand. She of all people should understand. "Do you know what she did Dottie? She was caught up in a drug sweep in one of the most notorious titty bars in Topeka."

That would shock her into siding with him. She knew about Colton's drug and alcohol problem in high school.

"I know that," she railed. "How do you think she ended

up here? I've worked with probation cases in the past, giving people second chances. Some worked out. Some not. Elaine was a dream come true. And yes, surprise, surprise – she was human and made mistakes. Mistakes she's paid *dearly* for. She's done everything right to get her life back on track. Now don't ruin it for her."

She ripped the flyer in two and shoved it back at him. "I should have stepped in years ago, and I regret that I didn't. Someone shoulda told you to get off your high horse when it came to Colton. I know you were young and full of yourself, running off to those missions, doing your duty to your country." She scowled. "But you had a duty here too. Everyone but you could see that boy was hurting, and all you did was come at him with crazy rules. So I'm gonna tell you what I shoulda said then." She gave him a blistering gaze. "You fix this Travis Kincaid. You fix it. And don't come around until you do." She spun on her heel and marched back down the hall.

CHAPTER 29

D OTTIE'S FOOTSTEPS ECHOED through the hall. Weston stared at him grimly. "Why don't you start with Lawson you dumbass? Did you ever look at the dossier I gave you?"

Motherfucker.

Shamefaced, Travis shook his head.

Weston pushed open his office door. "How the hell you became police chief when you're so stubborn and hard-headed is beyond me." A moment later he came back with a folder. "Open it."

Travis shook his head. "Elaine first. I want to know everything."

Weston eyed him critically. "Are you sure? I don't want you using this shit against her."

Weston might as well have kicked him in the balls for the pain that burst through him at his accusation. A tendril of fear curled through him. He wanted to know. Wanted to believe her. At the same time, confirmation that he'd been played would break him.

"Well? What's it gonna be?"

He clenched his jaw so hard his molars squeaked.

Weston's voice softened a fraction. "The truth will set you free, man. You'll know for sure, and you can figure out how to move forward."

He scrubbed a hand over his face. "Fine, fine. Make the call." Weston was right. If he knew definitively, he could deal with the fallout. He wanted to puke.

"Mac, I need a favor." Weston's voice bounced off the wall as he walked down the hall.

Travis walked into his office and sat down, tossing the folder back on his desk. He propped his head in his hands, trying to control his churning stomach. If Dottie and Weston were both right and he was wrong, that made him the biggest asshole outside of the US Navy. And if he'd been wrong about Elaine, did that mean he'd been wrong about Colton too? Dottie sure as hell thought so. Had he been too hard on his little brother? His stomach gave a growling answer to the question. A weight pressed down on him. He'd always looked out for his team. How could he have failed his brother? He'd let the rigor of his training spill over into his personal life, and it hadn't mixed well with a seventeen-year-old trying to find his way. Fuck him.

Footsteps sounded at the door, and Weston's polished boots came into view. "Check your phone."

Travis raised his head. He hadn't seen Weston's face that taut since… he shuddered. Not for a very long time. "I really don't wanna know what connections you have, do I?"

Weston shrugged, mouth a rigid line. "Probably not."

Travis's phone beeped. He pulled up the email from what he presumed was a dummy account. Elaine's mug shot flashed on the screen and then a summary. He skimmed through the bullet points. A runaway at fourteen, juvenile detention, repeated failed attempts at fostering, a group home, underage drinking, pot possession. A baby at seventeen, likely father a known criminal five years her senior, who died in a prison gang riot when she was nineteen.

His stomach churned. Good riddance. No wonder she'd turned to cutting at some point. Guilt stabbed through him as everything he'd learned about dealing with self-harm came slamming back to him. Weston was right, what kind of a hack cop was he? He continued scrolling through the summary.

After Dax was born, a string of low wage jobs but no criminal activity – until the night she was arrested in a drug sweep at Naughty Nellie's. According to the document, she'd submitted a request for a hearing to have her probation reduced. Hearing set for the day after tomorrow. He raked a hand through his hair. "I've really fucked this up, haven't I? With Elaine?"

Weston frowned and leaned in the doorway. "Elaine's a good woman, Travis. You know that. You have to fix this. This is all Lawson's doing. You want someone to pay? Make it him. Elaine's paid enough."

He reached for the file and opened it. Lawson's formal police chief photo smiled back at him. His hand twitched. God, he needed a heavy bag. But he wasn't going to drive all the way home just to release the energy stuck inside him.

Everything Weston had hinted at was there, right on the page in black and white. And the farther down the page he read, the hotter he grew, blood pounding in his ears.

Lawson was shady. The kind of cop you heard rumors about but didn't quite believe could be true. Or that they only happened in big cities like Chicago and New York. The man had questionable connections with drug dealers and prostitution rings, but no one could ever seem to pin anything on him. Twice, he was accused of assaulting a female suspect in holding, but nothing was ever proven.

He flicked a glance at Weston. "You knew this? And you've been sitting on it?"

Weston raised his hands. "I tried to tell you, but you were more concerned with doing things by the book. Honorable trait in a police chief."

For all the good it did him. He glanced through the last page, eyes catching on the words *Naughty Nellie's*. "Did you see this?" He quickly scanned the last paragraphs, heart racing. "Lawson was the arresting officer at Naughty Nellie's the night Elaine was arrested."

Weston's eyebrows shot up. "Huh."

"Did you know this?"

Weston shook his head. "Nah. There was enough on the first page to convince me the guy's scum."

Travis's mind raced. He was missing something. And then the missing link dropped into place. The abject fear on Elaine's face when he'd seen Lawson talking to her after the 4th of July parade. The look that had made him spontaneously decide to jump in the race for sheriff. He slammed a hand on his desk and stood. "Holy shit, Wes, Lawson knows her. He knows Elaine."

"How do you know?"

"I just know," he growled. "And I'm going to get to the bottom of this once and for all." He tossed the folder on his chair and brushed past Weston.

"If you're going to confront Lawson, be careful," Weston called after him.

Adrenaline pumped through him, narrowing his focus. All he could see as he slipped into his vehicle was Elaine's terrified face. The entire drive over to Marion he replayed every encounter with the man, honing his anger. He took the police station steps two at a time and smiled politely at the gray-haired front office lady just inside the door. "Lawson in?"

He walked silently down the hall, pausing just outside the

open door. Lawson's voice drifted out. He was on the phone with someone. A quick glance around the corner showed an office similar to his, with the desk facing sideways into the room. Lawson was behind it with his feet up on the desk, at an angle to the door.

Travis slipped into the office and silently shut the door, turning the lock. As Lawson turned, he ripped the phone out of the bastard's hands and slammed it on the receiver.

"Whaa?"

Before Lawson could say more, he'd pulled the man out of his chair and shoved him against the wall. "Right now, you sonofabitch," he bellowed. "This stops right now. Tell me how you know Elaine."

Recognition bloomed on Lawson's face, and he sneered. "So you finally figured out the bitch was playing you?"

Travis punched him in the gut. He'd start with the soft spots first.

Lawson wheezed and squirmed, but he had six inches on the guy and rage fueling him. Lawson was going nowhere. "You'll pay for that, Kincaid," he choked. "Once this gets out," he gasped, "Your career is over."

Travis punched him again. Harder. It felt entirely too good. "I don't give a shit you asswipe. You're scum. What did she ever do to you?"

Lawson's eyes lit fanatically, full of hatred.

Of course. The locked door. "Wait. She turned you down didn't she? You wanted a piece and she told you to get lost. So you tried–"

"She's nothing but a whore," Lawson spit.

Red hazed his vision and he came unleashed. This time, hitting higher. "Don't." A fist to the ribs and an accompanying crack. "You." Another fist to the ribs. Upward, punctuating each word with a blow. "Ever. Call. My. Future. Wife. A. Whore. Do. I. Make. Myself. Clear?" He took aim and slammed his fist into Lawson's nose with a sickening crunch.

Lawson gave a strangled cry and went limp, sliding down the wall and collapsing in a heap when Travis let go. He stood a moment, letting the shaking in his body dissipate, then flexed his hand and silently left the office closing the door quietly behind him.

Calm settled over Travis. All his years in the SEALs, he'd saved his fighting for the battlefield. But he'd learned an important lesson today. There was something deeply, *viscerally* satisfying about delivering cowboy justice to an asshole. He parked his vehicle back at the station and gave the roof a pat as he shut the door. Keeping his pace measured, almost leisurely, he climbed the stairs and pushed open the glass door. Acknowledging Jeanine with a wave, he didn't stop until he reached Weston's desk. "Congratulations, you just earned yourself a promotion." He tossed his badge on the pile of papers scattered in front of him.

Weston swiveled around, eyes moving back and forth between his bruised knuckles and his face. "I should see the other guy, huh?"

He nodded once, not trusting his voice.

"What next?"

He took a deep breath, releasing it slowly. "I find Elaine and beg her to forgive me."

"Prepare to grovel."

"Yep."

"Lots of groveling, Travis."

He nodded again.

"Unprecedented groveling."

"I get the picture," he growled. Leaving Weston with a two-fingered salute, he hit the locker room for the last time. He hung his vest and stowed his weapon in the lock box. He pulled on his Wranglers and slipped into his boots, buttoned up his favorite flannel plaid and secured his belt buckle. He gave a last look around the bare room and tossed his uniform in the laundry.

He stopped at Jeanine's desk. "I probably haven't told you as much as I should've, what an asset you are to us. I'm sorry about that."

Jeanine tilted her head giving him a funny look. "Aww you're sweet, Travis. See you tomorrow for the party?"

The party. Weston had organized a watch party at the ranch. There would be no victory for him now. But it would be sad to waste Mike McAllister's victory brew he'd created just for tomorrow night. "Yeah. See you tomorrow."

Travis crawled into his SUV, tossed his phone on the passenger seat and sat, hands on the wheel. If he breathed deeply, he could still detect the faint residue of Elaine's perfume. He couldn't bring himself to start the vehicle. He'd never been a full-fledged civilian. He'd gone right from the military to the police academy, and from there, straight home to Prairie. Apprehension fluttered at the edge of his conscious. His new life started the second he pulled out of the parking space. The cell phone taunted him from the middle of the seat. Thoughts spun in his head like they were on a wash cycle.

Don't be a chickenshit.

Letting his head fall back, he shut his eyes, mustering the courage to pick up the phone. "Fuck it." He reached for the phone before he could psych himself out, or come up with a million reasons why what he was about to do was a bad idea.

He scrolled through his contacts, thumb twitching when he reached the name. His pulse raced, sounding like a drum in the small space. He hit the call button, stomach tightening with each ring.

And voicemail.

Clearing his throat, he waited for the brief greeting to end. "Colt. Travis. Look… I know this is long overdue, and I've been an ass." He laughed harshly. "Hell, worse than an ass… I'd like to properly apologize. Call me?"

He clicked off and stared at his brother's contact information. The lost years, the countless missed opportunities hung before him like a banner. His throat closed, remorse washing over him. He took a shuddering breath. He'd made a start, and it might not come to anything, but it was a start. He started the engine. One down, one to go.

CHAPTER 30

HOPE FLAMED TO life in Travis's chest as he pulled away from the Grace home. There were only four places Elaine was likely to be, and she wasn't at the first three. It was unreasonable for him under any circumstance to hope that Elaine would be home, waiting for him. But as he made the turn onto his own drive, hope was there, burning inside him. And when he saw her sitting on the front porch with Dottie, who bristled like a prairie chicken defending its turf, it spread like a grass fire down to his toes.

The urge to race to the porch and sweep her in his arms was powerful. But instinctively he knew that would only make it worse. What had Weston said about unprecedented groveling? Worry niggled at him, but he brushed it away. He was a man on a mission and defeat was not an option. His heart slammed into his chest as he kept his pace unhurried and stopped a few feet from the bottom step.

He kept his eyes laser-focused on Elaine, even though the mistrustful look in her eyes gutted him. With a jolt, he recognized her expression. She looked just like that in her early days at the diner. Scared yet determined. What an idiot. Beating was too good for him. He alone was responsible for putting the hurt there, the mistrust.

"Where's Dax?"

"Over at Hansen's with Hope and Gunnar. They'll bring

him home after dinner." Dottie answered with a note of accusation in her voice.

Still keeping his gaze riveted on Elaine, he opened his hands. "It's okay Dottie. I've been an ass. I know. I reacted and I couldn't listen."

Something flickered in Elaine's eyes, feeding his hope. "I took care of Lawson."

"I don't understand."

He rolled his fingers, flexing his hand. "Let's just say he's not gonna look too pretty in his election day victory photo."

Dottie snorted and threw up her hands. "What's that supposed to mean?"

"I can't serve as sheriff if I'm not currently holding a law enforcement position."

"Talk plain, Travis." Dottie snapped, having clearly run out of patience.

"Fine, you want plain talk?" He stayed focused on Elaine, watching for any signs that she might be softening. He'd work with any opening she gave him "I read your file."

She winced and looked down, two bright spots slashing her cheeks.

"All of it. I also read up on Lawson and put two and two together. I paid him a visit and took action that cost me my job as police chief."

She gasped, covering her mouth, eyebrows at her hairline. "Oh no, Travis. You shouldn't have. He'll come after you." Fear filled her beautiful blue eyes.

That was a good sign, wasn't it? That she was worried about his safety?

"Nope. He won't. Weston has put his source in touch with the attorney general. I think we'll see an investigation opened." He hooked his thumbs in his belt loops. "But I resigned. It wouldn't be right for me to stay police chief after what I did. Especially because it felt damned good to punch his lights out."

Elaine let out a strangled noise tinged with hysteria.

"On the drive back, I realized what's most important in my life is right here. You and Dax. That is if you can forgive me." He offered his hand, hope pounding in his chest. "I also remembered that the night of the First Responder's Ball I told you that you didn't have to tell me anything about your past until you were ready." He took a deep breath. "And obviously from my behavior, you were justified. I failed you and I'm sorry."

Her eyes darted to his outstretched hand then back to his face. Once. Twice. She worried her bottom lip between her teeth, clearly distressed. He couldn't breathe in or out. Like bailing wire had been wrapped too tight around his chest.

"I'm so sorry I didn't trust you enough to tell you. Dottie was the only person who knew, and she promised to keep it to herself."

Everything in him itched to go to her, wrap her in his arms and kiss the pain from her face, but he couldn't. Not until she met him halfway. He'd laid everything out for her, and if he'd blown it because he'd been an assfuck, then so be it. He'd have to live with the consequences.

She took a ragged breath, eyes searching his. "I wanted to start over here. To give Dax a safe and stable place to grow up. And Dottie gave me that chance. I didn't want to blow it."

"You didn't, I did," he murmured.

She looked at him sharply, but continued. "I know how small towns can be. I was afraid that if word got out, people would treat us differently – would treat Dax differently – if they knew that my past was… less than pristine. And you…"

Her cheeks turned the prettiest shade of pink as her voice turned husky. "Always made me feel like a lady. I didn't want that to go away. I didn't want to disappoint you, and I'm so sorry I did."

His feet disobeyed a direct order from his brain to stay put. He was on the porch in three steps, clasping her shoulders. "You didn't, sweetheart. I'm the disappointment. I'm not happy you didn't confide in me, but I understand why, and I'll do better, every day, to earn your trust. To show you how much I love and value you." His mouth was on board with his feet too, completely ignoring his brain's command to stop talking before he ruined things again. "Your strength, your kindness, your patience, your–"

"Travis," Dottie interjected. "If you don't ask this girl to marry you right now, I am never serving you coffee again."

Elaine laughed, tears spilling out of her eyes.

He kissed her wet cheeks, salt from her tears sharp on his tongue. "I'm stubborn and set in my ways."

"I break rules," she spoke barely above a whisper.

"Break them all, I don't care. As long as I can come home to you and Dax every night."

Her eyes filled with worry. "What are you going to do now that you don't have a job?"

"I'll figure it out. Right now, I don't care. All I care about is right here."

Dottie sighed loudly. "Well, you two kids are gonna be just fine." She gave them both a quick embrace. "I'm gonna get on home and check in on Cassidy. She's been helping Parker with his physical therapy. I think they're about to set a wedding date. You kids these days, not a one of you has had a decent engagement. And now Carolina's making noise about getting married by Christmas. Expect us all to make a celebration overnight."

Dottie reached up and clasped his chin. "You're a good man, Travis. I'm real proud of you."

Warmth spread across his chest. His voice grew rough. "Thanks. For always being there." The remaining words stuck somewhere in the back of his throat.

She patted his cheek. "Love you too, sweetie pie. See you two tomorrow night."

When her truck disappeared down the drive, Travis turned to Elaine. "Well?" Her eyes turned to dark pools and he held her gaze for a long moment. He could lose himself in her. Hell, he was already lost. "Will you make a life with me? Here?" He couldn't keep the gravel out of his voice. Or the hope.

A thousand emotions crossed her face while his stomach did jumping jacks. "I want to..." Her voice was full of hesitation. Not the enthusiastic response he'd hoped for. He tried to tamp down the feelings of despair. "But?" He wasn't going to give up easily. Not if there was an outside chance for them.

"I think we need to ask Dax what he thinks."

"Done."

"And I don't want to commit to anything permanent until I'm free and clear."

"I can't say I like that, but I get it."

"With any luck, all of this will be behind us on Wednesday. Would you ask me again?"

He'd keep asking. But a man could only live with so much uncertainty "Only if I already know the answer."

She tilted her chin, eyes glowing. "If you haven't figured out that I'm crazy about you, I don't know what else to do."

"You can kiss me for starters."

CHAPTER 31

TRAVIS LOOKED AROUND his crowded living room with a sense of satisfaction. The last time it had been this full was at his dad's wake. Tonight, instead of casseroles and jello molds, Jamey Sinclaire and Dottie had driven the food truck over and set out platters of sliders, French fry cups, and a fancy kind of coleslaw. In the spirit of election night, they'd invited everyone to cast votes for their favorite slider. The winner would be featured on their menu and called *The Sheriff*.

A small group was gathered around the television he'd brought downstairs, others were checking their phones as the results trickled in. Dax stirred in his lap and burrowed deeper into his shoulder, lightly snoring. He eyed Elaine. "What do you think? Should I take him upstairs?"

She nodded. "His teeth are brushed and it's a school night. I know he didn't want to miss anything, but let's tuck him in."

"I've got it. You stay right here." Before she could object, he'd stood, draping the boy over his shoulder. Bedtimes were fast becoming a favorite part of his day. Tucking in Dax, reading him a story, and receiving goodnight hugs and kisses hit a place deep within him. A place where everything was right with the world. After pulling up the covers around his chin, he brushed a kiss on Dax's temple, and quietly shut the door, tamping down the pang of regret as he caught sight of Colton's posters on the wall. It had only been twenty-four hours. He was silly to hope Colton would call back right away. He slipped back into his chair and caught Elaine's hand, twining their fingers and bringing the back of her hand to his lips.

Elaine's eyes lit up. "No matter what happens, I'm proud of you. You ran a good campaign."

"Even if I lose?"

"Even if you lose."

"I still think you should have hit Lawson with mail." Weston flopped into a chair next to them, and shoved two bottles of Mike's root beer their way.

"My fist was so much nicer," said Travis flexing his hand with the bruised knuckles.

"Speaking of." Weston leaned forward, eyes gleaming. "Have you given any thought to what's next?"

Travis scoffed. "No. I spent the day playing with Dax and Elaine. Time enough to think about it when the results are finalized."

Weston pulled a pen from his breast pocket and grabbed a paper towel lying in the middle of the table. He started to sketch. "So I've had this idea rolling around my head for a few weeks. And now that you're done with law enforcement..."

Travis groaned. "Oh no. Not another one of your crazy ideas."

"Hear me out."

Travis eyed Elaine. "This is how I ended up running for sheriff."

"That turned out okay, didn't it?" Elaine teased with a wink.

"Fine. Lay it on me."

Weston kept drawing. "You've always said you can't be a ranch of one."

"Right."

"How many would you need? To run your ideal operation?"

"Depends on what you're looking to do. Minimum five, but maybe more."

"Who's your family?"

He didn't have the patience for this tonight. "Are you going to explain or put me through twenty questions?"

"Go with me. Who's your family?"

"Colt. But he's a lost cause."

"Give him time." Elaine squeezed his hand. "He hasn't heard from you in years."

Weston nodded. "It's not like he's going to come running back and sing kumbaya the first time you call. Hell, maybe never."

Hearing Weston put it like that, stung. But it was a truth he'd have to live with. Colt might never come back. He stowed his regret. Plenty more time for self-examination after tonight.

Weston continued, an enthusiastic light in his eye. "Who else is your family?"

"You. Cash. Braden."

"Count me out because I have a new job that suddenly taking up a lot of my time. That gives you three."

"I'm four," Elaine offered shyly.

Hearing her say that warmed him to his toes. "You're going to start community college soon though."

"I can still help."

"Fair enough. So we have four."

Weston pushed the drawing in front of him. "Resolution

Ranch. Where healing and husbandry come together."

Travis made a face. "I don't get it."

"That's because you're not thinking. What do we have right here in Prairie? Land. Hope Sinclaire helping people like you and Cassie train wild mustangs. We've got buildings, and people who can build more. You've got a fixed-up barn, and space for bunkhouses." Weston's face grew more animated as he spoke. "You think we're the only ones who've struggled returning to civilian life? Why not create a safe landing space for our brothers in arms? A place to get physical and emotional help? We could ask Dr. Munger if he'd consult with us. I'll admit, he has some harebrained ideas about physical labor and sensitizing our triggers, but I think we can both agree he's helped us. Why not help others?"

Travis rocked back in his chair, chewing on the idea. He chuckled, shaking his head. "I'll hand it to you, Wes, you never think small, do you?"

Weston's face lit up. "Go big or go home."

Elaine squeezed his hand, eyes bright. "I think that's a wonderful idea, Travis."

Travis's thoughts raced. Would they come? It had been months since he'd talked to either Cash or Braden. He still had some of his nest-egg left. "It might be worth a few calls to gauge their interest."

A collective groan came up from the group gathered in front of the TV. Someone cursed, and it grew unnaturally quiet. He brought the chair down with a thunk and Elaine shot him a worried look.

Gunnar Hansen spoke up, disappointment clear in his voice. "Final count has you down by thirty-six votes. Sorry man."

Even though he'd prepared for it, disappointment stabbed

through him. Not because he lost, but because Lawson won. "Damn."

Elaine wrung her hands, face scrunched. "Oh, this is all my fault. I'm so sorry."

"Shh." He draped an arm around her pulling her close. "We're not going to kick that dead horse. Yesterday's mail didn't help, but it was already close. And I didn't play the endgame right. I could have hit Lawson and I didn't. But I have to look my friends and neighbors in the eye when this is all over, and I couldn't do it. *Wouldn't* do it."

"My new boss is going to have it in for me," Weston smiled grimly shooting him a heavy look. "I hope the AG goes after him. I may have encouraged my friend to share his information."

Whatever it took. Maybe the attorney general could get something to stick.

Elaine's brow creased with worry. "Do I need to worry?"

Travis shook his head. "I'm quite sure Lawson will be avoiding this part of the county unless absolutely necessary. He knows we're onto him, and eventually he'll slip up, if he hasn't already."

Weston's face grew tight and a muscle twitched high on his cheek. "Good news is, we only get his sorry ass for eighteen months, and I will file to run against him tomorrow. I won't be such a nice opponent," he said with a hard glint in his eye.

Travis stood. "Thank you all for coming, and most importantly, for your support." He gestured to Weston. "I have no doubt Prairie's newest police chief will do an excellent job, and I'm committed to helping Prairie make a full comeback. Together we can make Prairie the most vibrant town in the Flint Hills."

A cheer went up from the small gathering.

"Thank you, Travis, for all you've done for us," Jamey Sinclaire added sincerely. Echoes of her words rippled through the group. Six months ago, he couldn't see himself doing anything but law enforcement, but so much had changed. In spite of the loss, he felt more hopeful than ever. Complete.

Dottie clapped her hands. "Listen up. You'll hear it at the food truck tomorrow, but we might as well end this evening on a high note. Cass and Park have set a date. Clear your calendar three weeks from Saturday."

More clapping and cheers went up. Travis wrapped Elaine in his arms. "Maybe we'll have an announcement of our own soon?" he whispered in her ear, heating at the pretty pink that tinged her cheeks when she nodded.

Weston clapped him on the shoulders. "Think about what I said? I think it could work."

Travis nodded, a flicker of excitement rippling through him. "Wes?" his voice grew thick. "Thanks for everything, man." He hugged his best friend.

When they were finally alone, Travis shut the door and locked it behind him. Then pinning Elaine with a look, began working the buttons on his shirt as he stalked toward her. "We need to talk."

"Oh?" Her eyes lit with anticipation, and she licked her lips.

He tossed his shirt to the floor and pulled her close so he could slip his hands underneath her shirt. She gave a little sigh when his fingers skated across bare skin. He buried his face in the satin skin of her neck, breathing her in. "But we can't have this conversation with our clothes on."

"*Oh.*" Her hands came to his belt, working the buckle free.

"How do you feel about being a ranch wife? Hypothetically?" Her shirt floated to the floor.

She dropped her head, exposing the creamy column of her neck. He followed, tasting a trail from the hollow of her throat to the sensitive spot beneath her ear. The noise she made in the back of her throat went straight to his cock. As did her words. "I'd be open to that," she ended on a gasp when he nipped her.

Pants jingled to the floor joining shirts.

He traced the swell of her breasts with his thumbs, finding her nipples through the thin fabric and driving them to hard peaks. "And hypothetically, how do you feel about ranch babies?"

"Babies?" She moaned as he rolled her nipples between his fingers, arching into him. Her hand slipped between his legs, skating up to stroke his balls through his shorts.

"Lots of them," he grunted as he thrust his hips, need spiraling through him.

Her throaty laugh made his cock jerk, and he groaned as she slipped her hands inside his shorts to firmly clasp his length. "You have ideas, cowboy?"

"Yes," he hissed out as she gave a little tug, thumb circling the sensitive head. "Sooner the better," he grunted, hooking a finger inside her panties and giving a tug. A second later his shorts joined hers. He slid a finger back and forth through her wet folds, drawing a needy whine from her.

"Oh, yes," she panted.

"Yes to babies? To ranching?"

She lifted her head, eyes dark and glazed with desire. "Yes. All of it."

His heart filled to bursting as he lowered them to the rug and settled himself between her legs. "Tell me again."

"Yes," she cried out as he drove into her slick tight heat,

filling her up. She clasped his cheeks, gazing straight into his eyes as he began to thrust slowly, "I want your babies, Travis."

That was the hottest thing she'd ever said. Heat pulsed through him, building with each slow thrust. Her hips rocked against him and he kissed her deeply, thrusting into her mouth. Tongues tangling and moving together in time with their hips until she cried into him, shaking with release, pussy clenching in waves and pulling him along with her over the edge into sweet ecstasy.

CHAPTER 32

MORNING SUNLIGHT STREAMED through the curtains as Elaine drifted into awareness. Travis stretched out against her backside, arm loosely draped over her belly. His grip tightened as he nuzzled her neck. "Happy Thanksgiving."

"Mmmm, you too." She smiled, appreciating the calm before the storm.

"Happy wedding."

She wiggled her toes and grinned, angling her neck for a kiss. "Mmmm. Happy wedding."

His hand skimmed over her belly. "How's our little person this morning?"

She shrugged, delighted at Travis's excitement. "So far so good."

He moved behind her, planting a kiss on her shoulder. "I know it's early, but can we tell everyone at dinner?"

She shook with laughter rolling over to study him. "I'm barely pregnant." She bit her lip, a tendril of worry twisting her insides. "What if something happens?"

Concern flickered in his eyes. "Then we don't grieve in secret. And we have friends to help us through it." He tucked a tendril of hair behind her ear then traced a finger down her jaw. "But that's not going to happen. I have a good feeling about this. Besides, Dax is excited too. We can't ask him to keep a lid on that today."

Contentment settled over her. She could never have imagined feeling this happy. Some mornings, she still had to pinch herself. "It's settled then. We'll let the cat out of the bag." She pressed a hand to his chest, enjoying the prickle of his hair against her palm. "Have you heard from your brother?"

Travis's face clouded, and he shook his head giving her a pained smile. "I've gotten pretty good at talking to his answering machine though."

Her heart ached for him. "We'll set an extra place, just in case." She brushed a kiss across his lips. "It's only been a few months after years of silence. He may not be ready."

Travis puffed out a breath, nodding. "You're right. I hope someday I get the chance to make things right with him."

She tucked her head under his chin. "You are a good man, Travis. I'm proud to be your wife."

He kissed the top of her head, chest rumbling with laughter. "Don't you have primping to do before that happens?"

"Posse's on their way over to help with that and dinner."

He landed a light smack on her bottom. "Then get going, woman."

"And what are you going to do while we slave away in the kitchen?" She grinned up at him.

"Smoke cigars and fry up some turkeys."

"Thank God you'll have half the fire department here."

"No one's gonna get hurt," he kissed her forehead.

"Mom, mom, mom," Dax pounded on the door. "Someone's here, can I let them in?"

"Yes, we'll be right down." She drew a finger down Travis's chest. "I could stay here all day."

"Tomorrow, and the rest of the weekend." He kissed her nose.

A knock sounded at the door. "Elaine. It's time to boot

your man out," Dottie hollered through the wood. "We've got work to do."

Smothering a laugh, she hopped out of bed and threw on a pair of leggings and one of Travis's flannel shirts. "Coming. I promise." Blowing Travis a kiss, she hurried into the hall and down the stairs. Eleven smiling faces waited expectantly at the bottom of the stairs. Jamey, Hope, and Maddie Sinclaire, along with Hope's mother, Martha Hansen. Next to her stood Gloria McPherson and Peggy Hansen, the newest Posse member and Parker's mom. Emmaline Andersson and Millie Prescott stood holding trays of mimosas. Finishing the group were Dottie and all four of her daughters – Cassidy, Lydia, Lexi, and Carolina. Lydia held out a shoebox. "You can't open these until later, but I made you a little something to go with your wedding dress."

"I don't know what to say." What could she, when there was so much love directed at her? Her chest grew tight. "I promised I wouldn't cry today," she squeezed out, blinking rapidly.

Dottie enveloped her in a great hug. "Oh sweetie, there are gonna be happy tears all day. I hope you bought water-proof mascara."

She laughed against Dottie's chest, settling into the woman's strong, steady embrace. "I did."

"You're set then. Now, have a mimosa."

Crap.

She lifted her head, brushing at her eyes. "How about some juice instead?" she said brightly.

Dottie's eyes narrowed.

There was no way she could keep a lid on this. Not with her cheeks flaming.

"Are you?"

She nodded.

Dottie whooped and squeezed her again. The others followed suit as Travis clamped down the stairs, buttoning a shirt. "What's this?"

Martha handed him a mimosa. "We couldn't be happier for you two."

Travis caught her eye and winked, downing the glass in a long gulp. "Why thank you. We can't wait. Now if you ladies will excuse me, I have to supervise a turkey fry."

The morning flew by, and the smell of frying turkeys wafted in the front door, mixing with the aroma of pumpkin pie, mashed potatoes, and stewing cranberries. Before she lost her nerve, Elaine struck a glass. "I know it's just about time to get ready, but I wanted to thank you all for being here this morning." She met each woman's gaze. "All of you have been so kind to me, and to Dax. I came here afraid and alone, and now I feel like I have a family."

"You've always had a family here, Elaine, sweetie." Dottie gestured to the women. "You might not have known it, but we've been here rooting for you the whole time."

The women nodded and murmured their agreement.

"Lydia," Dottie called. "Grab your box. We won't all be able to fit upstairs."

"Sure, Ma."

Lydia retrieved the box from the couch and handed it to Elaine. Elaine loosened the satin ribbon and slowly lifted the lid. "Oh," she breathed. "These are beautiful, Lydia. How can I ever thank you?"

Lydia beamed. "Wear them. That's thanks enough."

Nestled in the silver and white paper, were a pair of white satin slippers with a curved heel embroidered in silver and white. Across the top of the shoe and along the outside were tiny silver embroidered branches topped with tiny white embroidered flowers. "How did you think of this? They're perfect."

She shrugged, obviously pleased with the praise. "Mom showed me a teacup you liked. I thought it would make a nice pattern on a shoe."

"I can't wait to see what they look like with my dress."

"Well, let's get you upstairs then, hon. Emmaline and Millie have offered to help with your hair and makeup. The rest of us will help ourselves to more of Millie's *champagne*." Dottie made quote marks with her fingers.

Elaine tilted her head. "I don't get it?"

Millie giggled. "The technical term is Methode Championése. But that's a little too hoity-toity for out here and no one would want it. But I can't legally call it champagne, not that it matters right now," she rushed on. "I'm not selling it."

"Why not?"

"It's a big undertaking, and with running the market, I don't have the time. But someday I'm going to put Prairie on the map for winemaking." Her face turned dreamy. "In the meantime, it's nice to share at local parties."

"We'll hold back a bottle for after the baby comes." Dottie winked at her. "Now upstairs with you. I'll make sure your men are ready by three."

Elaine, Emmaline and Millie headed upstairs. When it was finally time to slip into her dress, she'd been buffed and puffed from head to toe. Elaine wiggled her fingers. "You did a great job on my nails, Millie."

"Thanks." She beamed. "One of my side jobs growing up on the road. I could always find ladies who wanted their nails done."

A knock sounded at the door and Lydia popped her head

in. "Have you tried the shoes on? How do they fit?"

"Let's find out." Elaine pulled them from the box and slipped them on. "I don't know how you did it, but they're perfect."

"Shoemaker's secret." She winked. "Everyone's waiting downstairs, it's time."

Emmaline slipped the dress off the hanger and over her head. The satin lining cascaded over her body, soft and cool. "Shut your eyes," Emmaline suggested.

Elaine shut her eyes as the dress tightened around her ribs and the buzz of the zipper sounded in the quiet room. But they flew open as something cool touched her collarbone. "What's this?"

"Dottie sent her family pearls up. Something borrowed," Millie cooed.

Elaine blinked hard, determined not to spoil her makeup with happy tears. She didn't recognize the glowing young woman smiling back at her in the mirror. Emmaline's dress was a work of art. Simple in its glory. A princess bodice of white silk satin slightly flaring at her hips and falling in soft folds to the floor. On top, a wide vee neck and simple three-quarter sleeves. She wore a little crystal and pearl bracelet that Dax had given her this morning. Travis must have taken him to pick it out when they picked up their wedding suits.

Millie had braided white roses into her hair and clipped a short veil below the flowers. "You've outdone yourself Emmaline. And I felt like a princess in the last dress. Now I guess I feel like a queen."

"Mom?" Dax poked his head in, eyes widening as he saw her. "You look like the lady in the fairy tale."

"Thank you. And you look like a fine young man. So grown-up. Are you ready?" She kissed his head, then held out her hand.

Dax nodded eagerly. "So does this mean I have a mom *and* a dad now?"

She melted at his sweetness. "It does."

"And I can call Travis *Dad*?"

"If you want to. I'm sure he'd love that."

He nodded seriously. "I want to."

She gave his hand a squeeze. "Let's go then." She turned, extending a hand for her bouquet. Emmaline handed her the bouquet of white roses and hydrangeas and slipped out the door.

Dax helped her down the stairs and she paused on the bottom step, taking it all in. The smiling faces spilling into the kitchen, Travis and Weston looking smashing in gray suits at the fireplace next to Judge Brewer. Travis caught her eye and smiled. Only she could see the faint disappointment lingering in his eyes. She smothered a little sigh. Even Colton's absence couldn't ruin today. Nothing could.

Keeping her eyes trained on Travis, she stepped off the stair, taking his hand as soon as she reached him. He leaned in, brushing her cheek with a kiss. "You look stunning."

"So do you." She kissed him back setting off a smattering of applause and catcalls.

"No kissing until the I-Do's," Weston ribbed.

"Then let's get this show on the road," Travis grumbled good-naturedly.

Judge Brewer cleared his throat. "We're gathered here today, not just for Thanksgiving turkey, but to celebrate the love shared by Travis and Elaine. And to recognize and witness their decision to journey forward together as husband and wife."

Judge Brewer looked over the gathering. "Is there any

legal reason why this couple cannot wed?"

A knock sounded at the door and Elaine's stomach dropped like a stone. She looked from the door to Travis, failing to quell the panic rising through her. He looked as surprised as she did. The knock sounded harder.

"Someone open it," Travis snapped.

Brodie Sinclaire, who was in the seat closest to the door, stood. He gave Travis a sardonic grin. "You sure you don't want to seal the deal before I open up?"

Nervous laughter rippled through the group.

Travis's mouth flattened. "Open it."

The door creaked open, and a figure in a black Stetson towered in the doorway. He took off his hat and Travis gripped Elaine's elbow. Murmurs rose up around them, but Elaine couldn't stop staring at the man in the door. On second glance, he was obviously younger and his hair was a shade darker, but he could easily be mistaken for Travis's twin. When he spoke, he sounded like he'd had too much smoke and whiskey. "I hope I'm not interrupting."

For a split second, the young man's bravado slipped. He was nervous. But then the swagger was back and he flashed a grin to the room.

"Say something," she whispered to Travis. He blinked and stepped forward, eyes guarded.

"Colton."

"Travis."

The tension between the two men was palpable. Someone in the back coughed. A chair squeaked. Then Travis pulled him into a hug. "You're just in time," he said hoarsely. "Just in time."

Colton's arms slowly wrapped around Travis, giving him a pat, then he extracted himself. "I'll just stand in the back."

"Wait." Travis laid a hand on his arm. "Stand with me?"

Elaine's heart shot into her throat. Travis would be crushed if this went badly. After a pregnant pause, Colton nodded once, face a mask. The tension swept out of Travis's shoulders and out of the room. Like the whole place breathed a collective sigh of relief.

Weston moved over to make room for Colton and Travis resumed his place at her side taking her hand in a vise-like grip. But when she met his eyes, there was only burning elation.

Their vows were exchanged in a blur, and Travis's mouth was on hers in a searing, joyous kiss. "Now I have a dad *and* an uncle," Dax shouted gleefully.

Applause and shouts echoed around them, but all that registered was the heat of their kiss and the rapture in her heart.

CHAPTER 33

T RAVIS SAT DOWN, draping an arm around his wife. Elaine snuggled into him and covered a yawn. "Tired?"

She smiled, eyes aglow. "We can sleep in tomorrow."

Kissing her head, he glanced around the table filled with the last of their friends. At the far end of the table, Colton sat playing tic-tac-toe with Dax. They locked eyes over the boy's head. He was a man now. Filled out and broad. It shouldn't shake him, but it did. The last time they'd seen each other, Colton had been four inches shorter and half a man slimmer. There was a hard edge to him now, too. To the uneducated eye, he looked relaxed next to Dax. But Travis could sense the tension in him, coiled and ready to spring. He'd own his share in that, as soon as they could manage a little one-on-one. They'd hardly shared two words in the chaos. But the fact Colton was here, meant everything. They'd sort out their differences. He'd make sure of it.

Elaine squeezed his hand as if reading his thoughts. "It's enough that he's here. Save your talk for tomorrow."

His throat squeezed tight, stealing his words. She was right. Colton had come home, and that was what mattered.

Weston leaned in, swirling a glass of bourbon. "Have you given anymore thought to Resolution Ranch?"

Brodie perked up. "What's this?"

"Nothing." Travis waved him off. "Just a harebrained idea

232

of Weston's to get the ranch running again and turn it into a place to help veterans land on their feet." Right now, he wanted to celebrate with Elaine. Everything else could wait.

"Using animal husbandry, like what Hope does, and working with a counselor I know," answered Weston.

Hope leaned in. "You know, I've been thinking along those same lines. Using what I've been teaching you with others. Would you be interested in collaborating?"

"Heck yes," Weston said enthusiastically.

"Not so fast, Tex." Travis turned to Hope. "There are a lot of logistics to overcome. We don't have space yet, so we'd have to spend time building a complex of bunkhouses, not to mention acquiring livestock, and figuring out an income stream or three to keep the ranch in the black."

"Maybe you could start a non-profit?" suggested Hope's husband, Ben. He was usually pretty quiet, but rumor had it he was the reason Sinclaire & Sons ranch did so well.

"I hadn't thought of that," considered Weston, eyes lighting.

Travis shook his head. This was spinning out of control, just like running for sheriff. "We still need more capital than my nest egg will afford."

Emma Sinclaire's head popped up. "I'd be happy to volunteer my time working on your PR and helping connect you with sponsors. I could even organize a big fundraiser."

Brodie Sinclaire chimed in. "Take her up on that, Kincaid. Emma works for one of the biggest marketing and PR agencies in Kansas City."

"I know I'll get razzed to death for even *thinking* of helping a Navy boy," added Cassie. "But you should talk to Sterling Walker. Sterling was good at everything in high school, and his parents mentioned the other day he might be coming home. I'm sure he'd be an asset to the ranch. And I'll vouch for Dr. Munger. He's been very helpful to me too."

It was a nice idea, Resolution Ranch. But he couldn't see it getting off the ground without a significant influx of capital. Together, he and Elaine could handle a small operation if they hired seasonal help from town. Anything bigger would have to wait.

"I'd be willing to invest a portion of my earnings," Colton offered quietly.

Travis's stomach dropped as he locked gazes with his brother. "No way. I can't let you do that." All eyes swung from Colton to him, then back to Colton. He coughed, trying to clear away the shock that stopped up his voice. "I appreciate the offer. But you only just got home. I don't even know how long you're staying."

"Silent partner only. I'm not ready to settle down yet," Colton countered firmly, mouth thinning into a determined line.

Travis recognized the set of his brother's mouth. The *'once Colton decides on something don't even think about stopping him'* expression. Some things never changed. But if Colton was serious... maybe the ranch could become a reality.

Elaine squeezed his hand again, and placed a kiss on his jaw. "You know I can help with managing the books, among other things."

Anticipation thrummed through his veins as he surveyed the excited faces around the table. The kind of energy he'd only ever felt before big missions. "Are you sure?" He turned to his wife, amazed at her enthusiasm. "It would be asking a lot. Seven days a week. Fourteen-hour days. No time off. Always something that needs fixing."

"I already work like that now. I'd much rather do it with

you."

His heart swelled to bursting as he pressed a kiss to her forehead. His strong, beautiful wife. He'd never tire of calling her that.

Elaine gestured down the table. "And we wouldn't be alone. We'd have a family with us."

The nodding faces of the Sinclaires, Hansens, and Graces overwhelmed him. She was right. Together they could bring Resolution Ranch to life. Together they could overcome any obstacle.

Weston lifted his glass. "To Elaine and Travis, may your love infuse this ranch with new life, and bring second chances to those who need it most."

Travis bent to take her upturned mouth. "I'll seal that deal with a kiss."

THE BEGINNING OF HAPPILY EVER AFTER

Did you like this book? Please leave a review! Independent authors rely on reviews and word of mouth. If you enjoyed this book, please spread the word!

Want more?

A HERO'S HEART – Sterling Walker & Emma Sinclaire
(On Sale Jan 9th)

A HERO'S HAVEN – Cash Aiken & Kaycee Starr
(Coming 2018)

A HERO'S HOME – Jason Case & Millie Prescott
(Coming 2018)

A HERO'S HOPE – Braden McCall & Luci Cruz
(Coming 2018)

A HERO'S HEART (preorder your copy now!)

The town superstar has just met his match

When retired Army Captain and Prairie's favorite son, Sterling Walker, returns home to join Restoration Ranch, he finds himself face to face with his biggest rival – Emma Sinclaire, the sole daughter of Prairie's oldest family – all grown up, gorgeous, and glaring daggers at him.

Will it be winner take all in this battle of hearts?

A rising star at Kansas City's internationally acclaimed Royal Fountain Media, Emma agrees to personally oversee the marketing and fundraising campaign for Resolution Ranch. But she never expected to come face to face with her high school nemesis, Sterling Walker, let alone have to work closely with him. As they face off across the boardroom, she can't deny her attraction to the smart, sexy, soldier who engages her in battle at every turn.

When a moment of carelessness threatens to shut down the fundraiser before it starts, Sterling will put everything on the line to protect Emma's reputation. Will it be enough to win Emma's heart for good? Or will the fallout be the ruin of Resolution Ranch?

WHERE IT ALL BEGAN:
THE COWBOYS OF THE FLINT HILLS SERIES

PRAIRIE HEAT – Blake Sinclaire & Maddie Hansen
(on sale now!)
PRAIRIE PASSION – Brodie Sinclaire & Jamey O'Neill
(on sale now!)
PRAIRIE DESIRE – Ben Sinclaire & Hope Hansen
(on sale now!)
PRAIRIE STORM – Axel Hansen & Haley Cooper
(on sale now!)
PRAIRIE FIRE – Parker Hansen & Cassidy Grace
(on sale now!)
PRAIRIE DEVIL – Colton Kincaid & Lydia Grace
(coming in 2018)
PRAIRIE FEVER – Gunnar Hansen & Suzannah Winslow
(coming in 2018)
PRAIRIE BLISS – Jarrod O'Neill & Lexi Grace
PRAIRIE REDEMPTION – Cody Hansen & Carolina Grace

COMING IN APRIL 2018 – PRAIRIE DEVIL

He's the Devil she shouldn't want

Colton Kincaid has a chip on his shoulder. Thrown out of the house when he was seventeen by his brother, Travis, he scrapped his way to the top of the rodeo circuit riding broncs, and never looked back. Until a chance encounter with hometown good girl Lydia Grace leaves him questioning everything and wanting a shot at redemption.

She's the Angel he can never have

All Lydia Grace needs is one break. After having her concepts stolen by a famous shoe designer, she returns home to Prairie to start a boot company on her own. But when her break comes in the form of Colton Kincaid, Prairie's homegrown bad boy and rodeo star, she wonders if she's gotten more than she's bargained for.

They say be careful what you wish for

To get her boot company off the ground, Lydia makes Colton an offer too good to refuse, but he ups the ante. Will the bargain she strikes bring her everything she's dreamed of and more, or did she just make a deal with the devil?

Help a Hero – Read a Cowboy
KISS ME COWBOY – A Box Set for Veterans
Six Western Romance authors have joined up to support their favorite charity – Heroes & Horses – and offer you this sexy box set with Six Full Length Cowboy Novels, filled with steamy kisses and HEA's. Grab your copy and help an American Hero today!

Subscribe to my Newsletter for updates and release information for Prairie Storm and the rest of the Cowboys of the Flint Hills Series.
http://tessalayne.com/newsletter
Join my reader group on Facebook – The Prairie Posse this is where I post my sneak peeks, offer giveaways, and share hot cowboy pics!
facebook.com/groups/1390521967655100

ACKNOWLEDGEMENTS

This book series would not have been conceived but for an article I read over a year ago about the groundbreaking work of Heroes & Horses. My heartfelt thanks to this organization for their tireless support of veterans. Especially to Mackenzie Fink for the many conversations about military life and H&H.

To my mentor Kimberley Troutte, I am grateful to you every day.

To Genevieve Turner, Kait Nolan (aka blurb doctor) & Kara, for both your feedback, sense of dramatic arc, and for wine and chocolate.

To Amanda Kelsey, whose visual talent has brought my heroes to life on the covers. Seeing these heroes puts a smile on my face.

To Mr. Cowboy, for your smiling face, words of encouragement, wine at the end of the day and coffee in bed. I love you.

Lastly, to my readers in the Prairie Posse. You are an incredible group of women and I'm grateful to spend time with you almost every day. I'm especially grateful for the days when you send virtual supplies of chocolate, wine, and hawt cowboys :D

Made in the USA
Lexington, KY
30 June 2019